FAMOU$ & $HAMLE$$

Bev Dulson

Published in 2016 by FeedARead.com Publishing

A CIP catalogue record for this title is available from the British Library.

Also By Bev Dulson

BETRAYAL

TWISTED SISTER
(Sequel to Betrayal)

LOVE
OVERBOARD

READ ALL ABOUT
IT

THIS CHRISTMAS
(A Novella)

Find me on Facebook: - Bev Dulson (Books) on
Twitter @bevster69 and on
Goodreads – Bev Dulson

ACKNOWLEDGEMENTS

Thanks to my lovely colleague, Nathan Elsdon for my fab cover. You're right it is 'totally Bev.' To my 'filth-o-meters' Kate & Louise, if it got passed them it was going in the book! To my proof readers, Clare Ibbotson and Zoe Dingwall and obviously my writing partner in crime Cat Batty who always helps me out with the old writers block!

Massive thanks to anyone who has read my previous books and even bigger thanks for leaving reviews, it all helps me to build my name as an author.

Thanks to my amazing friends and family, just for being you...in particular, The Shone's, The Dawson's and the Bradley's you are all truly 'special fings'

Finally, thanks to My Hubby, Mr D, for
your unwavering support in everything I do.
I love you and our beautiful girls so much.
You are my world!

For Cat – The bestest writing buddy ever, it wouldn't be half as much fun without you!

PROLOGUE

January 2013

The two bodies fumbled with each other's clothes as they clashed together with urgency, shirt buttons ripped off, the zip of a dress yanked down such was their desire for each other. Weeks of pent up sexual tension and missed opportunities culminating in this moment. Now as they crashed through the suite door they didn't even make it to the bedroom, they fell clumsily over the coffee table knocking over a bottle of whisky as they landed on the sofa.

'Sshh', she giggled drunkenly, placing a finger on his lips.

'Don't worry, everyone's too busy downstairs to miss us,' his mouth came down on hers again, his hands hungrily pushing up her skirt. Her breasts were exposed now that her dress had slipped off her shoulders. He rolled his tongue over an already erect nipple, as his hands disappeared further up her skirt. His cock throbbed as he felt the dampness of her knickers, the foreplay had been the weeks leading to this moment. She wriggled out of them as he undid the zip on his trousers, she lifted her hips and wrapped her legs around his waist, pulling him into her. Her hands grasped his firm buttocks pushing him even further. He grabbed the back of the sofa to gain a quicker rhythm. This was hot, fast, urgent sex. Their bodies building up to a crescendo, both of them needing this release. They were slick with sweat. This wasn't about a marathon, it was a sprint to the finish. They went limp with exhaustion and he collapsed on top of her, nuzzling her neck.

'I wanna do that again, properly.'

'There was nothing improper about that.'

He lifted his head so he could look into her eyes. 'I wanna take my time, feel every inch of you, kiss you all over...'

She sighed. 'Time is something we don't have, we'll be missed.'

He stood up, pulling her with him. 'We can make some excuse, c'mon you know we need to do this.'

She nodded. 'I know.'

'No point standing here chatting is there? We're wasting time,' he led her by the hand towards the bedroom.

Pushing open the door a scream stuck in her throat as her hand flew to her mouth.

'Shit.'

On the bed, naked, on blood-stained sheets was a body, a quite clearly dead body.   'That's my husband,' she gasped.

Chapter One

Six weeks earlier

The Liver Bird Hotel November 2012

Gathered in the small staffroom in the basement of the grand hotel that was the Liver Bird, manager Tim Smith was holding a very important meeting with the staff he considered to be the best of his team. Their faces were expectant, it was almost December, there was never normally time for a quick briefing as the festive season approached, never mind a scheduled meeting. Tim was a tall, skinny man who was perfect for the role of manager, not so much for the staff but for the customers, he was an expert in brown nosing. He clapped his hands together to get their attention, he could already see they were starting to get distracted by the two people standing next to him.

'Right team, before I begin can you all please turn your mobiles off. What I am about to tell you is on a need to know basis only,' he waited a few moments while they switched off their phones. 'You may be wondering why I've called you here today, you are the elite few. You are the people who will put The Liver Bird firmly on the map. Our beloved song bird, Ms Magenta Valentina has decided that our humble hotel will be hosting the launch for her next album, now obviously I cannot go into too much detail as you can understand, discretion is required in this delicate situation. However, I can tell you that after the launch party here at the hotel, where a bevy of stars will be in attendance, and we are talking 'A' list here, there will be a separate secret party. A helicopter will whisk a select few across the river and over to a Manor House. This is where you come in, the Manor House will be staffed by you,' he allowed himself a triumphant smile as the excitement grew in the room, this was huge news.

'May I introduce to you two more members of the team, firstly we have Jody Stanley who will be the liaison between you and Ms Valentina if any issues occur, secondly we have Hunter Cole who is my opposite number from the Boston hotel, he is here to assist our American friends. Any questions?'

Magenta Valentina flicked her long glossy auburn hair over her shoulder as she sat perched on a bar stool of the residents bar in the luxury Liver Bird hotel. It was good to be home. She'd just finished a very successful meeting with her agent and the hotel management. Normally she'd leave her PA Jody to deal with everything, but this particular meeting she wanted to be heavily involved in, she wanted the final word on everything, it had to be perfect. Now she was in the bar, having a celebratory glass of Cristal. She was on her own, which was rare, but she took pleasure in these quiet moments when she had time to herself and she could actually think.

She was excited about the release of her second album and knew coming back to her roots was the right way to go. She'd had an eventful career so far and had come a long way from the girl from The Dingle, the inner City area of Liverpool which had a very tight knit community and was made famous by the TV series Bread. Most people from that area didn't grow up to be models or singers but that's exactly what happened to Maggie Vale when she was fourteen.   She was shopping in town with her friends and they wandered into the department store, George Henry Lee's admiring stuff they couldn't afford. They were at the perfume counters, getting free samples when a lady tapped Maggie on the shoulder. She'd introduced herself as Leila DuPree a scout for Lightening Models International. She told Maggie she had just the look they were after and was her hair naturally that colour? She was of Irish descent, of course her auburn hair and pale complexion was natural. Leila gave her a business card and asked her to visit the London office. She'd put the card in her bag and forgot about it, she was sure it was a joke. When she mentioned it to her mam a few days later she thought the same.

'People don't rescue people like us queen, we have to rescue ourselves.'

Maggie was inclined to agree but her best friend Trina, thought otherwise. She was convinced the DuPree woman was genuine. Maggie's boyfriend Jason, was less convinced, he pleaded with her not to go, said it sounded like a scam. In the end the two girls bunked off school and one Friday morning found themselves at Lime Street heading down to London. Listening to Trina paid off. By the summer of '95 sixteen year old Maggie had become Magenta Valentina. Newly single Magenta. Her relationship with Jase was over, largely due to two reasons, one her agent and two, Jase's family moving back to his dad's home town of Chicago. She'd never seen him again, but no one ever forgets their first love do they?

Whilst her career had never quite reached the dazzling heights of Kate Moss or Naomi Campbell, Magenta hadn't done too badly, she had some lucrative shampoo contracts, launched a perfume, posed in the LFC football kit for the new sponsors and got some catwalk work. By the age of twenty nine her star was slipping, she was getting older, her face not so fresh or in demand. Everything changed overnight when she was asked to sing on a charity single with the scouse comedian, Danny Diamond. The single went straight to number one and the biggest surprise of all was that the scouse bird could sing, and not only that but she could sing beautifully. Her agent was fighting off calls from music companies desperate to sign her. The two she was most interested in were the ones from Simon Cowell and the American music mogul Max Maxwell, the power behind the hit show 'Starmaker' which had indeed made many stars. She signed with Max, she would often laugh in magazine interviews that she picked him because he was cuter than Simon Cowell. That answer was in fact the truth. Max was ten years older than she was and the most enigmatic man she had ever met. She was attracted to his power, he seemed just as taken with her and after three number one hits, they married. Yes, she knew it was all very 'Mariah Carey', marrying her manager, but she was totally under his spell. At the time, that didn't seem a problem...but now she wasn't so sure. His power soon became very apparent that it was just arrogance and as for the magical spell, that appeared to have been broken.

Her singing career had gone from strength to strength, her début single had been a cover of Blondie's hit 'Atomic'. This was the perfect choice for her, she was nearly thirty, she needed an edgy image. She wasn't some teeny bopper singing about waiting for some guy to call her up. Being from Liverpool helped, the city that gave the world the Beatles. She was often asked during interviews if she'd ever met John Lennon, she was sure he'd never popped into her Auntie Flo's in The Dingle for a cuppa, besides she was two when he'd been killed, so if she ever had bumped into him, she certainly wouldn't remember. Every single since her first had hit the top spot. Men loved her, woman wanted to be her, she had the perfect fairy tale life, being married to the magnificent Max Maxwell. In hindsight, she'd been naïve to have even married him in the first place.

She sighed as she took a slow sip of her champagne. Max was digging his heels in over the plans for the launch of her new album, titled 'The Liver Bird' which was why she wanted the launch here. That was only part of her plan, she wanted to whisk a selected few over to The Wirral and use a secluded Manor House for a weekend of fun and debauchery. Max hated the idea when she broached it to him a few weeks ago in their New York Brownstone, their home when they weren't in their London town house or in their LA beach house. 'Why Liverpool?'

'It's my home town Max, I need as much support as I can get and scousers always get behind their own. Think of The X Factor, whenever a Liverpudlian is on the live shows, they always get to the final.'

A grimace crossed her husband's face, firstly, she imagined because she'd mentioned the X Factor which was a reminder to him that Starmaker had never quite been the hit he'd expected in the UK and secondly because he hated to be reminded that his wife was from a poor upbringing. Despite the fact that he'd always maintained to love her soft scouse lilt when she spoke, he would gloss over her upbringing. They were a power couple, her coming from a terraced house in Liverpool didn't fit the image he'd manufactured for them.

'Baby, think of the logistics, we're never gonna get the LA contingent on board, c'mon planes from the States don't even fly into that freakin' city.'

'Manchester airport is forty five minutes away.'

'You're crazy, this will never work.'

'You forget how persuasive I can be,' she walked towards him, letting the silk dressing gown she was wearing fall away from her body, revealing a black baby doll nightdress, trimmed in pink lace.

She sank to her knees, never once taking her eyes of her husband as she unzipped his jeans, releasing his dick which had already been straining through his trousers. She opened her mouth, taking him fully inside. Her eyes still locked on his, she had him.

The next day the private jet was booked for her trip to Liverpool. Her home town was almost unrecognisable, it was a cosmopolitan city in its own right, she could feel a buzz about the place and for the first time in years she felt like she was in the right place.

She looked down at her glass, it was empty. Before she could catch the bar tenders eye, a glass was placed in front of her as an arm stretched out from behind her. She spun round and to her surprise she was looking straight into familiar blue eyes.

'Jase!'

There didn't seem to be any surprise in his face. 'It's Hunter now.'

She screwed her eyes up in confusion. Why the name change? She hadn't expected the American accent when he'd spoken either. What hadn't shocked her was how utterly gorgeous he was, she knew all those years ago that the cute sixteen year old lad would grow into a sexy man. What on earth was he doing here? She found her voice, which was just as well as her mouth was about to drop open and drool at him. 'Why Hunter?'

He shrugged. 'Why Magenta?'

'Seems like it's not just our City that's had a bit of a makeover,' it was then she noticed his uniform. 'You work here?'

He nodded. 'I'm kinda in between jobs, but at the moment, anything you need, then I'm your guy.'

She couldn't take her eyes off him, couldn't form anymore words to come out of her mouth.

The last thing she expected when she came home to Liverpool was to bump into Jason Lomax.

This wasn't just crazy, it was insane.

He began to speak but his phone beeped. He looked down at the message, frowned, then shoved the phone in his pocket. 'I've gotta go, but let's catch up soon, hey Mags?'

She nodded, a warm buzz went through her body at the familiar way he used her old nickname. Looked like things were about to get interesting.

CHAPTER TWO

Maxwell Residence NYC

Max Maxwell was in his element, on his back, a beautiful blonde riding him. He reached up to squeeze her oversized breasts, fake of course. The only problem with false boobs was they never jigged up and down. That was the only time he was grateful of Magenta's refusal to go under the knife, her tits bounced around when she was on top of him so much, he could come just watching them. He closed his eyes tight, freakin' Magenta getting into his head when he was supposed to be enjoying himself. He opened his eyes again, refocusing them on the giant boobs above him. He moved his hands to her narrow waist, bucking against her as he gripped her hips. Her head was tipped backwards so he couldn't see her face. It didn't bother him, he didn't wanna look at her, he just wanted to be inside her. He could feel himself on the brink, he lifted her off him and spun her onto her back. He didn't mind a woman going on top, but he'd be dammed if he'd ever let one make him come like that, exerting power over him. He slammed straight back into her, pushing her legs up over his shoulders. Those damn boobs still didn't move. She arched her back into him, making noises of enjoyment. He wasn't really listening, too focused on himself. He was almost there, he slammed into her one more time, exploding into her. He rolled off her and lay back on the bed panting.

She leaned over him, stroking his chest with her long perfectly manicured nails. 'Baby, that was the best.'

He nodded, verification, like he needed it! He was indeed the best. Did she come? He didn't know, was he bothered? No. She obviously enjoyed it, they'd been lovers for months. Everyone wanted a piece of Max, but he was careful not to spread himself too thin. Besides, Brooke was at his beck and call any time he wanted. It was even easier at the moment, with Magenta out of the country in that stupid Liverpool place. He was dreading the thought of going over there. It'd be all grey, raining and miserable plus the people all talked funny there. He could just about cope with Magenta's accent, he'd tried to get her to have elocution lessons, but along with the cosmetic surgery, she'd refused. Man, she was a feisty bitch. She called it Northern soul, whatever the hell that was. God, he had to stop thinking about his wife, this was his down time. He felt Brooke's nails drag across his torso and down towards the wiry hair between his legs. He felt his cock stirring as she ran her finger tips across it. Seconds later her tongue was running up and down it, tantalizingly slow. He was hard again faster than you could say 'blow job'. He may have been sailing a bit too close to home with this affair, but the blow jobs were worth it, but God knew, Magenta would have him by his balls if she ever found out he was shagging her friend. He knew they were pretty safe over here, and the fact that Brooke was married to his business partner, Logan gave them plenty of cover as they were expected to be in each other's company. It wouldn't be so easy in the UK, the British press were a nightmare. He knew from experience when one of his UK acts got caught stumbling out of a night club in London and was pictured with cocaine around his nose. Wouldn't have been so bad if he was in a rock band, but the guy in question had been the lead singer of a holier than thou boy band who didn't drink, didn't have sex and didn't do drugs. Well, not in public anyway. That one picture had almost ruined his career. He leaned his head back against the pillow as Brooke's tongue brought him close to his second orgasm in ten minutes. He was easily distracted today though, his mind wandering when he should be feeling totally relaxed. All he should be thinking about was the tongue that was currently wrapped around his cock. Once he let his mind back on the job in hand, or mouth, he was all systems go. He pushed her head down and thrust into her mouth all it took then was her to tickle his balls and that was it. She sat up, her long blonde hair flicking behind her as she wiped her mouth with her hand.

'Baby, I'd love to stay and go for a third big O, but I gotta go. Promised Logan I'd go for dinner with him and Michael Buble tonight, chat to his wife while Logan sweet talks Michael into performing at that benefit gig.'

'More like Logan will have to stop you flirting with Mr Buble. I got a meeting with those One Direction boys management when I head over to the UK, gotta go down to London a few days before Magenta's launch. I need that freakin' weekend in Liverpool like a hole in the head. My wife doesn't seem to realize the amount of work involved in organizing this benefit, it's the weekend after her launch. Logan and I need to be here or in the LA office not in some freakin' little ole English town. God she drives me crazy.'

Brooke laughed. 'That's what you get for marrying a crazy Brit. Look, it'll be fun, just see it as a weekend to let off some steam before the main event. Everything will be organized by then and any last minute hitches will be sorted by the people you pay the mega bucks to, to sort that shit out.'

'Yeah, I'm just trying to think of any excuse to get out of this thing, but as Magenta's manager, I should be there.'

'As her husband, you should be there,' she winked at him as she wrapped her dress back around herself.

He laughed. 'Get out of here kiddo, I got work to do. You have distracted me for long enough.' She reached for her Birkin bag. 'Didn't hear you complaining before.'

'Well, you coulda licked my balls.'

She grinned. 'Max, has anyone ever told you, you're an ass?'

'All the time, baby.'

She headed for the door. 'Laters.'

'Oh, Brooke?'

She turned back round. 'Yes, Mr Maxwell?'

He felt movement between his legs at the naughty schoolgirl look she was giving him and he loved it when she called him Mr Maxwell, highlighting his importance. He tried to push the horny thoughts out of his head, he was trying to be serious.

'You do know we gotta be careful in England, right? Might have to cool it a bit, the press are animals over there.'

'Whatever you say, Maxie baby.' She spun round on the heel of her Jimmy Choos and was gone.

'Say hi, to Logan for me.' he called after her.

Maxie baby, he hated being called that, but at least that stopped his cock from thinking any further thoughts.

Brooke Hudson found her husband sprawled across the sofa in his entertainment room. Cigarette in one hand, bottle of Bud in the other, he was watching the first cut of Magenta's new video. She smiled to herself, she'd spent the afternoon locked in Max's bedroom, whilst her husband was spending the afternoon with Magenta. All be it technically speaking. And they say Americans don't do irony. She plonked a kiss on his head. 'Hey, sweetie.'

Logan didn't look up, his eyes totally glued on the screen. 'Hey, gorgeous. She's looking good isn't she? Song sounds amazing too.'

'Yes, Logan. Oh, by the way, Max says hi.'

'Ah, I wondered where he was.'

'I'm just gonna grab a shower. Didn't get time to have one at the gym.'

'Cool, babe, we don't have to leave for an hour. Max wasn't still at the gym was he? I need to give him a call.'

'He left just before me, should be back at the office or home by now.'

Brooke sauntered out of the room and into the huge reception area of their duplex penthouse. She wandered up the curved staircase to her en-suite bedroom. Bless Logan, he was so trusting. It made it so much easier. She loved Logan, he was totally hot and just like Max and Magenta they made a perfect couple. She met Logan on the set of her last movie, he was visiting her co-star, the English actor Rupert Seagrove, and apparently they were good friends. She wouldn't say it was love at first sight the first time she saw Logan, but she there was a definite attraction between them. She'd just come out of a messy divorce from a reality TV star who thought by being associated with her, his star would rise. He just became known as 'Mr Carrington, (her then maiden name), Brooke's other half'. He didn't like it, she didn't care. As long as the sex was good she was happy. She always thought she had a bit of a sex addiction, undiagnosed of course. So after she'd dumped Mr Reality TV, once his consistent moaning finally got the better of her, she was on the lookout for a replacement. Enter stage right, the luscious Logan. At 6ft 2 and dazzling Daniel Craig type blue eyes, she was hooked. She invited him to her trailer, if she remembered rightly he never did get to pop in on Rupert. They were married as soon as her quickie divorce came through. She soon learned that Logan and Max came as a package, they'd been frat bros in college and started Maximum Music in the basement of Logan's mom's house almost twenty years ago. It was now the biggest music company in the States, if not the world, as Max was fond of saying. Logan was the creative one of the two, he was the one more in tune with the artists whereas Max was all about the bottom line. It was a perfect partnership.

So, being married to Logan meant spending a lot of time with Max and Magenta, they fast became best friends. Well that's what the media thought, they were the fabulous four. The real story was that she and Magenta tolerated each other, in any other walk of life their paths wouldn't have crossed but because they were married to two of the most powerful men in America, they formed an unlikely friendship. A friendship that was often laced with too much forced smiling, too many patronising comments. They were wary of each other, they were both strong women, both fighting to see who was the strongest. Privately Brooke often wondered why Max had married her, he was well known for his strong dominate persona and Magenta was not the type of woman who easily gave in. Max seemed concerned about this trip to the UK, she was looking forward to it, she'd googled Liverpool and there was plenty of designer shops, she would be fine. He seemed concerned about the press over there, well she wouldn't be doing anything to draw attention to their little fling. Magenta's bad side was not somewhere she wanted to be, so if that meant cooling things with Max for a bit, then so be it. She should probably pay some attention to her husband anyway, he was after all voted one of the top five hottest men in the country for good reason. Although Max was voted number two, Brooke smiled to herself, she did however trump Magenta on that score as she got the best of both Max and Logan.

Chapter Three

The Liver Bird hotel, Liverpool

Magenta was in her hotel suite discussing the plans for the launch with her PA, Jody. She was convinced Max had been having a word in her ear, as she seemed to be Team Max on the whole 'let's launch the album in LA' argument. Jody sat opposite her, iPad in one hand, iPhone in the other and a pen behind her ear, she wasn't sure what the pen was for, there wasn't a single piece of paper in sight.

'Magenta, darling,' Jody began in her softly spoken voice, with just a hint of New Jersey in it. 'Max is very concerned about having the launch here when there is so much he needs to attend to back home and I have to be honest, I agree with him. Are we really gonna get Brooke and Logan over here? Not to mention Johnny and his band, he's unreliable at the best of times and that's before we get to the guest list for the Manor House.'

'Trust me honey. It'll be fine. You know how persuasive I can be. I had a text off Johnny this morning letting me know he can't wait to catch up.'

'In New York, maybe...but Liverpool?' The pretty brunette wrinkled up her petite nose. Magenta pushed herself up out of the chair and walked over to the floor to ceiling window, giving her a view across the Mersey that could rival any view in Manhattan. She sighed to herself. Why was no one getting this? Why did nobody understand how important this was to her? Jase would get it, or whatever his name was now...she pushed that thought right out of her head. Now wasn't the time to start thinking about Jason Lomax. She spun back round.

'I wish people would stop doing that, Liverpool is a great city, it can certainly hold its own. December 2007, Bon Jovi perform at the 'little old' Empire theatre in front of the bloody Queen, May 2012, Guns 'N' Roses perform at the Echo arena, all be it, three hours late and that was nothing to do with poor transport links, it was Axl refusing to get his lazy cycling short, rock star arse on the stage and in between that Green Day, Lady

Gaga, Beyonce....I could go on, but what's the point when it's falling on deaf ears.'

'Look, I get it, I really do. You wanna show those people who thought you were a nobody years ago that you've made it and there's no better place to do that than in your own back yard. But sweetie, you don't need to do that, you are the biggest star in the UK right now.' Magenta nodded slowly, that statement wasn't just to pacify her, she had outsold Adele last year, only just although Adele had beaten her in the American market. 'Jody, how long have you been my PA and about the only bloody person I can trust, which, I might add includes my husband in that statement?' 'Too long!'

'Yep, long enough to know I have never quite felt settled anywhere, well, here and now I do and I know I can't stay here forever, but just for now I'm home and I wanna enjoy that time. Yes, maybe I wanna show a few people that Maggie from The Dingle made it, but I also want to give something back to the people of this city who bought my records. I don't want to be the type of person who tries to hide where they came from or do a Ringo Starr and slag off my home town. I know Max has a problem with that, but that's not for you to worry about, I'll sort him out.'

Jody smiled at the person who was not just her boss, but also her friend.

'Ok, I'll back you on this, but you know I'm damn well gonna get my ass kicked by Max.'

She laughed. 'Let him kick away and have a tantrum, he's full of shit.'

'There you go again, I can never figure you and Max out,' she glanced at her iPad which was signalling the arrival of lots of messages. 'Look hon, I'm gonna head back to my room and deal with these messages. See you downstairs for dinner?'

Magenta nodded. 'Yeah, got some stuff to do myself.'

In fact, all Magenta had to do was think about Jason Lomax aka Hunter Cole who was somewhere in this building. She kicked off the Louboutin's and her fitted jacket, she really wasn't comfortable in this smart get up. She much preferred her rock chick image of jeans and DM's, but she was thirty three, how long could she pull that look off for?

It was 1995 when she last saw Jase, she was seventeen and had been back and forth from London for the past eighteen months doing various modelling shoots. She'd just completed her first advert, it was for a new brand of sanitary towel and she had to roller blade through a department store. Like she'd do that anyway, regardless of whether she was on a period or not. The money was good, so it was worth it. She'd headed back up to Liverpool on the train, beyond excited to see Jase, it had been almost a month. She knew he wasn't totally thrilled about her modelling career and it had caused a few arguments but she was convinced their relationship was strong enough to cope with the long periods of separation when she was in London. When the train pulled into Lime Street, he was there waiting for her. She could spot him a mile off. Jeans, Kickers jumper and a leather jacket. His chestnut coloured hair in the latest boy band style of 'curtains'. She always thought he looked a bit like Howard from Take That, he would tell her to 'do one' whenever she said it. Either way he was definitely the best looking lad in their year at school. She ran towards him, a big smile on her face. He hugged her tightly.

'You ok?' she asked, noticing that he seemed a bit quiet after she'd babbled on for five minutes about the ad.

He nodded. 'I've got a surprise for you. We're staying at the Adelphi tonight.'

'The Adelphi? Jase, me mam will kill me. She'd go mad if she knew we were sleeping together, I'm meant to be a good Catholic girl, remember? She won't let me stay overnight with you.'

'It's all sorted, she thinks you're staying at Trina's.'

She grinned, flicking her hair out of her face as the wind blew it into her eyes. 'What's the occasion?' she suddenly wished she hadn't asked as it dawned on her. He was going to propose, that's why he seemed a bit funny. He was nervous. She didn't want to spoil the surprise. 'It doesn't matter,' she reached up on her tiptoes and kissed him softly. He grabbed her hand. 'Come 'ead, you don't need anything, Trina got your stuff sorted.'

She remembered how excited she felt as they dashed to the hotel, it was literally moments away from the station, but for some reason every second seemed to matter. They checked into The Adelphi, the oldest hotel in the city, as Mr and Mrs Lomax. She knew the receptionist wasn't soft, they looked too young to be let out, never mind married, but she gave them their room key, no questions asked. She didn't want to ask him where he got the money from, he'd never take any of her modelling money from her. That was often a cause of arguments, Jase was proud, quite old fashioned when it came to money. He wanted to provide for her, not the other way round. So, she didn't even mention how much the hotel must've cost. As soon as they got into the room they headed straight for the bed, sitting side by side on it, holding hands. She could tell there was something he was nervous about, she wished he'd just come out and ask her, but knowing Jase, he'd have something totally romantic planned for later on when he popped the question. She was only seventeen but she knew she wanted to spend the rest of life with him. Who wouldn't want to wake up to him every morning? She was saving her modelling money and hopefully they'd have enough for a deposit on a nice house, maybe even on The Wirral. She'd been to Parkgate as a kid and always had dreams of living in one of those big houses.

'Mags?'

She looked up at him his blue eyes looking down on her

with so much love in them. God, she loved those eyes.

'Yes?'

'Y'know I love you? More than anything?'

'Course I do, soft lad. I love you an all.'

'Good,' he leaned in towards her, kissing her lips and pulling her close.

Although they had been sleeping together for a while, they were still in the early stages of their physical relationship, learning how to pleasure each other. They didn't always have the time to spend on sex like they wanted as it was generally rushed sex sessions in the bathroom at his mam's house. That night had been different, the whole night stretched ahead of them. Thinking back on that night made her shiver with delight but also with sadness. The first part of the evening had been amazing. Jase had taken her to a place of pure ecstasy, in their usual rushed sex session she had never had an orgasm, it was always a quickie, but that night, wow. He'd laid her down on the bed, slowly taking off her clothes, kissing every newly naked part of her, cupping her small breasts with his warm hands, placing her nipples in his hot mouth. That alone made her want to scream out loud. She lay on the bed naked, but he was still fully clothed.

'Jase, get naked with me, I never get to feel your skin against mine.'

She hadn't even finished her sentence before he began to strip off. He lay on top of her, pulling her into his arms as they stroked each other's skin, exploring parts of each other that they normally had to ignore. He ran his fingers across her stomach and over her hips, leaving a trail of goose bumps. She kept stroking the area where his hip bone jutted out, at seventeen he hadn't yet filled out to the man he would become but that hip bone was almost like a sneak preview of when the rest of his body became more muscular. She leaned over, kissing his neck, listening to the moan that made his throat vibrate. His light touch all over her body made her feel like she was being touched for the first time, she knew his body intimately, just like he knew hers, but this felt so different, like they'd taken it to a whole new level.

She flicked the hair that had flopped into his eyes out of the way, his hair felt damp with sweat and there was a small trickle of perspiration running down his chest. She followed the trickle with her fingers. He took her face in her hands, looking her straight in the eyes.

'I will never love anyone like I love you, Mags.'

Before she could question the weirdness of that comment he'd moved his hands to her hips and lifted her easily on to his erection. She gasped with pleasure as she rocked against him, feeling him in complete rhythm underneath her and as she moved, he rubbed her clitoris. She dug her nails into his shoulders as he brought her to climax, her whole body shuddered as she collapsed on top of him. That was the first of many orgasms that night and she fell asleep blissfully happy, safe in the arms of the lad that she loved, knowing he loved her just as much.

Magenta couldn't help the thoughts of the next morning flooding her mind. Whoever said pain was so close to pleasure had that right. She'd woken up alone the next morning. She thought Jase was in the shower. She allowed herself a few moments to bask in the afterglow of the night before. If only it could always be like this instead of a quick shag in his Ford Fiesta or in his mam's bathroom. She suddenly realised the room was quiet, she couldn't hear the shower running. Rolling onto her side she could see an envelope on Jase's pillow, with her name on it. Her stomached flipped, whatever was in that letter was something he couldn't tell her to her face, it couldn't be good. She opened it slowly, it was written on Adelphi letter headed paper.

Mags,

I lay awake long after you fell asleep, trying to work out how to tell you this. I wanted to wake you so many times, but you look so beautiful when you sleep. (Not that you don't when you're awake). Tonight has been sound, far better than I could've ever thought and I hope you will carry tonight in your heart always. I know I will.

My dad has been working back in Chicago for the past six months, I never mentioned it to you, I didn't think it was important. I was too wrapped up in us. Turns out its mega important. We're leaving Liverpool, he wants us to move back to Chicago and nearer to his parents.

Me ma won't let me stay here on my own. So I have to go.

This is our last night together babe, I leave today. I am so sorry to leave you like this, I'll come back for you one day, promise.

Love ya la,

Jase xxx

P.S. Don't worry about the hotel bill, it's settled.

She'd lain in bed in the hotel room, all alone for hours, sobbing her heart out she clutched the pillow he'd slept on to her chest. Breathing in the smell of his Fahrenheit aftershave did little to comfort her. It was only when the manager came to kick her out that she dragged her sorry self round to Trina's. A month later she moved to London and threw herself into her modelling jobs. Her heartache made her lose a few pounds and suddenly she was hugely in demand.

Jase broke his promise, he never came back for her. So to say she was surprised when she bumped into him earlier was an understatement. Now she'd gotten over her shock she was desperate to see him again, but she was damned if she'd make the first move.

There was a knock at the door, she opened it to a bell boy who handed her a note. 'Sorry to disturb you Ms Valentina.'

She smiled. 'Don't worry, its fine,' she took the note from him, opening it up as she shut the door with her foot. Dinner at the Panoramic 8pm, J x

She shook her head, Jody's battery on her phone must've run out, she really must get her a second phone.

Chapter Four

Los Angeles, Bel Air - Johnny Kidd's Mansion

'Yeah man, lovin' that intro, that's the kinda start that'll get the fans clappin' along on tour the second they hear it. Reckon you've just invented our own Radio GaGa, Fly my friend.'

Fly MacFly, hit his cymbal in appreciation. Fly MacFly so called because his drumming was fly, the Mac because his surname was MacIntyre and the second Fly because he was always fishing for women. 'Cheers Johnny, with those lyrics you've got down, reckon this could be an amazing track, just need that lazy ass Sloth to get the chords tighter on the chorus and we're done.'

They both looked over to their guitarist Sloth, who was in his usual position of asleep on the sofa.

The band were in the recording studio in Johnny's house, laying down tracks for their next album. Their band, Broken Arrow were one of the biggest rock bands right now. Johnny Kidd was the enigmatic front man of the group. He always performed on stage in just his jeans, the ladies loved his denim clad butt and bare chest, the guys loved their kick ass songs. It was win win. Johnny had the typical rock star look going on, collar length messy dark hair (that actually took ages to style), he always had an American flag bandanna in. Tattoos on his muscular arms, if he was gonna be half naked on stage, he needed to look ripped, which included a superman tattoo in homage to his idol Jon Bon Jovi. Man, if he could even have half the career he'd had. He didn't even have his own jet yet, he was close, but no cigar. Despite being an international rock star, he didn't do drugs, often, or smoke, he left that to Sloth and Fly respectively. He wasn't a total wuss, he did love his Bourbon oh and his other weakness, women. This week, his current flame was Savannah, she was a finalist on Starmaker. He'd done a master class on the show as a favour to Logan. These talent show things weren't usually his bag, he'd worked his ass off to get where he was today. His career hadn't begun by going on a TV show for five minutes then having a number one album the following week. But he'd owed Logan one, so he'd gone along for 'rock week'. Fly had laughed his ass off, told him he wouldn't go near that show with his neighbour's cock. Still, Johnny was always the 'face' of the band, it was his name the fans shouted, so he figured no such thing as bad publicity.

Blonde, buxom belle of the South, Savannah Zagger caught his eye straight away and it wasn't because of her voice which was pretty mediocre. She was perfect one night stand material. He'd shagged her in the make-up room. Someone had then tweeted a picture of them coming out of the room looking a bit dishevelled. He thought he'd be in deep shit and crossed a line but Max couldn't have been happier. Savannah was the one Maximum Music wanted as the winner, she hadn't been doing too well in the public vote, obviously because her voice was shit, but now she was hanging out with the Rock God Johnny Kidd, she was number one in the (not so) secret public votes. Max wanted him to keep up this relationship until the final, Savannah's voice could be auto tuned on her records so that wouldn't be a problem and then he could ditch her, giving Savannah a whole album full of heartbreak, a la Taylor Swift. Instant best-seller. So Johnny had ended up in the audience for the live shows.

Again, Fly laughed his ass off. Sloth wasn't assed, he was too busy drinking and sleeping. Three weeks and counting till the final, he couldn't wait...freedom. Thinking about freedom reminded him of the text he had that morning.

'Hey, Fly, how d'ya fancy a trip over the pond in January?'

Still tapping away at his drums he nodded. 'Could do, what for? Interviews?'

'Nah, got a text off Magenta, she's invited us to her launch in Liverpool, wants to talk about a duet.'

Fly laughed. 'No way man, we don't duet with chicks, we fuck chicks.'

'Why not? Jon Bon Jovi did a duet with LeAnn Rimes.'

'Oh man, if I didn't know you so well I'd swear you were gay with your man crush on JBJ.'

Johnny snorted. 'I just admire the guy, he's a New Jersey boy, done good like me and wouldn't you love a thirty year career like his? Our own jet, you could be still be banging away at your drum kit when you're fifty.'

Dropping his drum sticks and reaching for a cigarette, Fly shook his head. 'The only thing I'll be banging when I'm fifty is a different twenty year old chick every night.'

'So, you aspire to be a dirty old man?'

Lighting his Marlboro, he shrugged. 'Sounds good to me.'

Johnny laughed. 'You ain't never gonna grow up are you Fly?'

'Who wants to?'

'Anyway, I talked to Logan and he said Max is real keen for this duet.'

'Ah, Max, smax. He's full of bullshit. Like it would even work, us and Magenta.'

'She's got a rock chick sound, I could see us doing some kinda rock anthem, not a power ballad, that'd be schmaltzy shit.'

'I ain't convinced bro, you haven't exactly made some great decisions lately...how is the lovely Savannah, by the way?'

'Bite me, you dick.'

Fly laughed, smoke billowing out of his mouth. 'Look, I just don't think our fans would be into a Broken Arrow, Magenta Valentina song. It doesn't even sound right.'

Johnny pulled his iPhone out of his pocket. 'Let's ask 'em then,' he tweeted an update.

@JohnnyKidd Thinking of releasing with Magenta Valentina, whaddya y'all think?

Fly shook his head. 'You and freakin' Twitter, that's what got you in the shit with Savannah.'

Johnny was too busy looking at his phone. 'Ok, here's some of the responses. 'Man she's dope. Go for it' 'Great voice, she'd rock with you guys' 'She's hot give her one for me, Johnny #luckybastard'

'All that proves is that people think she's hot.'

'Look, you know Max will get his own way, so we may as well get on board with it, at least we get to write the song.'

Fly sighed. 'Ok, but you can go to Liverpool on your own, I ain't goin' it'll be freakin' cold over there.'

'Fine with me, I'll happily go to the land of The Beatles...and somewhere full of English chicks...'

'Ah man. I could be tempted.'

Chapter Five

The Liver Bird Hotel, Liverpool

At ten to eight Magenta was heading down to reception, the building that housed the Panoramic restaurant was next door. It also happened to be the tallest building in the city and the restaurant had a prime space at the top. As she walked through reception the manager scuttled up to her, God he was such a creep.

'Evening Ms Valentina. I trust everything is to your liking?'

She smiled. 'Yes, thank you. I'm just off for dinner.'

'I won't keep you, but don't forget, if you need anything, don't hesitate to call me.'

'Thanks Tom.'

As she stalked past him he whispered. 'It's Tim...'

Although she didn't have far to walk, literally two minutes, it took her nearly ten minutes as she stopped for a few photos with fans. She walked into the building, the restaurant actually had a reception in the foyer as the restaurant was thirty four floors above her head. She spoke to the concierge.

'Good evening, Ms Magenta Valentina, I have a table reserved for 8 o'clock.'

'Ah, yes madam. Mr Cole is already waiting for you. I'll just call the lift, it will be a moment or so.'

He moved away.

'Shit,' she mouthed. J, wasn't Jody, it was Jase. Holy crap. She was woefully unprepared for this. She quickly tapped a text message to Jody. Sorry love, feel a bit sick, will skip dinner. It wasn't far from the truth. Her stomach felt like there was an Olympic gymnastics squad in there. Bloody Jase or Hunter or whatever the hell he was called these days.

'Ms Valentina, lift is ready.'

She stuck a smile on her face and nodded politely. Once the lift doors closed she breathed out and leant against the wall. Thirty four floors meant she had a bit of time to think. She'd gone through this moment so many times in her head, what would she say if she ever saw him again? Now she had the opportunity, everything was flying out of her head. She looked at her reflection in the lift mirrors. How did she look? How would he think she looked? Her long auburn hair was piled loosely on top of her head, strands falling down sexily to frame her face. She was wearing a simple black Victoria Beckham shift dress, matched with red Jimmy Choos...oh God red shoes, could that deliver a message anything other than, fuck me? The lift pinged. Show time, Valentina she told herself.

She strode with confidence through the restaurant, following a waiter who was leading her to her table. She knew she was attracting looks, she always did. As she neared the table, he stood up to greet her.

'Mags,' he grinned, a soft kiss landing on her cheek as he took her elbow, guiding her to her seat. He nodded to the waiter. 'Champagne, please.'

She looked out of the window. 'Nice view. The city looks beautiful lit up.'

'Yes, it does,' he replied looking straight at her.

She leaned forward slightly. 'Look, Jase...'

'Mags,' his voice became stern. 'You can't call me that.'

'But....but, you signed your note with a J.'

'I know, I was careless, I shouldn't have done that, its Hunter now, has been for a long time and you need to call me that.'

'So, why the name change and why Hunter Cole?'

He was silent as the waiter poured their champagne, only once he'd gone did he speak again. 'The reason is a bit of a long story and probably one for another time…the choice of name however, well Hunter was easy, it's kinda my job, again one for another time and the Cole...well that was simple. Where did we have our first kiss?'

'At school', she frowned.

'Which was on what road?'

Her green eyes flicked across his face as it dawned on her. 'Cole Street.'

He nodded. 'I'm sorry I ran out on you like that, that morning.'

'I never had you down as a coward Ja...Hunter,' the name sounded alien on her lips. He sighed. 'I couldn't watch your heart break Mags, not when mine was already shattering into a million pieces.'

She looked down at her glass, she needed to ask him something that had played on her mind for the last seventeen years. She looked back up, straight into his eyes, God they were so blue, how could she have forgotten what those eyes did to her? 'So, did you?'

A frown appeared across his handsome rugged face. 'Did I what?'

'Ever love anyone like you loved me?'

He tilted his head to one side, smiling slowly. 'You're the only one who ever broke my heart Mags.'

She laughed bitterly. 'Me? Break your heart? You were the one who left.'

'Kicking and screaming,' he took a sip of his champagne. As he set his glass back down he spoke again. 'Nobody else has ever broken my heart, although it's fair to say I've probably broken a few more. Never been big on commitment. Not since I lost the girl I thought I was gonna marry.'

'You didn't lose me soft lad, you left me. There is a difference. You said you were coming back for me.'

'Yeah, I noticed how you waited, how IS Max by the way? Wouldn't have had him down as your type.'

'Don't even start with that....do you have any idea how it was when you'd gone? I went off to London, lost loads of weight, 'cos I couldn't bloody well eat but as a result, got loads of modelling jobs. But suddenly the name Maggie Vale didn't fit, so my agency decided to change it and I became Magenta Valentina. I went along with it, I was only just seventeen, didn't know any better. I was miserable, my model shots looked great 'cos I had this 'look', the love sick look. So I just carried on along that track, learning to live without you, realising that you weren't coming back, that you'd lied. I used to get Trina to pop round to your old house in case you were there. Before I knew it, I had a number one record and I'd married my manager. Max is a lot of things, but he took care of me when there was no one else to really give a shit,' she'd said all this in a low voice so as not to attract attention, she'd even smiled a few times so anyone looking would think it was a normal conversation.

Hunter reached across the table, taking her hand in his. She snatched it back. 'You can't just do that, you can't pop up when I least expect it, kiss my cheek, hold my hand without a bloody explanation.'

'I'm so sorry, Mags ...'

'Magenta, now. If I don't get to call you by you real name, then you can't call me by mine. Even though I bloody well hate it.' she burst out laughing, in that uneasy way when people don't know whether to laugh or cry.

He also began to laugh. 'Oh honey, this is crazy. This isn't how this was supposed to go.'

The arrival of their starters caused their laughter to quieten down. She took the break in the conversation as a chance to look at him properly without him being able to interrupt her. His thick chestnut hair had a slightly wavy and dishevelled look about it, but kinda sexy too. Long gone was the 90's boy band hairstyle. She wondered idly if it would still feel the same to run her fingers through. His eyes, still just as blue, still having a strange effect on her, just looked a little older and maybe a touch wary. He had always looked fit but now his face had a craggy handsomeness about it, making him look even hotter than before. All this gorgeousness was even before she got to his body. He had on a crisp white shirt, highlighting his tanned skin and his muscles clearly visible through the thin material. The seventeen year old body she'd known so well had indeed developed into a fine specimen. His shoulders and chest were broad and strong and she'd bet her arse he had a six pack under there too. These thoughts running through her mind were enough to send her nipples into a frenzy, she just hoped to God he couldn't see them through the material of her dress, she didn't dare look down and draw attention to her herself. Instead she picked up the champagne glass and downed it in one. Setting it down she picked up a fork. 'So then, Mr Cole, how was this supposed to go? You know everything about my life. My modelling days, my singing career. I bet you've even downloaded some of my songs and I know you've googled my wedding pics.'

He looked slightly embarrassed. 'Yeah, nice dress by the way, shame about the husband. And your songs? Yep, got every single one on my iPod. I love the one that has the line 'If you walked back into my life tomorrow...'

'I'd love you like yesterday,' she finished, her eyes on him.

'Was that about us? Did you write that about me?'

She gave a throaty laugh. 'Honey, I sing the song, I have a team of writers who work on the lyrics,' she paused. 'But, the video for that song. It's fair to say you were the inspiration behind it. I was supposed to look all intense, broken hearted. It wasn't hard to find that place,' she shook her head sadly.

'Believe me, I wanted to stay.'

'It was a long time ago now, you think you know me 'cos you've googled me, listened to my songs, but you only know sixteen year old Maggie, you don't know the woman I've become. Although in fairness, you are the only one who knows my middle name. But I swear to God, if you ever tell anyone, I won't be responsible for my actions.'

He grinned. 'You ain't changed that much girl, you're still the same Mags who could always make me smile.'

'So what about you Hunter Cole, you still the same guy deep down? If I googled you, what would I find? Are you married? Kids? I know nothing about you,' she couldn't even get used to his American accent.

He sighed and looked out of the window for a few seconds as if to gather his thoughts. 'You'd find nothing on Hunter Cole, I suppose he's a stage name...'

'You're an actor?'

'I suppose you could say that, but not your usual run of the mill actor. I'm not famous. I guess, I just have learnt to live my life being someone else.'

'Why did you have to change your name? It sounds like you didn't want to...'

'It's a long story and one I really can't go into now, here. I will tell you what I can, when I can. But to answer your easiest questions. No, never married, never had kids...didn't ever seem on my radar and I guess I always thought...'

He was interrupted by her mobile ringing. She glanced down at the caller ID. 'Shit, its Max. I better take this,' she picked up her phone. 'Darling, hello. How are you?'

Hunter leaned back in his seat, casually watching her on the phone, watching her full lips move, her eyebrows as she frowned, her cat like green eyes roll as she talked. He tuned into the conversation, appearing to not be taking any notice. He was pretty good at stuff like that. Obviously he couldn't hear the other side of the conversation, but he concentrated on her body language to pretty much work out how it was going. Between that and the change in her voice, making it sound strained, it didn't take a genius to work out all was not well. 'Have you seen the new video? Logan loves it,' she nodded as she listened to the voice on the other end of the phone. 'Good, glad you like it. Has Johnny called you yet? She paused. 'Well he will do, think we're going ahead with the duet...oh and can you get Brooke to call me, can't seem to reach her at the moment... Good, good, yes everything's fine here. Just bumped into an old friend, just having dinner,' her eyes flicked back over to him. 'Yes I will do.'

'You OK? You sound a bit out of breath.'

'Well don't overdo it at the gym, you don't wanna give yourself a heart attack.'

'Next week some time, I'll see you then.'

She ended the call. He raised an eyebrow at her. 'What?'

He shrugged. 'Haven't seen your husband for over a week and there's no, miss you darling, love you?'

'We're not that kinda couple, we don't do lovey-dovey.'
'That's not the Mags I remember.'

She frowned.

'Love ya, soft lad...you never left to go to London without saying it, you never left me ma's to go home without saying it. Hell, if we'd have had mobile phones then, bet you'd have text me it every day,' he smiled at her.

She blushed. 'I...I said it 'cos I meant it.'

He raised an eyebrow. 'So, you don't mean it with Max?'

She shrugged. 'We're a business deal, it's complicated.'

'Does he make you happy?'

She let her finger trace the rim of her glass as she considered her answer. 'Probably not. No.'

He leaned forward. 'He doesn't hurt you does he? Or make you sad?'

She grinned. 'Ah, listen to you, coming over all knight in shining armour. I'd have to give one for him to hurt me and as for making me cry?' She shook her head. 'My mascara is far too expensive to be wasting it on tears for him.'

'Hmmm, the Mags I knew didn't have such a hard heart.'

'The Mags you knew hadn't had her heart broken.'

'We all make mistakes,' he lifted his glass up to hers. 'Here's to old friends and new beginnings.'

She raised her glass to his. 'Looks like things just got interesting, Mr Cole.'

After their meal Hunter insisted on walking her back to the hotel, seemed stupid not to when they were both going the same way. He took the opportunity to enquire about her family.

'So, I bet your ma and brothers are glad you're home?'

She looked up at him. 'Ma? Didn't take you long to return to scouse.'

'Obviously the company I'm in. So how are they? I used to love your ma's cooking.'

She shrugged. 'Wouldn't know, haven't spoken to them for ages. They don't like Max.'

'Ah, awkward.'

She nodded. 'Just a bit.'

They wandered into the foyer, still deep in conversation. She looked up to see the manager running over.

'God, I hate this guy, he's so smarmy,' she said through gritted teeth but still maintaining her professional smile.

'Me too,' he grimaced.

'Ah Ms Valentina, lovely evening I presume? And Mr Cole, what a surprise to see you fraternizing with our most important guest.'

'If you must know Tim, Magenta and I have a friend in common and we were catching up over dinner.' Like he was going to tell Tim he was Magenta Valentina's first love. He didn't trust that guy as far as he could throw him, although to be fair, he knew he could launch him across the foyer if the situation required it. He saw Mags frown slightly at the explanation he'd given, but then he saw her face soften. She thought he was protecting her, in a way, he was.

'Well, if there's nothing else you need, I'll bid you good night.' With that he scuttled off. She touched his arm lightly, he spun round to face her. 'Thanks....Hunter, I had a really lovely evening. We must do it again,' she reached up on her tiptoes, leaving a red lipstick mark on his cheek. She turned and walked off towards the lift.

It was only as she lay in bed that evening that it dawned on her that the only thing she'd discovered about Hunter Cole was that he wasn't married and didn't have any kids. Jase's new persona was still the mystery it was when the evening had begun

Chapter Six

Max Maxwell's Office, Maximum Music Corp. NYC

'I don't care if he's meeting the President himself, if that ass hole is not in my office at 9am sharp tomorrow he will find himself without a contract,' Max slammed the phone down, freakin' agents, who the hell did they think they were messing with? He gave the orders. Not them. He ran a hand through his jet black coloured hair, then realised he'd messed his perfectly styled hair up. He popped into his bathroom to fix the situation. Max Maxwell never had a hair out of place. Cowell had his trademark T. Shirts and jeans. He had his perfect hair, perfect smile and Armani suits. Cowell could go for the 'casual look' if he wanted but that wasn't for Max, he wanted the powerful and don't mess with me look.

When he came out of the bathroom he found Brooke sitting at his desk. Whereas Magenta took a lot of pride in her appearance, either nailing the Rock Chick look to a T, or dressing as Max's wife she always looked knockout. Brooke on the other hand, could sometimes look a little trailer trash. Today for instance, she had a dress that just covered her ass and boobs, he wasn't sure how Logan could let his wife dress like that. Although as a mistress, he kinda liked it.

'What brings you here?'

'Well, I popped in to see Logan but he's in a meeting so I wondered if you had a spare five minutes?'

He could feel his cock twitching at the suggestive way she spoke. 'I've locked your door and I sent Delores on a break,' she grinned, referring to his secretary. He could rely on Delores to be discreet, she'd kept many goings on in his office to herself. The hefty bonus he gave her every Christmas probably helped.

She stood up, dragging her finger nails across his desk as she walked slowly towards him. 'So, I had a real naughty idea, something I know you'd get off on.'

'I'm all ears baby,' she looked down at his pants, his bulge very apparent. 'I'd say you're all cock. While I do something about that, why don't you give Magenta a little call? Bet you haven't spoken to her for days. Reckon she's all lonely in little ole Liverpool.'

'You are a wicked woman,' he grinned. He pulled his phone out of his pocket and unzipped his pants at the same time, releasing his cock. She sank to her knees, stroking him as he put a call into his wife. She could hear the conversation as she sucked away at him, like it was a giant ice cream.

'I'm fine, Magenta, sweetheart.'

'No Johnny hasn't called, I'm sure the call will come soon though.'

'Sounds perfect.'

'Yeah, I'll get Brooke to call, she kinda has her hands full at the moment though,' he stifled a groan as from underneath his desk Brooke squeezed his balls tight.

'Ok, you have fun with your old buddy,' that came out a bit strangled as he spoke.

'Yes, fine honey. Just too much over exertion at the gym.'

'Don't worry about me I'm as hard as nails. When are you flying home?'

'Ok, bye sweetheart.'

He ended the call and shot his load into Brooke's mouth. Man that was hot. On the phone to his wife, knowing that Logan was in the conference room down the hall. Brooke stood up.

'You all done now Max?'

'Do you have to rush off, I'm so unbelievably turned on right now, look I'm all hard again.'

She tutted. 'I can't leave you like that. I do have an urgent appointment, although I could squeeze you in. She sat back on his desk, opening her legs to reveal herself to him. 'Ah man, you're not wearing any panties.'

After leaving Max's office, Brooke thought she better pop in to see if Logan was done with his meeting. Last thing she wanted was office gossip getting back to him that she'd been in the building and hadn't gone to see her husband. She walked straight into his office without knocking, her husband was on a video call with Johnny Kidd whose beautiful rock star face was on the plasma screen mounted on the wall.

'Hey, Logan, the missus is looking hot,' Johnny grinned, winking at Brooke.

Logan turned his chair round, mouthing a 'Hi' at Brooke. She was too busy looking at Johnny.

She gave him a small wave, and a flick of her hair. 'Hey Johnny, looking good.'

Logan coughed. 'When you two have finished flirtin', Johnny we got some stuff to figure out. We need to get you booked in for some studio time with Magenta.'

'Yeah, reckon we could do with doing that before Sloth goes into rehab, he's due for his next stint any time now. Also, Fly ain't hot on the idea, so sooner rather than later is better.'

'I hear ya, maybe you can get some lyrics down and we can look over them when we're all in England.'

'Sounds like a plan, gotta split. Catch ya laters.'

Johnny disappeared off the screen.

Brooke sighed. 'He gets more handsome every day.'

'I'm counting on it, that face makes me mega bucks. Keeps you in the luxury you're accustomed to,' he grinned at his wife. 'What brings you here?'

'Just passing.'

'Glad you did, I've invited Max for dinner tonight, I worry about him when Magenta isn't here. Why don't you see if Lara can make it too, you won't be bored then when I'm talking shop with Max.'

'Jeez, Logan, baby. You're a workaholic. Can't you have a night off? We haven't had a night just the two of us for ages.'

'Tomorrow night, I promise. Book us a table somewhere nice.'

His phone rang. 'Fly, what can I do for you? No, no, I promise it's a great idea...'

Brooke left her husband, full of promises to do it. She felt a bit guilty for cheating on him, but if she didn't, she'd get no attention at all.

As she left the building she sent a text to Lara, a wicked thought running through her head. If she could get Logan drunk enough at dinner to pass out then she and Lara could do their speciality. Long before she'd been in movies and Logan Hudson's wife, she'd been a waitress, along with Lara who'd been her friend since High School. Waitressing was shit money, putting on an all-girl show for punters wasn't. She and Lara had their routine down and were making a decent amount of money. One night they were getting it on for this oldish guy, he was loaded. He liked what he saw so much that he offered them a part in the movie he was producing. Brooke had been sceptical, she had visions of it being a porno. How wrong could she be? It was a film with Ashton Kutcher. Their careers had begun. Albeit she'd had more success than Lara, but she put that down to bagging a husband like Logan. You were nothing if you weren't part of a power couple. Lara didn't seem to mind, she was rich enough now, that's all she wanted although the movie parts had dried up a long time ago. She tried not to dwell on that too much. She thought Max would get a kick outta her and Lara's routine, she reckoned he'd well be up for a threesome. She'd had loads of threesomes, but what she really wanted to try was with two guys, all her previous ones had been with Lara and a guy. Max wouldn't entertain the idea of her and another bloke and Logan definitely wouldn't...she sighed, what she needed was some down and dirty rock stars, Johnny and Fly flitted through her mind. No, that would totally be playing with fire. She'd just have to fantasise, one day maybe she'd get two hot guys and be sandwiched in the middle of them, let them lavish all the attention on her for a change. She felt her stomach constrict at the thought.. God she was horny again. Maybe she should see a doctor about this sex obsession, only if he was hot of course.

Later that evening Brooke was still feeling frisky as she sat around the oversized dinner table in their New York Penthouse. Logan was to the left of her at the other end of the table, Lara opposite him and she was opposite Max. She hated this table, it was too God damn big. They could just about talk to each other, she had no chance of sliding her foot up Max's leg. She glanced down at Logan, he was busy sending a text message, he really was twenty four seven when it came to work.

Lara was unusually quiet, again because of the freakin' table she couldn't whisper to her to see if she was ok. Max had hardly spoken to her, but by the look on his face he clearly appreciated the cleavage she had on show. She'd dressed carefully in a low cut red dress. It was classy enough but also a bit vampy, it was obviously having the desired effect.

'Right, sorry about that guys, just had to confirm some dates for Magenta.' Logan looked back up, sweeping his mass of blonde hair out of his face. Originally from California, he still sported his surf dude look. He was all about the blonde hair, blue eyes, deep tan oh and that megawatt smile of his. Whereas Max presented a professional look in his designer suits, Logan preferred the laid back approach, Levi's and tour T-shirts for whatever band he was currently working with. He saw it as another way to advertise. Max looked up, frowning. 'What is my little angel up to now?'

'The free concert? I thought she'd run it past you?'

Max pushed his plate away. 'What the hell?'

Logan sighed. 'Typical Magenta. Coming through good cop first,' he smiled. 'Well, buddy, she's decided to put on a free concert. Its next week before she flies back. She's playing some little theatre as a freebie.'

'The hell she is, what does she think we're running here? A charity?'

Logan shrugged. 'She wants to give back, you forget she's the nation's sweetheart over there. The press will love her for this. Giving a free concert when some people probably can't afford tickets these days.'

'Again, we are not a charity. What next, popping over to Africa to sing to starving kids?'

'Max!' Brooke shouted.

'What? You know I'm right. The world is in a freakin' recession and she wants to blow an opportunity to make our company some money by doing freebies. She's deluded,' he pushed his chair back and stood up. 'I gotta make a call.'

Chapter Seven

The Liver Bird hotel, Liverpool

'What the fuck is going on over there?'

Jody held the phone away from her ear as she listened to Max's rant.

'You are supposed to be keeping an eye on her, not letting her get into trouble. Firstly, you've failed to talk her out of this God awful launch idea and now you're getting her to have a free fuckin' concert,' he raged.

'Max, relax its only one night at the Empire theatre. Logan was on board with it. It'll be great publicity, album downloads should go through the roof.'

'Of course Logan's ok about it, the schmuck doesn't see the bottom line of our finances, I do and we cannot afford free concerts. Where the hell is she? I can't get her on her phone. I'm her fuckin' manager, why was I the last to hear about this? You have my private number Jody, you should have called me.'

She sighed. 'I'm sorry Max, I really thought you'd be ok with it, Logan said...'

'Fuck Logan...look, I'm sorry I'm ranting at you. It's Magenta I'm mad at, I know what she's like, I know she will have ambushed any concerns you may have had about this stupid idea of hers,' he sighed. 'I guess, I just miss you.'

'It's ok.'

He grinned to himself, man, women were so easy to play. Of course it was the stupid broads fault, but he had to keep Jody on side, he needed her to be his eyes and ears when he wasn't around.

'Let's forget it for now, I'll take it up with Magenta when I can get her to answer her freakin' phone. Listen, why don't you take the afternoon off? You've got the company credit card, go and treat yourself to something nice, maybe something sexy you can show me when you get back over here?'

'Whatever you say Max, I gotta go, there's someone at the door.'

'Ok baby girl, I'll speak to you later. You're doing a great job.'

Jody flung the phone onto the bed, and followed it by flinging herself onto it. She'd lied, there was no one at the door. She was all alone as freakin' usual. God she hated Max, but she also knew she was head over heels in love with him too. He knew exactly what buttons to press. He could have her raging one minute then begging him for more the next when he flung her over his desk in his office.

63

She'd been Magenta's PA for five years, and Max's lover for three. He and Magenta had only been married for six months the first time she'd accidentally fallen onto his cock, like she couldn't miss the thing, it was huge. But somehow or other, she ended up right on top of it, she blamed the tequila, it never was a good idea to drink that. But what could she blame the remaining years on? She was twenty seven now, she'd given her twenties to some guy who was never gonna leave his wife, never loved her, just loved having a mistress. She wasn't the type of woman who would take any shit, she was a PA for God's sake, she had to have balls of steel, but when it came to Max, he just had this power. She saw it all the time, women just fell at his feet and he loved it. He thought his was more powerful than Barack Obama. Then there was Magenta, lovely, sweet Magenta, who seemed wary of most people, unsure who to trust, with good reason. Magenta who she'd been friends with for such a long time, what would it do to her if she ever found out she'd been sleeping with Max? She probably wouldn't give a damn about him, Magenta wasn't blind, she must know that her shit of a husband wasn't faithful, but she knew it'd really hurt her if she discovered he'd been shagging her. She was a terrible person. Magenta paid her to be her PA and Max paid her to be his spy, not that she told him everything...there were some things she would never tell him.

Hunter was pacing one of the tiny rooms at the back of the hotel where the staff quarters were. He thought he'd worked off the nervous energy that morning with his usual two hour work out. It took time and effort to keep this body in the condition it was in. He had the time and he needed to make the effort, it was part of his job. It surprised him that Mags hadn't questioned his role of 'hotel manager', did she really think he didn't have greater ambitions than that? The dreams they used to have. Ok, so he hadn't been overly happy about the modelling and the travelling down to London, only because he'd been stuck in Liverpool. He'd wanted to drop out of school and go with her, his strict dad wouldn't hear of it. But after he left school, they had plans. He'd been playing for Waterloo Rugby Club and had dreams of running out at Twickenham to captain England, they weren't just school boy dreams, he had a real chance. Rugby was his passion, after Mags and he could see a bright future for them. Him a rugby star, she a star of the catwalk.

Not only did he lose Mags when his dad uprooted them back to his dad's home town of Chicago, he lost rugby too. The nearest thing over there was American Football, he played it, he didn't want to lose his fitness for when he returned home. He didn't really fit in, his natural impulse was to play the way he'd always played, he couldn't get his head around new rules. He found himself hanging around with a load of drop outs, more out of boredom and to annoy his dad more than anything else. Revenge for taking him away from everything he loved. He thought about Mags every day, hoping she was ok. His dad had given him a cell phone when they'd settled in their new home. He wasn't really sure what to do with it, no one he knew had a cell phone, he couldn't call Mags from it, the credit wouldn't last five seconds. They seemed pointless. He couldn't imagine them ever catching on. He smiled to himself, if seventeen year old Jase knew then what thirty four year old Hunter knew now, he'd have gone and bought some shares in Apple.

Still pacing in the stupidly small hotel room, Hunter frowned. Everything in his life had gone wrong the minute he'd left Mags alone in bed in the Adelphi. If he told her now what had really happened to Jason Lomax she wouldn't believe him, that boy was long gone. He knew exactly the date that Jason became Hunter, but if he thought about it, the transition began long before that, it began as his plane left Manchester Airport and the anger and resentment began building up inside him. When you're seventeen and you have nowhere for that aggression to go, you're bound to end up in the shit, or at least in the Army which is where at nineteen he ended up.

Hunter shook his head, he'd trained himself not to go down that route. Jason was gone, he had been for ten years, once he'd left the Army under a cloud and emerged as Hunter Cole. The night that had changed the course of his life for good and turned him from a soldier into a hunter, meant he now rubbed shoulders with people who could arrange for new passports, driving licences, whatever he needed. Training became more important, he was physically in the form of his life. He trained every morning without exception. He made a lot of money from the bigger jobs, now he was his own boss. He'd laid low and was able to leave freely from the States, the first flight had been a nightmare, he was convinced they'd spot his fake passport a mile off, but it'd all been fine. The guy who did his passports was an ex government official who hadn't got the pension he thought he deserved, now he topped it up selling state secrets and fake passports. The enemy within.

If he'd eradicated everything to do with Jason a long time ago, then why did he feel more like Jason now than ever before? The answer was simple, Mags. He hadn't been surprised to see her, he knew she'd be at the Liver Bird, that was the reason he was here too. He sighed, there was so much he wanted to tell her, but so much he couldn't. His head was not the calm and controlled place it usually was. She'd told him he didn't know her anymore, but the truth was he did. He could recall every inch of her body, the way she used to look at him, the feel of her lips on his. Those things don't change, or do they? The thought of her with that gobshite Max made his blood boil, she'd deserved so much better. Had he hurt her so much when he left that she'd just settle for anything? That didn't sound like the girl he knew, maybe she was right, she had changed. Didn't stop him from wanting to take her in his arms and kiss her like there was no tomorrow. He could get rid of Max, make it look like an accident then swoop in and rescue Mags like he was a hero. He laughed, like he was some big hero? Couldn't be further than the truth. How had this happened? How had the boy who was going to play rugby for England got to this point in his life? Probably the darkest place he'd ever been to. All he knew was that he had to keep his head, if he let his heart even take over for a minute then it could be a disaster. It was vital he kept his wits about him, otherwise the wrong person would die.

Downstairs in the hotel restaurant Magenta was having afternoon tea with Trina, her oldest friend. They didn't see each other as much as she'd like, Trina and her husband Dean had been out to stay in their Bel Air mansion, but Max hadn't been especially welcoming and it had been even worse the following year when they'd bought their kids with them. Max had told her in no uncertain terms that they were never to be invited back. They had of course, just when Max was away on business and she'd enthused that he was terribly sorry to have missed them. She knew Trina wasn't soft and could see right through her, even so, she'd never hurt her friends feelings. Trina had always been excited to hear her stories of the showbiz world and was so proud of her friends' success, the only thing they'd argued about was when she married Max. She had been convinced she should try and find Jason before she headed off down the aisle.

Ignoring her friends' advice, she'd gone off and got married. She'd never regretted not taking Trina's advice more than she did right now. She knew she was only half listening as Trina told her about being made supervisor in Boots, how Dean junior was in trouble at school, but little Jade was an angel and how Dean's shifts were getting cut back at the car plant he worked in.

Her ears pricked up then.

'I can give you some money,' she reached for her Gucci handbag.

'Oh God, love, no, that's not what I was getting at. We'll be fine. I was just filling you in on my news.'

She smiled at Trina, noticing the lines around her eyes and the ones around her lips from smoking, they definitely didn't look the same age anymore. Poor Trina looked well on her way to forty. 'Look babe, I'm supposed to be Dean junior and Jade's Godmother and I'm well aware I've done a crap job. Let me give you some money, put it into an account for them if you want, or if there's things they need now, then get it. It's nearly Christmas, I'm sure you could use the spare cash. While you're at it, get yourself something.'

'Aah Mags, you don't have to do this.'

'I want to,' she frowned slightly, she wasn't used to hearing herself being called Mags so much.

'Why the frown, you ok?'

She opened her mouth to speak, then closed it again. She desperately wanted to tell her about running into Hunter, the artist previously known as Jase, but some instinct told her to keep it to herself. He'd been so mysterious about his new identity she didn't feel like she could say anything. Besides, what would she say? All she knew about Hunter Cole was he was as fit as fuck. As if to confirm her thoughts she spotted him coming into the room, then duck back out again when he saw who she was with.

'Everything's fine, just remembered I gotta call Max. Do us a favour Treen, order us some more drinks, I'll be back in a mo.'

She found Hunter in the cloak room. 'You hiding from me?'

He grinned. 'Sorry, just remembered I'd left something in here.'

She put a hand on her hip. 'That's a shame, I was gonna call you over. Trina would love to see you.'

She watched his face fall. 'Mags, nobody can know,' he lowered his voice. 'You have to forget Jason ever existed.'

She took a step closer. 'How can you ask me to do that? That would mean forgetting about us.'

'We were a life time ago Mags, a whole other life time.'

'Whatever's happened, whatever you've done...you can trust me.'

He stood looking at the floor, his hands in his pockets, it was the only way he could stop them from reaching out to pull her to him. He slowly looked up, her green eyes were on him, searching every bit of his face.

'Jason's gone Mags, he's never coming back and as for Hunter, you really don't want to get to know him.'

She was now right in front of him. 'He's there, in your eyes, how you're looking at me now, I've seen that look a million times before.'

He closed his eyes, ordering himself to not let his guard down, it was too dangerous. He opened them again, she took a step back, gasping. He knew what look was in his eyes now, the look that had given him his new name, that of a hunter.

'Go back to Trina, she'll be looking for you. Please don't mention me to her...' Your life may depend on it, he wanted to add but stopped short.

She backed away, still looking at him. 'I won't, but you need to be straight with me, this conversation isn't finished.'

She disappeared out of the cloak room, he leant against the wall, rubbing his hands across his face. Holy shit, he'd just given her 'the look' and yet she still wanted to talk, He'd had to summon every ounce of strength to look at her like that. Was she really stronger than he was? After all his training had he finally met his match? He left the cloakroom a few moments after her.

In the small rarely used office attached to the cloakroom, Tim Smith smiled to himself. What luck to find himself in here at the same time as that interesting conversation took place? He believed very much in fate and the only reason he was in that particular office today was to get some quiet time to plan out Magenta's weekend trip in January. It was only eight weeks away and needed planning meticulously. So, working away quietly had meant Hunter Cole had been oblivious to him even being there. He'd been about to go out to the cloakroom and reprimand him for skiving off, Cole may have been the same management level as him, but this was still his hotel, despite the transatlantic invasion. Then he'd heard Magenta's voice. He'd listened intently. Clearly there was more to Hunter and Magenta just being old friends and who was the mysterious Jason? What had Hunter done to him? Had he killed him? He didn't trust the guy. First of all he was far too good looking, the waitresses practically had their tongues out every time he passed them and secondly, there was a look in his eyes that he saw when he thought he wasn't being watched. Nothing got past Tim Smith. He had a friend who was a reporter at the Liverpool Echo, he might ask him to look into the mysterious Hunter Cole.

Chapter Eight

JOHNNY KIDD'S MANSION, BEL AIR

Johnny was lazing by his pool, strumming his guitar, jotting down lyrics for future tracks. He was under a shade, tanned rock star wasn't the look he was going for. There was no point living in LA if you didn't take advantage of the sunshine every now and then, be at one with nature, sitting amongst the palm trees. Or some shit like that. Fly came wandering out of the house with a couple of beers, he handed one to Johnny and plonked himself down on the sun lounger next to him. Fly had his own house, but seemed to spend most of his time at Johnny's pad, he wasn't great with his own company. Sloth was probably asleep somewhere in the house, again he very rarely went home either. It was what made them such a good band, they still liked each other's company. Although he and Fly could still have a humdinger of a row or 'creative differences'. Fly began absent-mindedly tapping his hand on his thigh in time with Johnny's guitar.

'Hey, I like that riff, get the drums on it straight away, it'll sound rockier.'

Johnny nodded. 'This track needs a really strong intro, got some real powerful lyrics.'

'Why not go for a softer intro and the kick the ass outta the song when you get to the verse?'

'Yeah, that could work too,' he scribbled down some notes. 'Reckon we get into the studio with this later, when Sloth wakes up.' Fly laughed. 'Yeah, good luck with that.'

'Hey, how's my favourite rock Gods?'

The boys looked up to see Max walking towards them.

'Great, who invited him?' Fly rolled his eyes.

'He doesn't need an invitation, you know Max, just turns up like a bad smell.' Max stood in front of them, dressed in his usual suit, despite the Californian heat.

'We were fine till you showed up.'

Max looked down at Fly. 'Fine way to speak to your manager.'

'Logan is our manager.'

'Logan is my business partner, ergo...' he took his shades off and flashed Fly his million dollar smile, which actually cost him two million dollars, but that was inflation for you. 'I am your manager.'

Sensing Fly was about to fly off the handle, another reason behind his name was his short temper, Johnny took command of the conversation. 'What brings you out here? Flying visit?' he asked hopefully.

Max shook his head. 'Semi-final week of 'Starmaker', thought I'd call in on my guys on the way to the studio and invite you to Spago for dinner, with your own little 'Starmaker,' he winked at Johnny.

'One, we don't do Spago and two, I aint doing the 'Starmaker' anymore.'

Fly laughed. 'Ah c'mon man, you can never resist a nice juicy...'

'Thank you very much Mr MacFly, that'll be enough for now,' Max interrupted.

Fly grinned. 'Ah, well, on the home straight now John boy. Not long till you can dump her mighty fine ass.'

'Count down is on.'

'Yes, well, about that...' Max began.

'What?' Johnny glared at him

'Well, this little trip we're all taking to England is a perfect opportunity to market Savannah over there. I wanna get her on some shows, that This Morning show is always a good start and what better way to promote her with you by her side, Johnny. The king of rock.'

'No way man, you said it'd be over after 'Starmaker',
anyway what if she doesn't win?'

'Oh she will, she's been top of the voting polls since
she hooked up with you and do you know nothing about
how my talent show works? I always choose the
winner.'

Johnny stood up. 'I aint doing it, I'm a rock star not a
babysitter. You're asking too much.'

Max laughed. 'What? To be photographed with a pretty
girl? Who knows, this could be the real deal and you'll
thank me for it in the end.'

'Whatever, this stops now.'

Max's face changed from all smiling to aggressive in a
split second. 'You listen to me Johnny, I made you and I
can break you. I could drop your little band in a
heartbeat. You guys are too thick to make it on your
own. I will do it and Broken Arrow will be history.
You're barely holding it together anyway, Sloth's a
mess.'

'You don't know shit. We're your biggest money
spinner. You wouldn't drop us.'

'Just try me Johnny, there are plenty more young rock
groups out there just ready to step into your cowboy
boots. I could finish you like that,' Max snapped his
fingers.

Fly stood up. 'Look Max, just get the hell outta here.'

Max held his hands up. 'Gotta split anyway boys.' he placed his shades back on his face. 'See you tonight, reservations are at 8pm.'

Johnny was fuming. 'Man, I hate that Son of a Bitch.'

'We signed with Logan, not him. Logan won't let him drop us.'

'I wouldn't be too sure. Max sure as hell wears the pants in that relationship.'

'We don't need him, maybe we should call his bluff and dump his ass. Anyone'd sign us up and besides it does nothing for our rep to be tied to the management team behind those stupid talent shows.'

'Trouble is, he's got too much on us, he's right, he could ruin our career. Few leaked stories to the press and that's it.'

Fly shrugged. 'So what? So people find out Sloth once got locked up on a drugs charge, big surprise and they find out about me shagging a bunch of famous married women,' he laughed. 'Although not at the same time, I'm talented, but not that talented. And you, blue eyed boy can do no wrong. We'd be fine.'

Johnny looked away. 'It's not just me though...he's got shit on my family. Insurance, he told me at the time. Trust me, you do not wanna get on the wrong side of Max.'

Fly looked confused. 'Insurance? What the hell for?'

'In case we left the company.'

'That's bullshit. Why would he do that then threaten to drop us?'

'Cos, either way, he's got us over a barrel. We'd have been better signing with Satan.'

'Logan won't be happy about this.'

Johnny laughed bitterly. 'Logan knows, he's not gonna go against Max is he?' He turned to walk away.

'Johnny?'

He turned back to face Fly.

'What has Max got on your family?'

Johnny shrugged. 'Some other time, my friend. I need some space. Gotta think things through.'

Chapter Nine

The Empire Theatre, Liverpool.

Magenta strode confidently onto the stage.
'Good evening, Liverpool. It's good to be home.'
A loud cheer went up. She stood on centre stage, one
hand on her hip, the other holding the microphone. She
knew she looked good, tight fitting black leather jeans,
a Rolling stones T-shirt and her long red hair flicked
over her right shoulder. She let the cheers and clapping
die down before she spoke again.
'Thanks for coming out tonight, I wanted to do this for
you, my fans. I'd be nowhere without you. My new

album is out soon and here is the title track from it, Liver Bird. I hope you all like it.'

She nodded to the band behind her and the opening chords filled the theatre.

Hunter stood in the wings, watching. She'd seemed surprised to see him at the Empire, he'd told her he was there on behalf of hotel security, she was a VIP in the hotel, they wanted to look after her. Her face had fallen at that, she thought he was here for her. He was, he just couldn't tell her that. She'd thanked him and said it wasn't necessary, she had her own security team. He said he was just following orders. She stormed off on to the stage, within seconds her game face was on and she was wowing the crowds. He watched in slight awe, he'd spent hours on you tube watching her videos, but nothing prepared him for the real thing. She had the audience in the palm of her hand, laughing and joking with them, belting out her back catalogue of hits and she looked so sexy on the stage. She was full of confidence, he felt his heart swell with pride as he watched her. She was still his Mags, always would be, he just couldn't let her know that, at least not yet. He let his gaze spread to the other side of the stage, in the opposite wing was her PA, Jody. He needed to get to know her a bit more. Reading people was one of his many skills, and that girl was definitely hiding something, she had an anxious look on her face when Mags' attention wasn't on her. Something was on her mind, Hunter needed to start his hunt somewhere and she seemed the obvious choice. He wasn't going to able to get close to Max or anyone one else until they came over after Christmas, he'd have to do some background checks from this side, so for now his priorities were Mags, Jody and he had an inkling Trina may cause him a bit of a problem. Nothing that couldn't be dealt with.

Jody was aware she was not her usual self, she was stressed to hell. Max had been on the phone again earlier, bawling her out again, over this concert. He'd demanded to speak to Magenta, for some reason she wasn't answering her cell. She hadn't let him speak to her, she didn't want her upset before the gig, she knew how important it was to her. So she'd told Max she was having a massage to relax her. She could almost hear the steam coming out of his ears. He wasn't a happy bunny. She knew she'd be in deep shit with Max when she got home, she had a hunch that it was more than a quick blow job would fix. His temper was worse than normal at the moment, maybe he was just a bit frustrated, what with both herself and Magenta away, he must be noticing the lack of sex. She was sure that was the root of his bad mood. She watched Magenta strutting her stuff on stage, all her inhibitions disappeared when she hit the stage. She was aware that the guy from the hotel was watching her from the other side of the stage. He was really hot. It would teach Max if she came over here and found someone for herself. She couldn't see his face properly as the stage lights put him in the shade, but his silhouette filled the wings. He was so tall and muscular. She wouldn't mind getting to know him better.

Magenta came off stage, on a total high. The first person she saw was Hunter, she momentarily forgot she was mad at him. She was jumping up and down on the spot. 'Well, what do'you think? Was it good? They were an amazing crowd. God, I love being on stage.'

'You were awesome. Totally rocked it,' he grinned at her. She looked more alive than he'd ever seen her before, her green eyes wide with excitement, her skin had a sheen of sweat on it, her smile was bigger than the Mersey tunnel and she radiated energy. Yep, he'd never seen her look so alive, or more beautiful. He reached out and pushed a damp strand of hair behind her ear, his hand suspended by her face as he realised what he'd done. Her eyes flew to his and he slowly dropped his hand to his side. 'I…I…I have to go back to the hotel,' he turned to walk away.

She grabbed him by the wrist. 'Wait!'

He turned slowly round, keeping her at arm's length.

'Thanks for watching, I guess that's what you really came here for tonight?'

He slowly nodded, best let her think that, he couldn't tell her the truth. He turned back around and walked away.

She hugged herself, married woman she may be, but she'd drop kick Max into next week for Hunter. She knew she still loved him, she'd never stopped loving him, Jase was in there somewhere, Hunter kept slipping up with her. She just needed to be patient and let him come to her and clearly he needed to deal with whatever demons had led him to change his identity. She'd help him, she needed to find a way to let him know it was ok. She wanted to banish the look in his eyes, the one he gave her in the cloakroom.

Jody sat in the residents bar, it'd been a long day, but she wasn't ready for bed yet. Who wanted to crawl into bed on their own? Hotel rooms were made for illicit sex, not sleeping on your own. She'd thought about heading out into town, there were some good bars on Mathew Street and the Cavern Club for starters or maybe to the more upmarket Albert Dock, she might meet some footballers there. However, she didn't fancy wandering round the City on her own, she needed a partner in crime and Magenta was her only option. She certainly couldn't just pop out for a few drinks and pick up guys, she'd be mobbed and Max would go ballistic. So, there she was drinking alone in the bar, well apart from her and the bar man although technically he wasn't drinking. She wasn't sure how much she'd drunk, she just knew she was drunk.

'Can I get you a drink?'

She turned toward the voice. Well, well, things were starting to look up, it was only the hot hotel guy. 'Shure.'

'Or maybe you've had enough?'

'Ah, who's countin'?' She shrugged.

'Two vodkas please, mate,' Hunter sat down next to her.

'Ain't you workin'?'

'Just clocked off, been a long day.'

'Saw you at the gig, you like Magenta, huh?' She slouched toward him.

He took the glass of the barman. 'I like her music.'

She giggled. 'Didn't have you down as a lover of girlie music.'

He shrugged. 'Why would you, you don't know me.'

'I shoulda known, everybody loves her, it'sh me, they forget.'

Damn, he knew he shouldn't have got her another drink, her slurring words were getting worse. He wasn't going to get very far tonight. Still all he needed was to get into her room.

'C'mon,' he stood up. 'Let's get you to your room, you don't want a stinking hangover tomorrow do you?'

She tried to stand up, but stumbled. He caught her. 'S'ok, I'm ok, s'ok everybody.' He put her arm around her shoulder and his arm around her waist and headed off towards the lift. He hoped the movement of the lift wouldn't make her throw up. They reached her floor without incident and he got her into the room. She was practically asleep on his shoulder. He laid her down on the bed, taking her shoes off and then covered her with a spare blanket. She was snoring lightly, she was well away. Now for the job in hand. He searched her bag for her phone, it wasn't there. He looked back at sleeping beauty and groaned, He frisked her body with just the gentlest of touches, it was in her pocket. He removed the phone quickly. Then he went into the bathroom, he closed the door over so the light wouldn't disturb her. He noticed there was a text message off Max, he opened it.

Keep me updated on M, want this launch cancelled. Miss ur sweet cheeks (ass cheeks that is) lol.

He deleted the text then took the back off the phone and lifted the battery out, he slipped in a tiny chip so that he'd be able to monitor her calls. After that text message it seemed his initial hunch that he was onto to something was right. He put the phone back together and snuck out of the bathroom, replacing the phone in Jody's pocket. Quietly he left the room.

Magenta was coming back along the corridor to her room when she saw Hunter come out of Jody's room, his clothes looked dishevelled. She quickly ducked into her room so he wouldn't see her. Jody and Hunter? No....it couldn't be. He wouldn't do that to her, or would he?

Hunter exited the lift at reception. He was met by a glaring Tim. 'Hunter, did I see you escort Miss Stanley to her room?

'Maybe.'

'May I remind you of our strict rule of no fraternizing with the guests? It might be free and easy in the Boston hotel, but we do things differently over here.'

He laughed in the little man's face. 'Oh Tim, you do make me laugh. Our guest just had a little too much to drink and she needed taking back to her room, safely.'

Tim scrunched his face up. 'Well, as long as that's all you did.'

'Listen man, I'm knackered, if you've got an issue, let's do this in the morning. I need some sleep.'

He walked away. Sleep would have to wait, he needed to digest the information he'd just learnt and also work out how he was going to bug Mags' phone. He needed to know where she was at all times.

Chapter Ten

Spago, LA

Johnny's mood had not improved during the day and finding himself in Max's company again was just rubbing salt in the wound. Fly looked about as happy as a nun in a brothel to be there too. Max was filling in the awkward silences with his inane rambling about 'Starmaker'. Johnny was sick of it, sick of him and sick of this stupid hold Max had on him. There had to be a way out of it. He needed to talk to Logan, he'd feel better then. He drained the JD that was in front of him, he'd worked his way through quite a few of them. It was the only way he could stand being around Max.

He stood up. 'I need a smoke,' he grabbed Savannah's hand. 'Comin'?'

She smiled up at him. 'Sure thing, sugar.'

He saw Fly throw him a look. He felt bad for abandoning his friend and leaving him with Max, but not that bad.

He took Savannah by the hand and led her through the restaurant, not even giving a second glance to all the other famous faces in there. He headed towards the kitchens. He was almost stopped by a waiter when he opened the kitchen door, who quickly back tracked when he realised who he was.

Yep, he was Johnny Kidd, he could go wherever the fuck he wanted. He strode through the kitchen, smiling that rock star smile of his at anyone who looked like they might question what he was doing. He could hear Savannah's giggle behind him. 'Johnny, baby. Where are we going?'

He exited the kitchen and pulled her into a small linen room off the corridor. 'Getting laid, that's what's happening.'

He lifted her up, setting her down on a table top that was just the right height. He pushed her short dress up towards her hips as he stood in between her legs. She was already pulling his T-shirt over his head. She looked at him, her blue eyes filled with lust, for a moment he paused, that was all that was there, lust. No other emotion, this was just a quick fuck to her, her 'this one time when I shagged Johnny Kidd', moment. Not that there was anything other than lust driving him either, he didn't feel anything for Savannah, other than she seemed like a nice girl, until you got her knickers off – his kinda girl.

'What's the matter, sugar?' Her southern drawl more prominent when she was playing Little Miss Seduction.

'Nothing, baby girl. Come here and kiss me.'

Her lips were on his, her teeth pulling at his bottom lip as his hands roamed over her body, pushing the skin-tight dress she was wearing over her head. He stood in just his jeans, but she quickly freed his hard cock, he moaned into her mouth as he felt her tight grip on it, moving rhythmically backwards and forwards. He removed her bra, her large breasts were desperately trying to escape from their constraints. He buried his head in them, rude not too really. She wrapped her legs around his hips and arched herself backwards. She removed her hand from his cock slid them round to his butt. His cock didn't need any help, it knew where it was going, it nudge forward towards her lips.

'Johnny, baby, I want you in me now.'

She didn't even finish the sentence before he was thrusting away inside her.

Neither of them seemed to care that they were in a linen cupboard, in Spago. Savannah was especially vocal and appreciative as she called out Johnny's name over and over.

Logan put a call into Johnny as soon as he saw the video on his Twitter news feed. 'What, the fuck, Johnny?'

He knew he was in serious shit, Logan rarely swore at him, he was the golden boy. He'd been alerted to the video about two seconds before Logan's call.

'We could always say it wasn't me...'

'Your tattooed ass tells the world otherwise. How many times do I have to tell you about this? We live in an age that anything you do, good or bad can go global in a nano second.'

'Hey, I'm only doing what Max wants, he wants this little relationship with Savannah rammed in people's faces.'

'Yes, but that doesn't mean we have to see your cock rammed in her...' Logan stopped himself just in time. 'You know what I mean.'

'Loud and clear, boss.'

'Look, I'm not saying don't get laid, that's what rock stars do...I'm just sayin', don't do it in Spago's linen cupboard. They could sue our ass over this.'

'You know fine well they won't. There aint no thing as bad publicity, right?'

Logan sighed. 'I know you aint happy with this Savannah thing, but it'll be over soon.'

'Yeah right, you out of the loop on Max's latest plan? I gotta take her with me to England, for Magenta's launch.'

'What? That wasn't the deal.'

'You're tellin' me. I don't do dating.'

Logan's laughter rang down the phone line. 'Johnny, she's got tits and a mighty fine ass, don't know why you are complaining.'

'What I mean, is, I'm not into this arranged relationship shit.'

'You'd be surprised how many high profile couples are together just for their career.'

'Yeah well, I don't want to be one of them.'

'I gotta go, we'll talk later. In the meantime, don't speak to any press and don't update your Twitter. I'll sort it this end and don't worry about Max, I'll sort him too.'

Logan ended the call, as he looked up Brooke sauntered into his office, wearing the shortest skirt he'd even seen and an even shorter crop top. He wondered how she was never cold.   'Hey, honey. How's it going?'

'It's just hit the fan.'

She giggled. 'Johnny's video?'

'You seen it too huh?'

She shrugged as she plonked herself down on the corner of his desk, flicking her blonde hair over her shoulder. 'Who hasn't?'

'That boy frequently gives me one headache after another, I swear he's gonna turn me grey before my time.'

'You'll still look sexy,' she leaned over, running a hand through his floppy blonde hair. He swatted it away. She jumped off the desk and stood behind his chair, resting her hands on his shoulders.

'Was thinkin' it'd be kinda fun to make our own home movie.'

'Brooke, baby, I am so busy this video is a nightmare. Just look at my inbox since it went viral.'

'Fine, I'll see you at dinner, if you can make it,' she stalked away, never mind his inbox, it was her inbox that needed attention. At least Max was home tomorrow, he'd sort her out.

Broken Arrow were in their favourite place, Johnny's recording studio. Sloth was actually awake for once and he sat strumming his guitar. 'Looks like I missed a helluva lot today.'

'Yeah, if you sleep all freakin' day, you'll find that happens,' Fly turned his attention back to Johnny. 'Man, I keep tellin' you about the Twitter thing and the internet. Do it, just don't get caught doing it.'

Johnny laughed. 'Says Saint. Fly MacFly over there.'

He held his hands up. 'I aint saying I'm a saint, I just didn't get caught...where are the videos and pictures of me with those married women? There isn't any, 'cos I'm careful.'

'Who ever heard of a careful rock star...this is rock n roll, man,' Sloth high fived Johnny.

'Go back to sleep, I prefer you that way.'

'What's rattled your cage Fly? It's me gettin' the shit off Logan.'

'It's you, what's goin' on with you right now? Max sure as hell got under your skin,' Johnny sighed. 'I need a beer if we're gonna do this.'

Johnny and Fly headed up to his kitchen, leaving Sloth to have a nap. He opened his massive fridge which was mainly just filled with beer. There was a small shelf with food on that his cook left, she was forever trying to replace the beer with food. Johnny didn't see the point. After grabbing a few beers they went into his games room and sat on the lazy boy chairs they used for playing on the Xbox.

'C'mon then, cockstar, spill.'

Johnny ignored the dig. 'Max got involved in something that didn't concern him.'

'Sounds like Max.'

'Remember when Shane was in court after the car crash?'

Fly nodded, Johnny's little brother Shane hadn't followed his brother's lead, instead he'd found himself in prison after being involved in a car crash in which Johnny had been a passenger.

The official line had been that Johnny had had nothing to do with his brother after he'd been sent to jail and whilst he felt for the victim of his brother's crime, a cab driver who'd spent six months in a coma, he had nothing but contempt for Shane. That couldn't have been further from the truth. Johnny had wanted nothing more than to help his kid brother but the record label thought this level of publicity would do Broken Arrow more harm than good. Max had told him that he had his band mates' career to think of and should do the right thing. Publicly Johnny had washed his hands of Shane.

'Max said he'd take care of everything. I was pretty cut up, wasn't thinking straight but he promised me he'd get the best lawyers and Shane would only get a light sentence. I didn't really give any thought as to why he'd want to help, this was Max after all, Mr look out for number one.'

'But, he did it, Shane coulda gone down for longer if Max hadn't stepped in. Not that I'm biggin' the guy up. So what's the real story? Max didn't do that out of the goodness of his heart did he?'

Johnny shook his head as he lifted his bottle of Bud to his lips. 'Nope, Max did it to protect the Broken Arrow brand…to protect me…'

Fly frowned. 'What are you sayin, bro? Protected you? I don't wanna know this do I?'

'Probably not.'

'Man, that's some heavy shit, no wonder you hate the bastard.'

'I've always tried to have as little to do with him as possible, I always try and deal with Logan but lately Max is in my face all the time and this Savannah shit is too much.'

'If you wanna leave Maximum records, I'd understand, we'd get another deal. It's not worth his shit.'

Johnny smiled. 'I appreciate your loyalty, Fly, but it aint happenin' we leave Maximum, we won't work again, not like this anyway. All this would be gone,' he gestured to his games room.'

'Hell, your self-respect is worth more than this.'

Johnny shrugged. 'I got some ideas first, before we jump ship.'

'Care to share?'

He shook his head smiling. 'The less you know the better.' Maybe it was time to put a call into his brother.

Chapter Eleven

THE LIVER BIRD, LIVERPOOL.

      Magenta had hardly slept all night. Hunter and Jody, really? It's not that Jody wasn't pretty, she was, but she didn't think she was his type. She thought she was. Hell, there was definitely unfinished business between them, what the hell was he playing at? Maybe he'd been trying to make her jealous, get a reaction from her. But then, he didn't know he'd been spotted coming out of her room. Maybe it was just quick meaningless sex, had she got him all fired up and he needed an outlet? She was clutching at straws. In truth she had no idea what was going on in Hunter's head. She looked at him and he was her Jase, then he behaved like some guy she didn't know, like Hunter. God, this was doing her head in. It was one thing for her first love to come back into her life but it was another thing for him to come back as a totally different person. Where was her romantic, rugby playing, funny Jason now?

It only took a second for a memory to pop into her mind. She and Jason had bunked off school and gone into town for the day. He looked far older than his seventeen years, so tall and broad and she definitely didn't look like a school girl. As they wandered around town, they certainly didn't look like two kids bunking off, they probably looked like students from Liverpool Uni just mooching around the shops. They walked down Bold Street, holding hands and headed down through town towards Quiggins, a warehouse type building that pumped out rock and indie music and housed many quirky little stalls. She never knew what she was looking for in Quiggs', as it was affectionately referred to, but she always came out with some little treasure. In her DM's she was wearing the unofficial dress code of everybody else in the building. She and Jase planned on having a browse around the shops then some lunch in the café on the top floor of the building. As they entered Quiggs' they were instantly hit by the mix of various aromas of incense and jossticks burning away in the small shops off the main corridor. They wandered in contentment through the little shops, picking up scented candles, taking in their smell, looking at sloganed T-shirts, trying on bits of jewellery. There was a lovely silver Celtic ring that she'd admired, it was totally her taste. They spent a good hour in one of the music shops, she bought the Blind Melon single on CD, No Rain. She loved that song. When they eventually sat down in the Brook Café they were starving. They sat at a table waiting for their jacket potatoes to come over and chatted easily. Jase put his hand in his pocket.

'Got ya something,' he passed a small brown bag over to her.

She looked at him, smiling. She opened the bag, the silver ring she tried on downstairs was in the bag. 'What's this for? When did you get it?'

'I popped back when you were buying your CD. I got it, 'cos you liked it and it suited your hand.'

She laughed. 'It suited my hand? You nutter.'

He reached across and placed the ring on her third finger of her right hand. He then took both her hands in his and tapped his index finger across each of her fingers until he got to the third finger on her left hand. 'One day babe, when we've had time to explore all our adventures I'll find a ring that suits that finger too.'

She leaned across and kissed him. 'Love ya, la.'

Their kiss was interrupted by the waitress bringing over two cheese and beans jacket potatoes.

She reached out for her iPad, she needed a distraction from pondering on the summer of '95.

98

Things had changed, that boy was gone, their dreams just a distant memory and their adventures something that never happened. No matter how much she wanted to go back, she couldn't. She flicked onto her Twitter feed. #johnnykiddsexvideo was the worldwide number one trend. She smiled to herself. What had he gone and got himself into now? For all of his rock star shenanigans she had a real soft spot for Johnny. She was looking forward to the duet with him. She and Johnny would make an awesome combination. She flicked over some of the tweets.

@Hotgoss Johnny & Savannah's steamy sex session in spago linen cupboard #hotstuff

@Johnnyk'swife OMG Savannah is so lucky. Johnny has such a cute arse. #weljel

@brookeHuds Go, JK's butt. So hot and squeezable.

She rolled her eyes when she saw Brooke's tweet, she was an incurable flirt. She tweeted her back, to keep up appearances of a happy Maximum camp. @brookeHuds sounds like I'm missing all the fun.

She searched on her iPad for the local radio station, Radio City. She loved that station as a kid and always listened to it whenever she came home. The 'top ten at ten' was playing, with the DJ encouraging people to text or ring in to guess the year. She groaned when she heard 'Cotton Eye Joe' – the Gods were conspiring against her. The year was 1995. She used to love that song, Jase hated it, she used to play it all the time to wind him up. She was about to shut the iPad down when there was a knock at the door. She slid off the bed and padded over to the door. She opened it, expecting to find Jody, she was surprised to see Hunter. He was holding a tray.

'Got you some breakfast.'

'I didn't order any. I've already eaten.'

'Ok, so it was a ploy to come up here.'

She folded her arms across her chest. 'You sure you didn't get the wrong room, Jody's is down there.'

He frowned. 'You're talking in riddles. Are you gonna let me in or not?'

She stepped to one side. She tried not to look at his tight backside as he set the tray down onto the dressing table.

'Ah, bloody hell Mags, not that song again?'

She smiled, she liked how he lost that American twang when he spoke to her, she could hear some of his scouse accent coming through. 'Clearly, I must've sensed you were on your way here. So, to what do I owe the pleasure?'

He shrugged. 'Just wanted to see how you're feeling after your gig last night.'

She narrowed her eyes. 'I know you better than that, you're up to something. What happened with Jody last night? Have you come to ask me if I mind if you start seeing her?' Her voice began to rise at the end of her sentence.

'What are you talking about?'

'I saw you coming out of Jody's room last night.'

He threw his head back and let out a laugh. 'You think I've been shaggin' your PA?'

'Well, what else am I supposed to think?'

He looked at her and grinned, his blue eyes had a mischievous glint in them. 'Would you be jealous if I had?'

'Oh my God, listen to you. You never used to have such an ego.'

'You never used to have such an attitude.'

'I have not got an attitude.'

He grinned. 'Is it just me that brings out this feisty side?'

'I'm married to Max Maxwell, I need to be able to hold my own.'

His eyes clouded over with concern. 'Why? What does he do to you?'

'He does my head in, that's what he does.'

'I still don't get you being with him,' he took a step closer to her. 'You know, if you felt threatened by him, you could tell me. I could protect you.'

She wrinkled her nose up at him. 'What are you talking about?'

He stared at her, his deep blue eyes zeroing in on her. His gaze was intense, he didn't speak.

'What?' She nervously tucked a strand of her long red hair behind her ear. He was really spooking her out with the look in his eyes, although this was different to the haunted look she saw in the cloak room the other day. As she watched the expression on his face now, the look in his eyes...it took her back to the coffee shop in Quiggs'. 'Jase...'

He put a finger on her lips. 'Ssh...Don't say my name.'

It was all she could do not to part her lips and kiss his finger. His eyes were still on her.

'Oh, Mags. I wish, I wish things were different.'

She opened her mouth to speak, but found she didn't trust the words to come out. She wasn't sure how he'd managed to get so close to her, he was inches away. The tension between them drowned everything else out, even the radio. If he kissed her right now, she'd kiss him right back, their heads were already leaning into each other like a magnetic force.

There was a knock at the door. She didn't know if she was grateful or not, she broke eye contact and turned her back on him. She went to the door. She opened it to find Jody. 'Well, well. Is this what your plan was?' she turned back to Hunter. 'A Threesome?'

Jody blushed as she realised who was in the room with Magenta. She had a hazy memory from last night, but she did remember being carried back to her room in Hunter's strong arms.

'I, err, I'll come back later,' Jody mumbled.

Hunter held his hands up. 'No need, I'm done here,' he headed towards the door. 'I'll catch ya later Mags.'

He was out of the door before she could come back with the last word. It was only as he shut the door behind him that she realised she wasn't sure exactly what he'd come to her room for. Surely it wasn't just to give her breakfast? She spun back round to Jody. 'What d'you want?' she snapped at her.

'I've had Max on the phone this morning, he was just checking in. He said you haven't called him for days.'

'Since when did Max get all needy?'

'I think he just needed cheering up, he's pissed with Johnny over the sex tape.'

'My heart bleeds.'

'Why are you on such a downer with him?'

'You even have to ask? You know how unsupportive he's been of this project.'

Jody nodded. 'I know that, but he's your husband.'

'And as my husband, he should be supportive,' she sighed. 'I guess, being back home, well it just makes me think about what I've been missing.'

'I thought you had everything you ever wanted. Fame, money...'

'To quote the Beatles, which seems really apt right now. Money can't buy me love.'

'You don't love Max?' This was news to Jody, would it make her feel any less guilty about her affair though?

She laughed. 'Do I love him? I suppose I did once, maybe in the beginning, but probably not properly. I'm not stupid, or blind and neither are you, you know what he's like. He's a total womanizer.'

Jody felt her stomach flip, did she know about them?

'In fact, I know he's up to something, right now with someone and this time he's sailed too close to the wind. He doesn't know it, but that's part of the reason behind my secret weekend trip over to the Wirral, with our nearest and dearest closest friends. I have a surprise planned. Damn, I've said too much, still I can trust you to keep it to yourself can't I Jody?'

She could only nod. What the hell did she mean? Was she warning her to stay away from Max? Should she pre warn him? Why on earth did she get involved with Max in the first place?

Hunter was trying to piece the puzzle together, but so far this little mystery was about as clear as the River Mersey. He hadn't managed to get a bug in Mags' cell, but he had shoved a hidden speaker under her mattress when she'd gone to open the door to Jody. He sat in his room, jotting down some notes of what he knew so far. Max and Jody were having an affair, his first thought was that Mags was unaware of this, but having listened in to her chat with Jody it was clear she knew her husband was up to no good with someone. Did she know it was Jody? It seemed Mags had some plan of her own to get revenge on Max. Was it a coincidence that she had chosen the weekend retreat to expose her husband, when that was when he'd been given his orders to execute the plan? Someone was out to harm Mags, he didn't know who that person was, all he had was his orders from the handler, the person who was the go between, between the hit man and the person ordering the hit. He'd been trying to work out who was behind it all. So far his money had been on Max, he certainly didn't seem the type to get his hands dirty, but then if he was behind the plot to kill Mags, why would he be so adamant that he wanted the weekend trip cancelled when that was supposed to be the scene of the crime. Unless that was part of his plan, he could cry crocodile tears and tell the world's press that she wouldn't listen to him when he'd asked her to cancel the trip. He nodded slowly, yeah, that made sense. Jody was definitely on the list now he knew about her affair with Max, the main draw back with her being the one calling the shots was finance. He had no doubt that Mags paid her well, but he highly doubted that her wages would cover the price he charged to take someone out. Obviously his suspect list was short right now. He was yet to meet Logan and Brooke and then there were the Broken Arrow boys, but he would be very surprised if one of the guys had hired him. Hit men and rock stars didn't really go together. Still, he couldn't rule it out. It would be a very foolish error to discount someone just because they didn't fit the profile. So for now, everyone was a suspect. His plan was to play along, report back to his handler that everything was in hand, when really he'd be scouting out who wanted Mags dead, 'cos if there was one thing he was damn sure, it wouldn't be Mags with her name on a bullet, it'd be whoever ordered the hit.   He still loved her, had never stopped, she didn't know it, but as of now he was her personal bodyguard. He would see that no harm came to her. He could feel bits of Jason slipping back to him when he was with her, she made him remember the good guy he once was. The guy he used to be before he got involved with things way over his head. Well, this was it, one last job and he was erasing Hunter forever. He couldn't think like that now, he couldn't be distracted and let his feelings for her ruin his concentration. He had to be two steps ahead of everyone. He looked back down at the paper he'd written on, fortunately he had a photographic memory, so he took the information in, then ripped the paper to shreds. He couldn't have any bit of evidence lying around. Maybe it was time to put a call into his handler, see if he could get more information.

Mags was due back in New York in a few days' time, he didn't have much time. He looked at his watch, it was almost breakfast time in LA. He had time to do some press ups and planks before he made the call.

Chapter Twelve

MAX MAXWELL'S, DUPLEX PENTHOUSE NYC.

Mags was right about one thing, Max was up to something right then, banging her so called best friend in their marital bed.

'Ah, Brooke, baby. I've missed these tits,' he reached out and grabbed her ample breasts. 'And I've missed these.' His hands went to her butt and he squeezed each cheek.

'Ooh, Max, baby,' she purred.

'You missed me too?'

She nodded, twirling her hair round her fingers and then brushing it lightly over his bare shoulders. 'Of course, you know I don't like being neglected,' she pouted.

He grinned at her. 'Tell me what you missed the most.'

She knew how this game worked, Max liked dirty talk and she could play the slut pretty well.

'Your big cock.'

He groaned. 'Where have you missed it?'

She opened her mouth and ran her tongue over her top lip. 'In my mouth,' she lay back on the bed, opening her legs. 'And in my hot pussy.'

'You're a dirty bitch.'

'And don't ya just love it. C'mon Max. Don't leave a lady waiting.'

'A lady, is something you are definitely not Mrs Hudson, but I am a gentleman and I'd never keep you waiting,' he grabbed her ankles, pulling her down closer to him, she wrapped her legs tightly around him as he plunged into her. 'You know how to rock my cock, baby.'

She smiled to herself. Of course she did, sex was her speciality, her weapon of choice. Max would be hers, she just needed to get Magenta out of the picture. Unfortunately, Max wasn't as skilled, within seconds he was done. He collapsed, panting on top of her. 'God, I needed that.'

'Me too, baby.'

He rolled of her, got off the bed and headed to the bathroom. 'Back in a mo.'

Presumably he was off to pop a Viagra. She wondered if she had time to finish herself off, probably not. Instead she reached over to her phone. She clicked on to her Twitter account. She saw a tweet off Magenta. She tweeted back

@RealMagentaValentina – hell yeah. Missing it all. Catch up when you are back #winetime

She threw the cell on the bed. Stupid freakin' Magenta. She hated having to be all nicey nicey with her, just 'cos it kept the press happy. She briefly toyed with the idea of posting a selfie on Twitter, would Magenta recognise her own bed? And how pretentious could you get 'real' Magenta. She'd never need that on her own Twitter account, she had far less followers than the all mighty Magenta. Obviously, she was conveniently forgetting that Magenta was a worldwide star, whilst Brooke was just Mrs Hudson. She should've married Max all those years ago when she had the chance, before Magenta arrived on the scene. At the time she thought Logan was the main man, what an error of judgement that had been. Her plan now was to become the second Mrs Max Maxwell. He was the powerful one. Where was he anyway? She would've had the time to sort herself out. Just as she contemplated it, he came out of the bedroom, the Viagra had obviously had the desired effect. He was standing tall and proud again.

'Ready for round two?'

She tilted her head to one side. 'How about, we go in for a 69?' He pulled a face. Did he really just wrinkle his nose up at her?

'How 'bout you get down here on your knees and give me a nice blow job?'

She rolled off the bed. Freakin' men, if she was going to become Mrs Maxwell mark two, then she needed to teach him some manners. Starting off with, it's better to give than receive.

Logan was worried about Johnny, he always had the tendency to go off the rails but he seemed really pissed at the moment. Worse than he'd ever seen him. He'd sent him a text earlier that day and asked him to Skype him. Now he was looking at his troubled face on the big TV screen. Logan propped his feet up on his desk and placed his hands behind his head as he positioned himself to speak to Johnny. 'Hey man, thanks for getting in touch so quick.'

Johnny shrugged. 'No worries, it sounded urgent.'

'Just wanted to check in with you. You've been on my mind. Everything ok?'

'Why wouldn't it be? I'm a fuckin' rock star.'

This is what worried Logan, when Johnny got close to his self-destruction button it wasn't pretty to watch, although he had written some of his best stuff when he'd been a little bit too close to the dark side.

'Look, I promise I'll sort Max out and get him to lay off a bit. I'm heading over to see him later. I'll have a word.'

'I don't need you to fight my battles Logan, I can sort that dick out myself. What I need is for you to be my manager and keep Max the fuck away from me. I'd never have signed with you if I'd have known what an input he was gonna have.'

'Hey, he doesn't chose the singles, you and I do. He has nothing to do with production. The only thing he really gets involved with is promotion.'

'Yeah, well, feels like there's a rat in my kitchen...'

Logan smiled. He couldn't be too far gone yet, his humour was still there. 'I get it.'

'Do you really? I'm happy to duet with Magenta, but spending time in some old English town with that jerk off and dragging Crystal Barbie along for the ride aint filling me with joy.'

'After that weekend, I promise, you'll never have to deal with Max again.'

'Can I have that in writing?'

Logan pulled his Porsche into Max's driveway and parked up next to his Ferrari. He knew he had to have it out with him. Broken Arrow were his band, his clients. Max had no right sticking his nose in, especially if it was unsettling Johnny. Max probably thought he was helping but it was time for him to back off. He jumped out of the car and jogged up to the front door. Rosita, the maid answered on the second ring. He took off his Ray Bans as the door opened.

'Go straight into the Den. Mr Hudson.'

He smiled. 'Thanks, Rosita.'

'Would you like a drink, sir?'

'I'm good thanks,' he sat down on the sofa and made himself comfortable. He flicked on the TV whilst he waited. Max always said 'mi casa, su casa'. He may as well catch up on the sports news. Within a few minutes he was engrossed on the latest news on The Knicks, he didn't even hear Max come in.

'Logan, buddy, wasn't expecting you.'

He turned round, taking in Max's attire of lounging pants and plan white T-shirt. 'Clearly not. What have you been up to?' 'Just a little rest, LA was hectic.'

'Yeah, so I hear.'

Max raised an eyebrow. 'Let me guess, a certain Mr Johnny Kidd chucking his toys out of the pram?'

Logan was about to answer but was momentarily distracted by a car out of the window, he could've sworn it was Brooke's car heading out of the driveway. He squinted his eyes together to try and work out the registration, but before he could, Max stepped into his line of vision and placed a hand on his shoulder. 'He's asked you tell me to back off hasn't he? He needs to realise, we run this company together, the acts aren't exclusive. What's mine is yours, right?' Logan looked at Max, his buddy for years and business partner for almost as long. Did he really know him? Right now he felt he couldn't even trust him.

'Max, leave Broken Arrow to me. They are my act. I bought them into the company, we nearly lost them to Geffen records and if it hadn't been for me, we would've. You got your hands full with 'Starmaker'. Leave the acts to me and while we're at it, lay off Magenta too. This album launch is important to her, plus it makes sense, the tour kicks off shortly and Liverpool is the first date. Just put your ego aside for one minute and think things through, give your wife the support she deserves. This company is bigger than you or I Max, don't forget that.'

Max laughed. 'What's got into you? You threatening me, Logan?'

He shrugged. 'Why would I do that? We both want the same thing, don't we?'

Max nodded slowly.

'I gotta split, things to do, people to see.'

Logan left before Max had chance to have the last word. He had an uneasy feeling in the pit of his stomach. Something was going on, something he wasn't supposed to know about. He had a gut feeling that things were about to hit the fan and he wasn't sure why, but he had a feeling that a long overdue chat with his wife was needed.

Logan returned home to find Brooke relaxing in the hot tub on the private rooftop of their Penthouse. She was sipping champagne.

'Tough day?' He asked as he perched on the edge of the tub.

'Like you would not believe. Spent the morning in Bloomingdales and then I've just got in from lunch with Amber Gordon-Stevens, she'd back in town for a bit and I want her to redecorate this place.' she said, referring to the top interior designer in the country.

'Where did you lunch?'

She laughed. 'You can tell you don't check my twitter feed, just as well you're not a suspicious hubby, I could get away with anything. You're so trusting. Go on look.'

Logan pulled out his phone and checked twitter. His wife had tagged herself at the Four Seasons and posted a picture of her and Amber. It was an hour ago. She couldn't have been leaving Max's mansion then. He felt guilty for even thinking it. Brooke and Max? No way.

'So, when can she do the re-design?'

'Not for ages. Apparently Katie Holmes is before me.'

He shrugged and ran a hand through his hair. 'Ah well, we're in no rush.'

'Why don't you join me in here?'

He checked his watch. He didn't need to get back to the office just yet. Maybe he had time to have a quick dip. He started to get undressed.

Brooke breathed a quick sigh of relief. Thank God she had the foresight to stop outside the Four Seasons, quickly tag herself and post an old picture of her and Amber. She'd dived into the hot tub as soon as she returned home so Logan wouldn't question the different clothes. She pulled her husband towards her and wrapped her arms around his broad shoulders, pulling him close to her. His lips were on hers as they sank into the bubbles. If only it could always be like this, she wouldn't need Max then.

Chapter Thirteen

LIVER BIRD HOTEL, LIVERPOOL.

Magenta was in the reception of the hotel. It was a lovely winter's day outside and she fancied taking a walk down to the Albert Dock. She wanted to have a look at the Echo Arena where her tour would be starting next year. She'd piled her hair under a Yankees baseball cap and was wearing skinny jeans and an oversized jumper. Fortunately, due to the sunshine, she could get away with wearing her aviators so people wouldn't recognise her. Max would have a fit if he knew she was going out on her own, but she was in her home town, she felt safe.

'Whoa, nearly didn't recognise you there.'

She glared at Hunter. 'That's the idea.'

'You still pissed at me? What have I done wrong Mags?'

'Apart from Jody?'

'How many times, I'm not doing Jody. She was drunk and needed help back to her room,' he glanced at his watch. 'You off out? I'll come with you. Think we need to clear the air before our big meeting later on.'

'I'll be fine on my own.'

'Sure you will, until one person realises they're standing next to the great Magenta Valentina and they scream their heads off in excitement. Before you know it, you've got half of Liverpool chasing you around town.'

She raised an eyebrow. 'And you can protect me from that?'

'We'll just look like a normal couple going for a walk.'

The moment he got the sentence out an awkwardness hung in the air. A normal couple? Like they used to be?

She cleared her throat. 'Come on then.'

They walked down The Strand, the long road that took them past the world famous Liver buildings, the Liver Birds perched on top, one looking out over the river and the other looking over the city. The myth was that they protected the city and if they ever flew away the city would crumble. Mags smiled to herself as she thought about the old story. Jase had been her Liver Bird, she'd felt protected with him and when he'd gone, well, she fell apart for a while. But, now he was back and as they walked along the road, his arm linked through hers to maintain the 'normal couple' facade, she couldn't help those old feelings of feeling safe and secure resurface. They walked in a comfortable silence toward the Albert Dock, a set of warehouses that had been revamped in the 80's and was now home to lots of swanky restaurants, quaint little shops, the Tate Gallery and even the weather map was still there from the This Morning days.

'Wow, look at that!' Hunter pointed out across the river, she followed his gaze. A low cloud hanging over the river was the colour of a rainbow.

'How the hell can there be a rainbow cloud?'

They stopped and stared at it. 'It must be like some kinda prism and the water must be reflecting back onto the cloud, giving the illusion of a rainbow cloud. Or maybe it's just Mother Nature's magic.'

She took her phone to take a picture. She was about to upload it to Twitter, but stopped for two reasons, one it would give away her location and she was supposed to be incognito today and secondly, she didn't want to share this with anyone else but Hunter, he was right it did feel like magic. She turned back round to face him, he was no longer looking at the cloud, he was looking at her.

'What?'

'Aah, Mags, there is so much I need to tell you, but I wouldn't know where to start and there's so much I need to protect you from.'

'Protect me from? What are you talking about?'

'I don't know yet, but I will do. Until then, I need you to trust me.'

'You're scaring me, what's wrong?'

'What's wrong is that I ever let you slip away from me in the first place. Jeez, Mags. I shouldn't even been telling you all this. But I can't help it. All the barriers I've spent years building around myself, to protect me, just seem to want to come tumbling down when I'm with you.'

She reached out, placing a hand on his cheek. 'I don't think we were ever over. I just learned to live without you, doesn't mean I learned to stop loving you.'

He took her hand in his and kissed the palm of her hand.

'I can't do this to you. You think I'm someone else, you think I'm who I used to be. I've done bad things Mags and until I can put that right, by doing the right thing now, you shouldn't think of me with anything but disdain.'

She took a step closer to him, looking straight into his eyes that suddenly looked so tired. 'Everyone deserves to be happy,' she lowered her voice. 'I know my Jase is in there and I think you want to let him out. When you're ready, you can tell me what you've done. I'll try and understand. All I know is, I don't want to go home to Max. I want to stay here with you.'

He let her words sink in. He wanted that too, more than anything, but if she didn't go home then she could be in more danger than he could protect her from. It had to look like the plan was still on track. If they ran away together they would forever be looking over their shoulders. It was imperative he found out who was behind the hit. Once he did and he dealt with it, then they could be together. He thought he could keep his feelings for her at bay, keep them hidden, but his love for her had always been his Achilles heel.

'Mags, we can't be together right now. But trust me, we will be, one day.'

'I don't understand. I can leave Max right now, he wouldn't give a damn, unless he thought it'd damage my record sales.' she laughed bitterly. She'd drop her plan for revenge if it meant being with Hunter.

He pulled her close to him. 'Let's just think about the here and now.'

Before she knew it, his lips were crashing against hers. Her body automatically melted into his. She felt like a teenager again as the familiar taste of his lips hit her senses. She kissed him right back, suddenly not caring if anyone realised that Magenta Valentina was snogging some guy who wasn't Max Maxwell. Nobody did, they just looked like tourists, caught up in the moment.

Hunter couldn't think straight, which was really bad news. All he wanted to do was go right up to Mags' suite and spend the afternoon in bed with her. Tim had collared him as soon as they'd returned to the hotel and asked him to go through the agenda for the meeting later on that afternoon. He was sitting in the office, not even giving the agenda a second thought. He wanted to be with Mags more than anything, but the reality was, even when this was all over and he'd disposed of the person behind this, he could never be with Mags. Firstly, how would she cope with his past? Not just the arrest but being a professional hit man. It took a special person to deal with something like that. Not that he didn't doubt she was special enough. Secondly and more importantly, he'd spent so long living under the radar that if he came off the grid, he'd surely land his arse in jail. He had never gone to trial for the murder of his sergeant. He'd been given a way out and he took it, sometimes he thought it was the wrong choice. When he'd killed his sergeant at least it had been in self-defence, the people he'd killed since were just a target. Had he made the right choice that day? He sat in a holding cell on camp and two men in suits and bland faces came in.

'Corporal Lomax,' suit number one spoke.

'It would seem you are in a bit of a fix,' suit number two finished.

He looked up into their cold, stony eyes. He assumed they were Marine lawyers and were about the kick his ass all over the place till he confessed to killing Sergeant Travis. He had no problem confessing to killing him, his problem was the story the other soldiers had concocted making it out like he'd killed him in a fit of rage, when really he was coming to the defence of someone else and that someone else had done a runner at the scene so his version of events was just hearsay. He nodded wearily. 'You could say that.'

'So, let me get this straight. You stumbled on Sergeant Travis in a compromising position with a young lady, but the young lady was protesting?'

He nodded again. He expected to be told to speak up for the tape recorded conversation but then he realised it wasn't being taped which set him on alert.

'The story we have from the other three marines who arrived on the scene was that there wasn't a young lady in sight and they found you standing over Sergeant Travis' body.'

'I know how it looks…'

'How it looks is a murder one charge,' suit number one butted in.

The other suit began pacing the floor as he read from a manila folder in his hand. 'Excellent record you have here Lomax. Sharp shooter, best sniper in the regiment in fact and I see here you had put in a request to try out for 22 Regiment.'

He shrugged. 'I was thinking of going back to England, SAS seemed the logical step.'

Suit number two nodded. 'You'd be an excellent addition, one of the benefits of a dual nationality, you have your choice of two of the best in the world when it comes to being a serving soldier.'

'Yeah, well, the only place I'm heading to now is the inside of another cell.'

'Your defence is going for manslaughter, you'll never get that, a solider on trial for killing another soldier, it'll be lethal injection for you.'

'Can't I play my English card and get deported back home?' He tried to laugh.

Suit number one ignored him. 'There is another option. We can get you out of here right now. All you have to do is say yes.' 'Sounds too easy.'

'We are a secret Government agency that are so secret the President doesn't even know about us. We deal in handling terrorism and taking those terrorists out. We need a sniper like you on board. Whaddya say? Ready to fight the bad guys?'

Jason Lomax was still a wanted man in America, one minute he was in his cell, the next minute the security alarm had sounded for an escaped prisoner. The choices he'd made would probably cost him the one thing he wanted, Mags. It seemed like a good idea all those years ago to join the Marines, he was eligible due to his dual status from his dad being born in Chicago.

He changed his train of thought to the job in hand. He had an issue with Tim, not only did he not like the slime ball, he also thought he was up to something. Bugging Tim's phone was one of the first things he'd done when he got here. He had a plan of action if Tim caused him a problem. He took some photos out of an envelope in his desk. They were shots of Tim with a reporter from the Echo and also shots of Tim giving a chamber maid a good seeing to in one of the rooms. If Tim stepped even towards the line, never mind over it, then he'd get a warning, these photos would not only find their way to head office but also to his wife. That'd be his job and his wife gone in one hit. Sometimes you didn't actually have to take a shot with a gun to ruin someone's life.

In the conference room in the hotel Mags sat around the table, Jody was to her left, Tim to her right and Hunter directly opposite. She was finding it difficult to concentrate on anything but his beautiful face. She was to fly back to New York in two days' time and the thought of not seeing him till January didn't bear thinking about. She'd fallen hard for him, again. Although as she'd said to him before, she'd never really fallen out of love with him. 'So, confirmed for the weekend retreat are Magenta and Max, obviously,' Jody began.

'Obviously,' Hunter cut in.

Jody seemed put off by Hunter's interruption. 'Err, yes, obviously and err, Logan and Brooke Hudson. Then we have Broken Arrow, Max has advised it's just Johnny and Fly. Sloth will be otherwise indisposed.'

'Rehab again?' Magenta asked.

Jody nodded. 'Yep, but as far as the media will be advised, he'll have a stomach bug and will be unable to fly.'

'You got Trina and Dean on the list?' Jody nodded again.

'What?' Hunter asked.

Magenta's eyes shot back to him. 'Is that a problem, Mr Cole?'

He shook his head, a wry smile appearing at her off hand manner. Outside, he looked calm, inside he was quickly planning. Trina and Dean couldn't be at the retreat. They knew him as Jase, if there was one place he couldn't risk his cover being blown, it was then. He'd have to deal with Trina. If collateral damage meant Mags lived, then so be it.

'Oh and a late addition. Johnny will be bringing Savannah with him,' Jody advised.

Magenta rolled her eyes. 'Great, that wasn't part of the plan.'

Silently Hunter agreed, no it wasn't. Or was it? Savannah would also have to be checked out.

'Tim, I assume you've arranged for the helicopters to transport my guests to the secret location and staff have been arranged for the weekend? Obviously I will need your most professional and discreet members of staff.'

'Of course Ms Valentina. Only the best for you. The helicopters are arranged. Everything is right on track.'

Hunter stifled a smart comeback. Could that guy creep up her arse any further?

'Well, I think this concludes the meeting. It goes without saying that whatever has been discussed in this room goes no further. I want a weekend of absolute anonymity. I can trust you, can't I, Mr Smith?'

Hunter grinned. Well whaddya know, Mags had the measure of Tim all along.

'But, but of course,' he stammered. He turned to Hunter, expecting her to ask the same question.

'Mr Cole, I need some help with one of my suitcases, it's rather heavy and you look like you've got the muscles to help me move it. Would you mind?'

'No problem ma'am,' he glanced back at Tim who looked like he was about to self-combust.

He followed Mags out of the conference room. 'What was all that Mr Cole, shit?'

She grinned. 'I kinda liked it, made me feel like we were pretending to be other people.'

'So where is this problem suitcase that needs sorting out?'

'In my suite and it's not the suitcase that needs sorting out. It's me.'

He followed her into the lift, his throat suddenly went dry. Seventeen years of dreaming about holding her in his arms again were about to come true. Once in the lift, she went to put her arms around him.

'Cameras, baby,' he warned.

'God, this is frustrating.'

'You're telling me. I reckon it's a whole fifty seconds before we get into your suite.'

'A whole minute and ten till we're naked then,' she winked at him.

'Mags, you little minx.'

She smiled wickedly at him, her senses were overcome by the intoxicating scent of his aftershave, not the Fahrenheit of their youth but something equally manly, Hugo Boss. She thought there was something hugely sexy about being in a lift with a hot guy, who smelt divine.

As it was, it took longer than a minute to get their clothes off. They'd waited seventeen years for this, they were going to savour every moment. She raised her top over her head and flung it behind her. She slowly undid the buttons on the waistcoat he had on over his shirt. She pushed the waistcoat from his body, sliding her hands over his hard shoulders. He was staring at her, almost like he couldn't believe this was happening. She couldn't stop looking into his face, it was almost like they'd gone back in time. She unbuttoned his shirt and as it fell away from his body her gaze shifted.

'Wow,' she placed the palms of her hands on his shoulders and let them drift slowly down his hard biceps, across his tight abs and then up his well-defined torso, coming to rest on his cheeks. 'So, you work out then?'

He laughed. 'Ah Mags, you're still the same,' he let his eyes flick across her body. 'Only, more perfect.'

He reached behind her, undoing her bra strap, flinging her bra in the same direction as her top went. He pulled her close to him so they were skin to skin. She let her head rest on his shoulder as he held her tight. They fitted together perfectly, just like they always had. His skin still smelt the same, just as much of a turn on as it used to be.

'Mags?' He murmured into her hair as he ran his fingers through her thick red hair.

'Mmm,' she replied, totally lost in the feeling of being in his arms.

'Can I kiss you?'

She lifted her head back up to face him. 'Bit late to ask now, we're standing here half naked.'

He grinned. 'I didn't want to presume, thought it was polite to ask.'

'Let's forget our manners shall we?'

'Yes, ma'am,' taking her face in his hands he gently tipped her head to one side so he could angle her lips just underneath his. They stared deep into each other's eyes, only closing them the second before she felt his lips impact on hers. To say every sense was on high alert, every hair on her body standing on end would be an understatement. Her lips parted underneath the pressure of his lips, she sunk straight into his kiss. Some things don't change, some things get better. She never thought she'd top the feeling she got whenever she kissed seventeen year old Jase, but kissing him now, all these years later, blew her mind. The palms of her hands were on his bare back, pushing him closer to her. Even a millimetre of space between them was too much. She couldn't stop kissing him, stroking him or being totally consumed by him. As they kissed, he manoeuvred her towards the bed, they both crashed onto it, without breaking the connection between their lips.

She needed to catch her breath, he was making her feel dizzy. She moved her lips across his jaw and along his throat as she left a trail of kisses behind, she could feel his throat tighten beneath her lips. It turned her on even more knowing the effect he was having on her, she was giving it right back to him. She could feel his fingertips running up and down her spine, making her skin tingle. Within moments the finger tips were on the buttons of her jeans, undoing them. Mimicking his movements, her hands were now on the zip of his suit trousers, eagerly pushing them down his legs, over his hard thighs. Once the final pieces of clothing had been discarded, their bodies were wrapped around each other, enveloped in each other's naked skin.

She let out a happy sigh, she felt like she was right where she belonged. The last seventeen years disappeared in a flash, there was no awkwardness, they knew each other's bodies so well. He was already bringing her nipples to a point with the tip of his tongue, swirling around them in the way that he knew she loved. She titled her head back and arched her back, pushing her breasts further into his face. Her legs were already wrapped tightly around his waist and his hands were underneath her bum cheeks.

She could feel his erection pushing towards her, but she could tell he was trying to hold back before entering her, there was far too much fun to have first. She reached down with one hand and took hold of his erection, moving her hand tantalisingly slow at first, then increasing the rhythm. She felt him groan against her skin as his mouth travelled down from her breasts, across her stomach, his tongue dipping into her belly button as he moved lower. Her stomach tightened as his hot lips moved further down, she could feel his warm breath on her skin sending yet more shivers flying across her body. She felt his grip on her hips tighten as he pulled her up towards his lips, she collapsed back on to the bed as she felt his tongue on her clitoris.

'Oh my God,' she'd forgotten that was his specialist subject, within seconds she was on the brink, he repositioned himself and began kissing her inner thighs instead. She almost groaned, she'd also forgotten what a tease he was. His mouth was back on her clitoris again and every time she got close to coming he'd revert back to her thighs, until finally he gave into her writhing, screaming body. When he eventually let her come it was the biggest orgasm ever, it flooded her body in wave after wave, from the top of her head, to the tip of her toes. It was like a flash of fire had ripped through her body. She lay on the bed, panting, her body almost in spasm at the orgasm aftershocks. She could barely speak. He appeared above her, his strong arms either side of her. He looked down at her, grinning. She lifted her legs up, which felt like lead and wrapped them around his waist, pulling him into her.

'Do that to me again,' she whispered.

His hands slid along her arms, so he could hold her hands in his. 'With pleasure,' she gasped as he slid into her and rocked her, slowly to yet another orgasm.

She lay in his arms, her head on his chest. She couldn't remember the last time she felt this happy. She knew there and then that her future involved him, whether she got Jase back or had to accept Hunter as part of the new deal, she wanted to be with him. She was kidding herself if she ever thought she'd really loved Max. She'd left her heart and soul in Liverpool a long time ago and now she'd found it again, she wasn't going to let it go as easily this time.

'You're very quiet there.'

'I am just basking in the afterglow of this amazing sex I've just had.'

'Funny, that's exactly what I'm doing. I've been fantasising about this hot, sexy red head for years and finally the fantasy has become reality.'

She lifted her head to look at him. 'Why did we let those years slip by?'

He kissed the top of her head. 'Trust me babe, you wouldn't have wanted to know me back then,' still might not, he finished silently.

'We've got too much of a connection....Jase.'

He flipped her onto her back. 'Please, please don't call me that...it's too dangerous.'

The serious look in his eyes took her by surprise. 'I'm sorry, it's just...'

'I know, you feel like we've slipped back in time and everything is how it used to be. I wish it could be, but too much has happened to me...I am Hunter now. I always will be. I know it's a lot for you to take in, especially as I can't tell you the whole story.'

She stroked his cheek. 'You can trust me.'

'I know, but right now, the less you know the better. Please just trust me,' he stroked her hair away from her face. 'All I need you to know, is I will never let anyone hurt you or any harm come to you.'

She laughed nervously. 'I'm going on tour soon, what d'you think'll happen? An amp falling on my head?'

'Just know, I've got your back.'

'Ah, stop going all American on me, I prefer it when you talk scouse to me.'

He looked back into her eyes, this time, his eyes were burning with passion. 'Love ya la.' His lips were back on hers before she could say it back. Within moments, his talented tongue had distracted her.

Chapter Fourteen

LIVER BIRD HOTEL, LIVERPOOL.

Hunter was pacing in his room, the remnants of the bug he'd placed in Mags room, on the floor, smashed to pieces. He'd swiped it from its hiding place when she was in the toilet. He couldn't let it be found. He wasn't arsed about Max finding out his wife had been having wild sex, what bothered him was someone discovering his real name. Jeez, he was playing with fire here. How could he do his job properly when he was in love with the target? He was totally compromised. But then who better to protect her than a hit man, who was one of the best in the world, who also loved her. She couldn't ask for a better bodyguard. What worried him was his feelings might cloud his judgement and he might miss something vital. In his profession he couldn't afford to make a mistake, you cocked up, you were dead. Hell, if Mags really knew what was going on...well, he couldn't let that happen, it would only endanger her even more.

His cell rang. The initial S, alerting him to the fact it was his handler.

'Hey dad, whats up?' He slipped straight into their code.

'Just checkin' in with you. Making sure you're ok so far from home. I worry about you.'

'Nothin' to worry about. It's all good here.'

'How's work going?'

'Fine, got everything under control. It's pretty straight forward really, nothing I ain't done before.'

'Good, you ok for money, do you need me to send any?' This was code for can you handle the job on your own, or do you need reinforcements?

'Nope, I'm good, making loads of money.'

'Sounds like everything's workin' out like you planned.'

'Couldn't be better.' he paused for a second. 'Any messages from mom?'

'She's busy with all her clubs, she sends her love and says keep doing what you're doing, you're doing a great job.'

'Ok, gotta go, speak soon.'

He sighed as he clicked the phone off. 'Mom' was whoever hired the hit. He was hoping that the message would be, 'she misses you, pack your job in and come home,' meaning the hit would be off, but no, it was carry on. All systems go. He threw his phone on the bed. He couldn't get any information out of the handler about the person ordering the hit, it would look too suspicious. Especially as he'd never asked before with any other job. All his energies went into following his brief. He screwed his eyes up, why would anyone want to kill Mags? She wasn't doing any harm to anyone. If Max wanted rid of her, he could just divorce her, she was rich enough in her own right, she wouldn't fleece Max, besides, they had their pre-nup. He'd already researched lots about the Maxwell marriage. It frustrated him that he couldn't get close to the other main players till they came over in January, by which time he'd only have a weekend to suss them all out. The difficult part would be knowing that the person who'd sent him to kill Mags would be watching his every move. It'd be easy for them to work out he was the hit man, their only other choice would be Tim and he looked like he wasn't even safe in charge of a water pistol. He felt that gave him an unfair advantage, they'd know him and he wouldn't have a clue who he was really on the lookout for.

An idea popped into his head, hmm maybe he could use reinforcements. He could do with some tough looking waiters to take over to the retreat, just to keep the assassin options open, for whoever out there might be looking out for one. He had to be totally prepared. He'd normally sink into the background too, make himself look as unremarkable and as forgettable as possible, but this time round he was going to be in their faces, they wouldn't be expecting that, they'll assume he'd want to lie low. He needed to bring as much attention to himself as possible. He had to be two steps of them all the time. The one positive was that they wouldn't be on their guard, they'd just be sitting back, waiting to look shocked at Mags' death. If there was one thing he was sure of, she was going to walk out of that house very much alive at the end of the weekend. What he couldn't be sure of, was what would happen to them.

The following day was Mags' last day in Liverpool, she felt melancholy. Not just for the fact that she was leaving her home town again but she was also leaving the love of her life. The thought of going back to Max filled her with despair, the thought of being in his bed repulsed her, although that had been the case for a while. Did he really think she was stupid?

She he'd been shagging around and if there's one thing you don't do, its mess with a girl from The Dingle. She'd been biding her time, plotting her revenge but maybe the best revenge would be to leave him for

Hunter. That would damage his ego, the whole world knowing that the great Max Maxwell had been ditched for a hotel guy from Liverpool. A wry smile appeared on her face. She didn't know what had happened in Hunter's past, but she had a feeling it wouldn't be so easy to run off into the sunset with him. She was still going to put the question to him though, she was pretty sure he wanted to be with her as much as she wanted to be with him. Surely, whatever they came up against, it'd be better to face it together. They were so much better together than they ever were apart.

There was a knock at her door, her heart leapt, she hoped it was him, coming to say goodbye. Not that she wanted to say goodbye, she wanted to tie him to her bed and do all manner of saucy things to him and then let him do the same to her. God, her sex drive was never normally like this, but then she didn't normally share her bed with Hunter. Even just thinking back to those mind blowing orgasms yesterday was making her feel wet. The disappointment showed in her face when she saw Jody at the door.

'Sorry, you expecting someone else?'

'No, just a bit gutted I gotta leave Liverpool again. I assume you're coming to tell me the car is here?' She recovered quickly. She couldn't let Jody know about Hunter, she had an inkling she'd go running to Max.

'Well, it'll only be six weeks till your back.'

'Mmm,' she murmured. Six whole weeks till she saw him again, six whole weeks until she felt that powerful, strong body against hers. She couldn't bear it.

'I'll get Tim to send up a porter for your bags. You ready in ten?'

She nodded. 'Yep, let me just sort my hand luggage out.'

Ten minutes later she was in the reception. Tim was scuttling about as usual.

'Ms Valentina, I do hope you've enjoyed your stay at the Liver Bird, I hope everything was to your satisfaction.'

'Yes, I was very satisfied thank you.'

'Everything is already in hand for your return visit after Christmas. It will be truly spectacular.'

'Mmm, spectacular,' she was looking over his head, searching for Hunter, he must be around somewhere, surely he wouldn't let her go without saying goodbye. Yesterday he was in her bed telling her he loved her, now he was nowhere to be seen. 'You ok, Ms Valentina? You seem somewhat distracted.'

'Is Mr Cole on duty? I'd just like to thank him. He's been especially attentive.'

'Ah, he's err… in the office. I wanted him to wait for an important call.'

'Could you get him please?'

Tim snapped his fingers at a passing porter. 'Get Mr Cole for me please,' Tim could feel his face burning up, why was she so interested in Cole? He was so far beneath her, she shouldn't be wasting her breath on him.

Hunter appeared in front of her. 'Ms Valentina, you didn't think I'd let you go without saying goodbye, did you?' He smiled at her.

She felt her insides melt under the glow of his smile. She'd spent the last seventeen years building up her career, taking no shit, not even from Max and with one smile he totally disarmed her and made her feel seventeen again.

'I wondered if we could go someone more private,' her gaze flicked to Tim and then back to Hunter.

'Of course, we'll use the office. That's ok with you, isn't it Timbo?'

He nodded. 'Anything for Ms Valentina.'

Hunter chuckled as they walked away. 'He really needs to watch his blood pressure. He looked like he was gonna blow then.'

They walked into the office she shut the door behind her. 'If I didn't have to catch a plane very soon, I'd throw you over that desk and would not be held responsible for my actions.'

He leaned against the desk, folding his arms, stretching his long legs out in front of him. 'Let's get one thing straight right now *Mizz* Valentina, if there is any throwing to be done, it'll be me throwing you over the desk. For one thing, you couldn't even push me over, never mind throw me,' he laughed.

14

She stepped closer to him, so his legs were still stretched out between hers. 'Or,' she began an as she fiddled with his tie, wrapping it slowly around her fingers. 'I don't have to get on the plane. I could stay here with you.'

His eyes clouded over, radiating sadness. 'Mags, babe. I would love nothing more than to stop you flying back to New York and back to that git of a husband of yours and the fact that I am willingly letting you walk away from me is not what I want,'

She leaned in closer to him, pulling him to her by his tie. 'Then don't,' she whispered into his lips which were so close they almost touched hers.

'But, what I NEED to do, is let you go, for now. I know I keep asking you to trust me, please understand that for now, this is the right thing to do,' he gulped as her lips brushed his.

'I trust you, doesn't stop me wanting to stay with you.'

He pulled her tight to him. Her head buried against his chest as he held her in his strong arms. 'Just knowing that you trust me, without knowing the full story is enough,' he lifted her head up, holding it in both hands, he bent closer to her, so he could look right into her eyes. 'Love you la, I always have, always will and what I'm doing now is the right thing for us. Just don't give up on me. I promise, it'll all be over soon.'

'You do scare me when you talk like this, what do you know that I don't?'

'I know stuff that should never even be in your imagination, let alone your thoughts, which is why I can't tell you. I'm your shield Mags, everything that looks like it's coming your way, I'll deflect.'

'But, everything's fine. The only thing coming my way is divorcing Max and I can handle him.'

'Babe, just don't give anything I've said to you a second thought, it's for me to deal with.'

'What? So I can't think about you telling me you love me?'

He grinned. 'Well, yeah, that'd be ok,' he paused. 'As long as I can think about you loving me?'

She tilted her head. 'Do you even have to ask? I bloody well love you.'

He pulled her back into his embrace, kissing her hard, this kiss had to last six weeks and who knew what was going to happen then?

Her cell rang, interrupting them. She looked at the caller ID, it was Jody. 'She'll be getting stressed that we're going to miss the plane,' she flicked her finger across the phone to answer the call. 'I'll be two mins.'

She looked back up to Hunter. 'I guess this is it. I can't believe the coincidence that fate brought you back into the hotel I was staying in, but I'm so glad it did.'

He smiled at her. Trust her to think it was fate, she was so unaware of the darker forces at play and the fact that things were rarely a coincidence. 'Me too babe, me too.'

'See you soon, Hunter.'

14

He watched her walk away, out of the office. The romantic in him wanted to run after her and make her stay, the cold analytical killer in him knew there was no chance of saving her if he didn't let her go back to New York. He had six weeks to save her life. There was much to be done. He also had a small matter of Trina and Dean to sort out. He'd always liked Trina, but he loved Mags and sometimes you had to accept a little collateral damage on a mission. 'See you soon Magenta,' he whispered to the closing door. 'See you sooner than you think.'

PART TWO

Chapter fifteen

JANUARY 2013

Penthouse, West Tower. Liverpool

      Hunter stepped back, looking at the flip chart before him. He held a marker pen in his hand, tapping it loosely against his chin. He turned back round to look at the open laptop on the desk. The image he was looking at was being streamed from Max's office. He hadn't been lying when he'd whispered after Mags that he'd see her soon. Barely a day had gone past in these last five and a half weeks where he hadn't seen her. Albeit through the lens of a camera. He'd had one of his old contacts install cameras in Max's office, Logan's office, Max and Magenta's homes, Johnny Kidd's mansion and even Jody Stanley's apartment. He was leaving no stone unturned. He'd learnt lots of interesting things from these cameras. Frustratingly he was still pretty much in the dark where Broken Arrow were concerned. Those boys jammed so loud that any conversation between them was lost in music. What he had learned he added to his flip chart, which he then committed to memory, thanks to his photographic mind. He'd rarely left the building since he'd checked in as soon as Mags left for New York. Surveillance was a full time job. He was getting by on four hours sleep, during the daytime, when New York would mostly be asleep. He was doing his exercises on the large balcony so he could fill his lungs with the sea air and have his laptop on the table as he bench pressed and planked. Not that living in the Penthouse was exactly shabby. The wrap around balcony gave him great views across the river and out towards the Irish Sea and he could live with the minimal but trendy style of décor. Dark wood floors, offset with white furniture, including a white wood four poster bed. There were dashes of colour here and there, turquoise cushions on the white bed linen, a lime green vase on the white dining table and the floor to ceiling windows made it feel very light and airy.

He could totally live here, but the flash interior of the Penthouse wasn't the reason he'd picked the West Tower. Firstly, its proximity to the Liver Bird was of importance, on the rare occasion he left the Penthouse it was to sneak into the Liver Bird and replace the bugs in Tim's office. Tim was under the assumption he'd flown back to the Boston hotel and would be back just before Magenta and her posse returned. He had many disguises to choose from and had managed to sneak in and out undetected. And secondly, the Panoramic restaurant was directly below him, making him feel connected to Mags after their 'first date' there in November. He put his hands on his hips as he concentrated on the words on the paper. He wore grey jogging bottoms, which hung loosely from his sculptured hips and a tight fitting white training top, his muscles bursting out from underneath it. His hair may have suffered from his six week surveillance, but he wasn't neglecting his body. He ran a hand through his unruly curls, they definitely needed cutting, but he knew Mags had a thing about his curls, he smiled at the memory of her wrapping her fingers around them, pulling his face closer to hers just with her fingers in his hair.

He shook his head, this was what worried him, she was distracting him and she wasn't even in the same country. Back to business. He took the lid off the marker and drew a line on the flipchart, from Max to Brooke. The net of suspects were wider than he initially thought. He looked at the names written on the left hand side of the paper, for a guy, he had really neat writing. Next to the names were the strongest possible motives, He had a very full page in front of him. Max was at the top of his list and for him, his number one suspect. Not only had he been getting it on with Jody, he'd also been knocking Brooke off, who was supposedly Mags' best friend. Max seemed to have a real problem with keeping it in his pants. If Mags divorced Max, she stood to gain nothing financially as she'd signed a pre-nup. She didn't need his money, she was worth millions herself. He was pretty sure she'd walk away without making demands. Surely Max would know this. Putting a hit on her was a bit over the top. But then, having looked into some of his business dealings, he would put nothing past this guy.

Logan looked like the wronged man, oblivious that his business partner and friend was giving his wife one. On the surface he didn't look like he could be involved in this conspiracy. That was until Hunter had observed a meeting between him and one of the company lawyers going over Mag's insurance and increasing the pay-out to the company if she was injured or died. The pay-out was a phenomenal amount of money. He dug further, her employee's liability insurance was valid for another ten months, therefore there wasn't a need to update it until October. He took a look at the figures for Maximum Records and hacked into their computer. On paper the company was doing fine, but on closer inspection, it was leaking money faster than a sinking ship. They'd wasted millions on one hit wonder acts. The 'Starmaker' contestants won a one million dollar contract with Maximum Records but

Max had signed a few of them before the show was even over, they all needed money behind them to promote them. Angry emails had been flying back and forth between Logan and Max about the 'Starmaker' acts. In fact the only profitable clients where Magenta and Broken Arrow, both of which Logan had the most to do with. If either of those acts left, Maximum would go under, if one of those acts died, well the pay-out would see the company well into the next decade. Easier to see off one person than accidentally kill off a whole group. Was this behind Logan's sudden involvement in Mags' life insurance?

Brooke was definitely a suspect, she was certainly jealous of Mags' success, that much was obvious from the things he'd observed. She was very fond of defacing the promo CD's left lying around Max's office. That's when she wasn't shagging Max over his desk. Her husband seemed oblivious to his wife's extra marital activity. Mags, on the other hand seemed suspicious. He'd tapped into phone lines as well as hacked into emails. He'd listened to a conversation between Mags and her lawyer, telling him she wanted to meet up before her tour started to begin divorce proceedings. This wasn't headline news to him, she'd already told him she wanted to divorce Max before she'd left Liverpool. What was a surprise was her reference to a call she'd made prior to leaving New York, before they'd been reunited. She said. 'A further situation has arisen, I want the divorce dealt with quickly, I don't want to wait any more. Ignore my previous instructions that we are to bide our time. The ball needs to be rolling before my tour starts.'

He'd let that information digest, so, Mags had been thinking about divorce long before she came to Liverpool. He assumed, knowing that it was always very dangerous to assume, but without evidence he had to go with his gut, that he was the 'further situation' that had arisen. Hell, that woman did more to him than just make him 'arise'. Therefore, he could only conclude that the previous situation she was referring to was Max's adultery. Did she know he was a serial shagger? Did she know about both Brooke and Jody, or did she only know about one of them? It had been difficult to tell from any of the footage he'd watched of her, she seemed so guarded and closed. Not like how she'd been with him. He couldn't miss the look of distaste on her face whenever she was with Max. He knew for a fact they hadn't slept together since she'd been back in New York, he had all bases covered. Not that he could say anything if she did, Max was her husband.

He went back to making notes, he glanced at his Tag watch, he needed to be making a move soon and he had to get his disguise on. He still had Trina to sort out and he had to do it this afternoon. Timing was critical.

Two hours later Hunter was walking down Church Street heading towards the large Boots store in Clayton Square. He was dressed in jeans and had a dark winter coat on, he wanted to blend in and wear something non descriptive. He'd put coloured contacts in, so his eyes were now brown. He wore a baseball cap which flattened the top of his hair, resulting in bushy curls poking out, framing his face. Not a great look, but one that did the job. He wore thick framed, oversized glasses which hid his cheekbones. He hadn't shaved for a few days so he trimmed his beard into a neat goatee. He put one of his many sets of false teeth in, hiding his perfect teeth and leaving him with a set of crooked off white teeth. By his own admission he looked anything but the guy who usually took such pride in his appearance. He meandered along with the crowd, neither looking too hurried nor walking too slow that it would catch people's attention. He stood outside Boots for a few moments until he spotted what he was looking for, a homeless guy sitting outside Wetherspoons, an upturned cap in front of him. He walked past, and dropped a note into the cap and headed off into Boots. To the rest of the city the guy may have looked homeless, to Hunter that was one of his underground contacts that would help him carry his plan out.

He walked around Boots, idly looking at the shelves. It was a few minutes before he'd clocked Trina. She looked older, but as she smiled at the customer in front of her, he couldn't deny it was her. Even without the name badge he'd know that smile. He pushed all sentimentality to one side. Mags would thank him for this in the end. He worked his way over to her.

'S'cuse me, love,' he spoke with his native Liverpudlian accent, but made it softer and quieter, he couldn't risk her recognising his voice and to speak in an American accent would be more conspicuous.

She turned and smiled. 'Yes, sir?'

'I wondered if you could help me with something over here?' He began to walk away, so she would have no choice but to follow. He walked over to the furthest corner of the shop, where a stacker stool was conveniently placed. He pointed to the products on the top shelf. 'I'm having trouble reaching one of those, health and safety being what it is, I thought I best ask a member of staff.'

She smiled again, clearly oblivious to who he was. 'Not a problem sir, I'm insured if I fall,' she laughed.

Good, he thought silently.

As she stood on the stool and reached on her tip toes to get what he'd asked for, he saw the homeless guy out of the corner of his eye. Perfect, right on time. He ran straight past him, as if he was being chased, knocking Trina off balance. Hunter moved as if to catch her, which to any onlookers would look like that was his intention. Instead he angled his body so that she bounced off him, landing on her knees. She cried out in pain.

'We need help here,' he walked off in search of assistance as shoppers stopped to crouch down next to her. Without a backward glance he slipped out of the store. Job done, two smashed in knee caps. Trina wouldn't be going anywhere for the next few months. He felt guilty about her not being able to work, sick pay probably wouldn't be much. He'd find a way to get some money to her and Dean. Mags had told him she thought they were struggling a bit. He didn't want to

15

add to their money worries, he just wanted to save Mags. If Trina had been at the Retreat, his cover would well and truly be blown. He couldn't spend the whole weekend in disguise, Mags would wonder what on earth he was up to. He walked back up Church Street and towards the Waterfront back to his self-imposed exile. A feeling of unease in the pit of his stomach, he wasn't comfortable with what he'd just done to Trina but needs must. In less than forty eight hours Mags would be back and that's when the game really began.

Chapter Sixteen

Max Maxwell's Private Jet –
somewhere over the Atlantic

'For fucks sake man, why do we have to travel with that dick on his stupid Maxi Jet.'

Johnny laughed. 'Maxi Jet, you make it sound like some kinda sanitary towel.'

Fly snorted. 'Yeah, we're flying on a giant tampon. That man has an ego as big as my erections, fuckin' huge.'

'You said it buddy,' he passed his band mate a bottle of Bud, complimentary of course. He took it with one hand, whilst his other hand smacked the ass of the flight attendant walking past. She looked down, ready to glare at him, but when she realised it was Fly McFly smacking her ass, she was all smiles. 'Would you like anything else, sir?'

'Hell yeah,' he grinned at her.

Johnny rolled his eyes, Fly could score anywhere. He had his own distractions, Savannah was seated opposite him, her Louboutined foot running up and down his calf. Man, what was it with flying that made everyone so freakin' horny? He turned to speak to Fly, but he was gone, as was the flight attendant. He turned back to Savannah who was raising her perfectly sculptured eyebrow at him, suggestively. 'Seriously? You wanna shag on Max's jet?'

'Can't think of a better place.'

'I can, like in my own bed, in my own house.'

She frowned at him. 'Ah Johnny, baby, if only the world knew that this rock icon prefers to get it on in his own bed...'

She knew what buttons to press. 'Right, get up now. We're taking a trip to the bathroom.'

Brooke was always a people watcher and she certainly hadn't missed Fly going off with the flight attendant and she'd just watched Johnny's mighty fine ass retreating into the bathroom with Savannah. She sighed, she should've bagged a rock star instead. She was also very aware of Max sitting across the walkway, almost close enough to touch. She could smell his aftershave, she could see his eyes flicking to her every so often when he thought no one was watching. She didn't think she'd ever felt so sexually frustrated in her life, especially as he'd already pre-warned her there would be little to no chance of them hooking up on this trip. She glanced over at Logan, he was immersed in paperwork. She took her make-up bag out from her Marc Jacobs bag. She stretched out her long legs, for Max's benefit. Just 'cos she couldn't jump his bones right now, didn't mean she couldn't tease him. She crossed her legs at her ankles, giving him full view of her smooth tanned legs. She wriggled slightly in her seat, making her trademark almost non-existent skirt ride up even further. She took her reddest lipstick out and flipped open her compact, angling it above her head so she had to tilt her head towards him, slowly she parted her lips to form a perfect O shape, then she applied the colour, red roulette, to her lips in slow movements. She lowered her gaze so she could see his reaction. She could see the vein in his neck throbbing, she was pretty sure that wasn't the only thing throbbing right now. She smacked her lips together, then pouted at her reflection.

The problem with teasing Max was she was now even hornier. She leaned across to her husband, flashing her cleavage at Max. She had something that needed taking care of.

Mags stifled the grin that was attempting to get out, she took a sip of her Bellini to try and mask the look on her face. Brooke was so obvious and a terrible flirt. She could see Max desperately trying not to look. Mags wasn't sure if this little show of seduction was to try and tempt Max and show her that she could have her husband if she wanted or to try and drag Logan away from his paperwork and his constant companion, his iPad. She supposed she should care that Brooke was so blatant in trying to flirt with Max, but in all honesty she couldn't give a flying fuck. She watched Max's eyes bulge as Brooke led Logan into one of the two bedrooms on the jet. She really struggled to not laugh when just at that moment the Captain's voice came over the loud speaker advising that they may be coming up to some turbulence soon and they may be in for a bumpy ride.

The last six weeks, separated from Hunter had only confirmed what she already knew, she wanted to be with him, damaged or not, Hunter was ten times the man Max could even aspire to be. As the plane flew closer and closer to its destination she could feel her own body respond to getting closer to her own destination. She craved Hunter's touch, to feel his skin against hers, to feel his strong arms lift her onto him. She picked up the latest Jackie Collins she'd been reading and fanned herself with it, probably not the best book to be reading when she could feel herself getting into a heightened state of sexual abandon. Still, she could read a dictionary and wouldn't get further than A for arousal, without her mind going straight back to him. She picked up her glass again, this time she needed the drink in an attempt to cool her down. God, she couldn't wait to get back on to that delicious body, but it was more than just great sex, it was the emotional connection between them, the connection she'd spent her adult life denying. The sooner she could ditch her no good husband, the better.

Max was not enjoying the flight at all. Was he the only guy on this flight not getting laid? Well, apart from the pilot, and if he found out the pilot was getting some pussy, he'd fire his limey ass. Johnny and Fly, he could understand, it came with the territory. But Logan? Fuckin' Logan getting it on? Brooke may have been Logan's wife, but she was his mistress. He was mighty pissed at her for flaunting herself at him, then waltzing off with her God damn husband. He downed a JD, then held his glass out for the flight attendant. Thank God there were two on the flight, the other one seemed to be busy with in-flight entertainment. Why on earth had he thought it'd be a good idea for them to travel together? He'd arranged for the jet to fly straight into John Lennon Airport in Liverpool, so they could get to the hotel quicker, but realising he had to spend the next few days with these people, he wished he'd kept the jet for himself, and Magenta obviously, he couldn't fly without her. He looked over at his wife, who looked slightly flushed reading her book, no doubt it was one of those books filled with sex that all women seemed to be reading these days. No wonder he wasn't getting anything from her, she was too busy reading about it than doing it. Brooke was indisposed with Logan and Jody, sitting quietly near the front of the plane, well, he had no chance of slipping off for a quickie with her. Three women who he was central to and he couldn't even get a blow job from any of them. He was in a seriously bad mood. It didn't look like things would improve once they got to stupid old Liverpool either. He felt like he'd been slapped with a sex ban. God he wished he was slapping Brooke's ass instead.

Jody was pretty much aware of everything that was going on during the flight. Johnny and Savannah had just come out of the bathroom, his dark hair all ruffled and his t-shirt hanging, crumpled, out of his jeans. Savannah's lipstick was all smeared and her perfect hair do was now less than perfect, both had a satisfied look on their face. She buried her head in her magazine pretending not to notice, just like she was pretending to ignore the sounds coming from the bedroom. Trust her to be sitting right outside the door, she shoved her head phones in and put her iPod on shuffle. Fly still hadn't resurfaced, but she didn't think he'd be much longer. She kept glancing over at Max, he had a face like thunder. She knew he'd be pissed that he couldn't part take in any of the same activities as his fellow passengers. He kept glaring at Magenta who was engrossed in her book. If she was married to Max she certainly wouldn't hold out on him like Magenta did. She totally had the hots for him, what was not to like? He was very easy on the eye and always hard in her hand. Max was forever telling her, during their sex sessions that she was the light in the darkness and he could never get enough of her. She was already planning some time in Magenta's schedule when she'd be free to slip away and take care of Max. No one would notice if she wasn't there, nobody ever noticed her, why would they when they were surrounded by the rich and famous?

Three hours later, all the passengers were seated and the seat belt light was on. The Captain's voice came over the PA system. 'Ladies and gentlemen, we will shortly begin our descent into Liverpool, John Lennon airport. We expect to land in approximately twenty minutes. The weather outside is a rather nippy minus two, so I hope you've brought your woollies.'

'Woollies? What the hell are woollies? Minus two, where on earth have you brought us Magenta? The freakin' polar ice cap?' Brooke complained.

'I think you'll find the polar ice caps are a lot colder, babe,' Fly shouted down.

'Fuck you, Fly.'

'Any time, baby.'

'Now, now children, play nicely.' Logan pretended to tell them off.

'Sounds freakin' cold though, hey dude?' Fly lowered his voice and whispered to Johnny.

'Actually, I think things will warm up quite nicely.'

'Eh?'

Johnny grinned at Fly. 'Let's just say, watch out for some fireworks when Max discovers a surprise guest.'

Chapter Seventeen

LIVER BIRD HOTEL – LIVERPOOL.

Hunter hadn't stopped all day, he was back in his hotel uniform, playing the role of hotel manager and pissing Tim off at the same time, not that he knew how much he was responsible for Tim's current bad mood. He had discovered that Tim had been arranging to smuggle a reporter from the Liverpool Echo into the launch party tomorrow night. He'd left a brown envelope on Tim's desk with some of the photos of him and the chamber maid, with a little post it note on saying there was more where they came from and to un-invite his press friend unless he wanted his wife to get an envelope. He'd checked Tim's calls and he'd called off the reporter. Hunter wasn't stupid, he was pretty sure the hack would try and get in anyway if he knew there was a story to be had.

So, Tim was in a foul mood and was currently bawling him out in the office. 'Cole, where the hell have you been? The VIPs will be here any time soon.'

He'd been checking the perimeter, not that he was about to tell him that. 'Relax, I'm here now.'

'You could've got a bloody haircut. Don't they have barbers in America?'

'Timbo, you ain't my boss, so quit buggin' me. I gotta go, laters.'

He left the office before Tim could nag him about something else, he would not be sorry to see the back of him. Shame he couldn't get rid of him, but he was trying to get out of this with zero body count, unusual for a hit man, but what the hell, he liked living on the edge. He was thinking that this was definitely going to be his last job, or not job as he was planning on keeping the target very much alive. He was getting too old for this game. He was thirty four, if he'd made it as a professional rugby player, he'd be retiring round about now, so he figured the same rules applied for his equally athletic 'job'.

He was in reception when a large crowd bustled through the door, he looked up to see Mags walking through the door, arm in arm with Johnny Kidd. He took a step back, they made a striking couple. She was wearing tight leather trousers and a fitted black Basque, emphasising her cleavage and a fitted bomber jacket over it. God she'd catch her death in that outfit, Hunter shook his head, man he was getting old. Her flame red hair cascaded over her shoulders and her oversized sunglasses where perched on top of her head. Despite her height and she was even taller in her heels, Johnny Kidd was still taller than her. He wore skin-tight black jeans with a tight black t- shirt, just his silver studded belt breaking up the colour. He wore a biker jacket over the t-shirt and biker boots, loosely tied. His jet black hair had that dishevelled look, but probably styled within an inch of its life. His dark hair, next to her fiery red looked almost like elements had crashed together. As he watched them walk across reception Hunter couldn't help a feeling of jealously well up in the pit of his stomach. Whenever he saw Mags with Max, he felt nothing, he knew she felt nothing for him, but watching her with Johnny now, they looked like a couple. They radiated an aura of je ne sais quoi, he supposed it was what X Factor and 'Starmaker' was all about, finding people who could not only sing, but had the charisma to go with it. These two had it in abundance.

She hadn't seen him yet, he was partially obscured by a pillar. Tim was scuttling over to her, he smiled to himself, she wouldn't be very happy to see him, time he stepped in.

'Ms Valentina, s'good to see you,' Hunter stepped forward before Tim could begin his brown nosing.

'Ah, Mr Cole, such a pleasure to see you again. I like your hair a bit longer,' she grinned at him.

God, it was so good to see her.

'Let me introduce you to Johnny,' she gestured to the rock star next to her, who needed no introduction.

Hunter held out his hand. 'Nice to meet you, dude. Anything you need whilst you're here, gimme a shout.'

'Mr Kidd, I am a huge fan,' Tim stepped forward, not enjoying being out of the loop. His comment was met with blank stares from the two superstars in front of him and the annoying Hunter Cole.

Johnny smirked. 'Yeah, sure you are. Bet you have 'Livin' Loud' blasting out,' he laughed. He began to walk away, slapping Hunter on the back. 'Good to meet ya, man.'

Hunter was pretty sure Tim wanted to stamp his foot. He turned his attention back to Mags, she looked amazing. Her green eyes were brimming with happiness, she looked him up and down, her eyes staying for a moment on his waistcoat. He hoped she was remembering when she slid it from his body, 'cos he sure as hell was. He winked at her. 'Missed ya la,'

'Who the hell is in charge here? Why have I had to carry my own bag over?' Max gatecrashed the tender moment.

Tim grinned. 'Cole, I believe Mr Maxwell is under your care?'

Hunter could almost see the thoughts running through Tim's head thinking he'd got one over on him. He moved closer to Max. 'Mr Maxwell, welcome to the Liver Bird. I'll take care of your bags, but Timbo here, he's your main man. What he doesn't know about this hotel isn't worth knowing, he'll escort you to your suite.'

Again, Tim looked fit to burst, he couldn't work out how Hunter had flipped things around.

'Magenta, you coming now?' He barked.

'I'll follow you up darling, I have a few things to sort out first.'

She smiled as she watched her husband stomp off behind Tim. She turned to Hunter and lowered her voice. 'Sight for sore eyes seeing those two disappear.'

'You're a sight for sore eyes.'

'God, I've missed you,' she desperately wanted to fling herself in his arms, head off to a hotel room and lock the world away. Before she could let him know any of this Fly appeared by her side.

'Nice hotel this Magenta, not too shabby, but fuck me, I'm freezin'. I need to get to my room and warm up.'

She laughed. 'So rock 'n' roll Fly, you'll be asking for an electric blanket soon.'

'Look, my body temperature is set to California, I don't do cold.'

Hunter stepped forward again. 'No worries, come with me and I'll show you straight to your room. I'll make sure your heatings turned up.'

'Cool, man. I ain't a diva, I don't demand only red M&M's and shit like that, I just wanna be warm. Ya get me?'

'Totally.'

Magenta laughed as she watched Hunter lead Fly towards the elevators. Men, never as tough as they made out. Hunter, being the exception, he could certainly hold his own. She watched his retreating backside, nice and taut in the grey trousers he was wearing as part of his uniform. She liked him all dressed up, but she made a mental note to tell the staff that were coming over to the retreat to dress down a bit, she wanted to see him in jeans and a t-shirt, a tight t-shirt at that.

'Admiring the view too, huh?'

She had been so caught up in daydreams of Hunter's naked backside that she hadn't noticed Brooke sidle up to her. She nodded silently, damn, she didn't want Brooke to get onto Hunter.

'I know the whole world loves Johnny, but Fly could have me any day'.'

Fly. Thank God for that. 'Hmm, don't think Logan would be too happy.'

'A girl can window shop.'

She nodded in agreement, hell she was doing more than window shopping, she'd handed over her platinum credit card. 'Ok, if we're window shopping. Johnny has the best arse, but Fly has amazing shoulders and arms, so give me the drummer boy any day.'

Brooke's false laugh tinkled out. 'Arse? Oh, honey, ass is so much better. We've been in

England five minutes and you're going all English on us.'

She narrowed her green eyes. 'That, Brooke, my dear is because I am English.' Thank God, she wanted to add, who wanted to be like Barbie Brooke?

'Well, clearly, being married to Max, you prefer ass over arse.'

Watching Hunter disappear through the elevator doors she grinned to herself. Brooke couldn't be more wrong. Give me arse any day. 'Brooke, Logan's looking a bit lost over there, you better go and check in.' She walked away from 'best friend' Brooke and over to Jody who was busy with Tim, going over check in details. Max obviously hadn't been his usual demanding self if Tim was back already.

Chapter Eighteen

Email from M.Valentina@googlemail.com

To. Max@maximum.com , Logan@maximum.com, BrookeHuds@googlemail.com

Johnnyk@brokenarrow.com fly@brokenarrow.com Savannah@googlemail.com

CC.   JodyStanley@maximum.com, HunterCole@Liverbird.com ,

TimSmith@Liverbird.com

SUBJECT – IMPORTANT INFORMATION – TOP
SECRET

Ladies and Gentlemen,

You are invited to the Launch Party of 'Liver Bird', my
new album.

Thursday 8th January 2013. 7.30pm in 'The Den'

Dress code – black tie.

There will be many other celebrities at this event, but
you are the chosen few who get to carry on the party.

Please be ready by midday on Friday the 9th, in
reception, with a weekend bag packed. All will be
revealed then.

Until then, please enjoy the hospitality of the Liver Bird
and the party.

Yours, as ever,

Magenta

Chapter Nineteen

LIVER BIRD HOTEL – THE DEN

Hunter felt like he was in some parallel universe, he was in The Den, the nightclub in the basement of the hotel. Despite not having any windows, it didn't feel claustrophobic. The ceilings were exceptionally high as the hotel was built on an old warehouse and the huge basement was added into the plans. The room was as twice as wide as it was tall, so it was extremely spacious. The décor was black and different shades of red, with low lighting, he assumed it was to give it a sultry feel. He was wandering around, trying to make sure everything was in order, flitting in and out of the famous people already knocking back the free champagne. He'd already seen Steven Gerrard and his wife, Alex. Wayne and Coleen Rooney. There were some other members of the Liverpool squad. There were some stars from one of the soaps, he wasn't sure which, they weren't his bag. Ant and Dec were there as was the new boy band of the moment, One Direction, apparently they had been personally requested by Max. Some other presenters, Holly Willoughby and Philip Schofield. There were even proper 'A 'list movie stars, Daniel Craig, Samuel L Jackson and Jude Law who were filming in the city. There was also Ricky Tomlinson and Paul O'Grady. A very strange mix of celebs indeed.

One of the reasons he'd been so busy prior to Mags' arrival was because he was putting bugs into all of their suites and he'd already heard some very interesting conversations. He looked up to see Johnny and Savannah enter The Den, Johnny with the usual swagger of a rock star and totally adept at ignoring the eyes of the women in the room who had suddenly turned their attention in his direction and the jealous glances of the men in the room who wanted to be him. Savannah followed, she was dressed in a tight fitting cocktail dress, completely at odds with Johnny's dressed down, breaking the dress code rule and going with jeans and t-shirt combo. Hunter wondered idly if

Johnny's wardrobe consisted solely of tight fitting jeans and black t-shirts. He watched them with interest as they made their way to the VIP seating area, despite the room being filled with VIP's that evening, Johnny was clearly a VVIP. They held hands as they crossed the room, with Savannah planting a kiss on his cheek, obviously marking out her territory to all the other women in the room. He returned her gesture by squeezing her arse. This didn't sit well with Hunter at all. It was totally at odds with what they'd talked about in their suite earlier on. Listening in to their conversation he'd heard Johnny tell her that as soon as this weekend was done they were over, he'd completed his end of the bargain, she'd won the 'Starmaker' competition, by rights he should now be a free man. He'd heard her laugh, a laugh of disbelief as she'd replied that he should know by now that it was Max calling the shots and they'd be over when he decided. Besides, she wasn't ready to end their relationship yet, it was perfect cover. Hunter hadn't discovered yet what she was covering up, but it sent up on high alert and she was definitely someone he'd be keeping an eye on tonight. The conversation seemed over as it had gone quiet for a few minutes, until Johnny finally spoke and told her that Max didn't always hold all the cards. With that, it had all gone quiet as Savannah had disappeared into the bathroom.

The room was still only half full, the main star of the night was yet to arrive. Hunter knew she was still in her room, tutting to herself and wondering where the hell

Max was. He knew exactly where Max was, son of a bitch.

'Oh, baby, I've missed this. Come on, I'm nearly there,' Max looked down to see Jody, on her knees, his cock in her mouth and sucking away like her life depended on it. He knew he didn't have much time, he didn't want Magenta to come looking for him, but at the same time, he couldn't resist the temptation of Jody's luscious lips around his dick. She was far better at this than Brooke. He watched her head bob up and down, her hair falling over her breasts, which were on show in the evening gown she was wearing. 'You'd better swallow baby, don't wanna ruin that pretty dress do you?' She looked up at him through her eyelashes. God, he loved this, a hot woman on her knees making him come. He could feel her drag her nails across his balls. 'Jesus Christ.'

That did it.

One of the down sides to surveillance was having to put up with shit like that. Hunter was fuming. How could he do that to Mags? He treated her like shit. It made his blood boil. She was far too good for him. Within ten minutes of Max getting his rocks of with Jody, he made his grand entrance with his beautiful wife by his side. Again, Hunter lost his focus for a second as he watched her enter the room to a huge round of applause. Max was holding her hand and he held it out at arm's length to show off his trophy wife to everyone. She looked stunning, her red hair cascading over her bare shoulders, she was wearing a long red dress that sparkled as she walked. She'd give Jessica Rabbit a run for her money in that outfit. He noticed her smoky green eyes scanning the room and then settling on him, he raised an eyebrow and smiled at her, hoping she could see in his eyes what he was thinking, that she was the most beautiful women he'd ever known.

Mags was smiling on the outside, inside she was fuming. Max was up to something and she had a pretty good idea what it was. He was incapable of keeping it in his pants.

Fortunately, by arranging this event, the net was closing in and by the weekend, her suspects would be narrowed down considerably, which was of course the whole reason behind this little shin dig. She was going to catch her husband in the act, he couldn't deny her a divorce then, all the paperwork was good to go and then she'd leave the Manor House on Sunday night with Hunter. Not that he was aware any of this was actually happening, but she had no intention of letting him get away again. She looked around the room, finally seeing him over in the corner. He was wearing a tuxedo tonight, his broad shoulders filling it nicely, his rugged look making him look slightly uncomfortable in it, which only made him look even hotter. He was looking at her like he wanted the dress she was wearing to fall away from her body. She dropped her hand from Max's and placed it on her chest, she could feel her heart practically beating out of her chest. Hunter had such an effect on her. She held her other arm out gesturing to her guests, making it look like she was over awed by their applause when in reality, there was only one person in that room who had her full attention.

Brooke's hands were starting to hurt, would everyone just stop with the clapping already. It was only Magenta freakin' Valentina. Hardly Princess Kate, although the way this lot were behaving, it was like she was royalty. She maintained a perfect dignified face, with a slight smile, so anyone watching her would think she was nothing but happy for her friend and her phenomenal success. Bullshit, she couldn't stand the bitch. She watched as she stood next to Max, all full of smiles and thank-you's, she was so freakin' smug. Just 'cos she had everything.

Well, Brooke was determined she wouldn't have Max for much longer, that bad boy was hers.

She leaned over to Logan.

'So, what's with this cloak and dagger trip tomorrow?'

He shrugged. 'Haven't got a clue.'

'But, you hate not being in control.'

'Max said to trust him, so I am.'

'Ha, you trust Max?' She hadn't meant to say that the way it came out.

He turned and looked at her, giving her a cool stare. 'Just get some champagne down your neck and enjoy yourself. Don't spoil Magenta's night,' she seethed inwardly, why was it always all about Magenta?

Hunter was worried, he felt slightly like a fish out of water. The decadence that was going on around him was in danger of making him blush. He was by no means a prude but some of the shenanigans going on in The Den would make even that Mr Grey guy blush. The night had begun fairly sedately. He'd noticed the young curly head out of the boy band trying to chat Mags up, it made him smile, she'd eat him for breakfast and then spit him out. When he realised he wasn't getting anywhere with her, he moved on to Brooke. This also made him smile, typical Brooke getting Mags' cast offs. He truly thought Max and Brooke deserved each other, they were definitely out for what they could get. Logan seemed like a good guy, he was up at the bar, chatting with Johnny and some footballers. The DJ was belting out, tune after tune and the dance floor was rarely empty. He couldn't see Savannah so he took a wander around the room, looking at the dance floor, he imagined she'd be the type to be right in the middle of it, although so far he couldn't see her. He was so intent on what he was looking for that he didn't see Mags sneak up on him.

'Hey you.'

Shit, he really needed to sort himself out, if she could creep up on him, anyone could. He didn't belay his anxieties on his face, instead he just winked at her and replied. 'Hey, yourself. Looking extremely hot tonight Mags.'

'Could say the same about you.'

Desire was written all over her face and she had serious take me to bed eyes. They were going to have to be careful, anyone could pick up on the sexual tension between them. He groaned.

'This is so hard.'

She glanced down to his crotch. 'I'll say.'

'Well obviously, you're around, six bloody weeks without you, I've got balls of steel.' he paused for a moment, taking in the cheeky look on her face. 'I mean this situation. I want nothing more than to pick you up, carry you out of here, throw you on the bed and...'
'Give me a right old rogering?'

He burst out laughing, she'd just managed to diffuse the situation, a moment or two later and he probably would've acted on it. Instead, she had him laughing, which gave him a chance to try and refocus. Not that that was working out to good for him at the moment.

'It won't be long, I promise, but listen...' she lowered her voice, 'meet me in the cloakroom upstairs in half an hour, I can sneak out for five minutes.'

He was still smiling as she glided past him to greet Stella McCartney. He could do a lot in five minutes.

Twenty minutes later he headed out of The Den, past Fly who was shagging some bird up against the wall. Classy, these famous people really had no shame. He was still concerned that Savannah seemed to be AWOL. Everyone else was accounted for, Max was busy smooching up to his fellow celebs, playing the doting husband and telling everyone how proud he was of her and what a star she was. Brooke was still hanging off the boy band boy's every word. Bloody hell, they were called 'boy bands' for a reason. He had pubes that were older than that boy. Still, Brooke seemed to be enjoying her role as a cougar. Logan and Johnny were still at the bar, Logan looking a bit worse for wear, he was trying to keep up with Johnny's drinking pace and losing, badly. Jody was like a puppy dog, following Max around and Fly, well, the whole room knew what Fly was up to. So that just left the elusive Savannah.

He took the stairs up to the main reception two at a time, such was his rush to get to Mags, the way his body was reacting right now, his dick would get there five minutes before he did. His attention wasn't totally gone, he spotted one of the maid's storage room doors slightly ajar. Knowing that the maids went home hours ago, he knew the door should be locked. He slowed his pace and his breathing right down. The hairs on the back of his neck were on end and he reached for the gun he kept at his waistband. He could hear muffled sounds, sounds of a struggle? He wasn't sure, but best to be on alert. He took a step closer to the door, kicking it open with his foot, his gun was raised, he hid it just in time, before the people in the small storage room could see him. Well, there was the mystery of where

Savannah was, she was currently in the middle of some serious lip action and was nipple to nipple with another busty blonde. So that was what her relationship with Johnny was covering up. She didn't seem too bothered right now to be caught. Her eyes went from startled to laughing in the space of a moment, clearly she thought her secret was safe with him. She pulled the blonde closer to her, twisting their bodies slightly so all he could see was two magnificent pairs of breasts.

'Care to join us, sugar?'

He raised an eyebrow. 'Sorry to interrupt ladies, as you were,' he closed the door back over and headed back up the stairs. Not even a set of double whammys could keep him from his rendezvous with Mags.

Chapter Twenty

LIVER BIRD HOTEL – THE OFFICE

Mags was already perched on the edge of the desk when Hunter walked into the main office tucked away behind reception. One long leg exposed as the slit in her dress made it fall away from her legs just below the waist. Within two long strides he was in front of her.

18

'Oh, babe, I've missed you so much,' he pushed her long red hair off her shoulders and ran his hands over the soft bare skin of her shoulders. She let her head roll to one side as she relaxed into his touch and the way he was massaging her shoulders.

'Me too, all I've thought about for the past six weeks is you.'

She grabbed his tie, pulling him right to her, then locking her lips down on his. She arched her back so she was leaning backwards on the desk, pulling her with him as she clamped her legs tightly around his waist. As far as she was concerned, he was going nowhere. She felt his hands trail down to her cleavage, where her breasts were easily released from her dress. He took them in both hands, his head disappearing between her cleavage, his thumbs flickered over her already erect nipples as he lay soft kisses across her breasts. She groaned in pleasure. She couldn't wait, she needed to feel him inside her right now, six weeks was a long time.

'Baby, don't make me wait.'

He positioned himself above her and undid his zip.

Just as she prepared to lie back and think of anything but England he whisked her off the desk and told her to get under it. At first she thought it was some kinky sex game but then he told her to keep quiet. He was busily fixing his clothes whilst booting up the laptop on the desk. She just got under the desk and was tucking her boobs back into her dress when she heard Tim's dull voice.

'What are you doing in here, Cole? Shouldn't you be keeping an eye on your guests?'

'That's exactly what I'm doing. I'm checking the forecast for tomorrow. I heard someone mention snow. The helicopters won't be able to take off if it's too bad.'

Tim eyed him suspiciously and walked towards him. Hunter took a step closer so Tim wouldn't be able to see Mags' dress poking out under the desk. He turned the laptop round.

'Look, possible snow, but not till the early evening, we'll be over by in the Manor House by then, so it's all good.'

Tim looked down at the local weather forecast being displayed in front of him. 'Hmmm, ok, but please don't come into my office without my permission. It's not your hotel.'

Hunter grinned at him. 'Sure thing. You may wanna check out the laundry room off the main staircase, the door was open when I came up.'

Tim frowned. 'Well, why didn't you sort it out?'

'Ain't my hotel, buddy.'

Tim's face twisted in anger. He couldn't wait till he didn't have to see this stupid American with his megawatt smile, any more. 'Right, well, come and show me. I'm not leaving you in this office alone.'

Mags waited a few minutes to be sure Tim was safely out of the way before she crawled out from underneath the desk. Although she was pretty sure Hunter would get him as far away as possible. She smoothed her dress down, which fortunately fell straight back into place. How on earth had Hunter heard Tim? It was just as well he did, two more seconds and he'd have walked right into them doing it on the desk. It had been so good to feel Hunter's hands on her skin, she felt flushed with desire, but just as it had been great to get so close to him again, she was now more frustrated than she'd been in the whole time since they'd been apart. Her body was practically calling out his name. From the moment she'd clapped eyes on him yesterday she'd been in a permanent state of arousal.

She wandered out of the office and back across the lobby to where she found Max. Great, just what she needed, she thought he'd be spending the night stuck to some blonde, or brunette, it probably didn't matter as long as she had great tits.

'What are you doing up here?'

He smirked at her. 'I might ask you the same question. Your adoring public are wondering where you've got to.'

'I wanted to check with the manager to see if he had any messages from Trina. I can't get hold of her and she hasn't turned up. Her mobile is going to straight to answer machine.'

He rolled his eyes. 'I'm sure there's a good reason why she isn't answering her cell.' God, he hated the stupid

English words she used. 'Anyway, you have more important guests to be concerned with, like the 'A' listers downstairs. I'm sure Trina will be here when her bus turns up,' he laughed.

'God, you can be such a knobhead.'

He took her by the arm and led her towards the stairs. 'And you my dear can be a gigantic pain in my ass. There are a billion things I should be doing this weekend instead of being in this godforsaken place. So, be grateful I'm here and at least make a freakin' effort.'

They walked down the stairs in stony silence, only flashing their million dollar smiles when they met fellow party goers.

Mags was by the bar, being bought a drink by Daniel Craig, yet another famous North West star. His home town on the Wirral wasn't too far from where the Manor was. Despite having the full attention of James Bond, she was finding it difficult to give him her full attention. She hadn't been lying to Max before when she said she was worried about Trina. In fact, she'd wanted to mention it to Hunter earlier, after they'd fucked each other's brains out, but obviously they'd been interrupted before they could even get that far. She wanted to see if Hunter could find out where Trina was. She had a feeling that whatever he'd been involved in, which he still wouldn't divulge, would equip him with trying to find her missing friend. It wasn't like Treen to be late and she certainly wouldn't miss this party at least, not without letting her know first. Over Daniel Craig's shoulder she saw Hunter enter the room. She made her excuses and left. She smiled as she walked away, she was pretty sure not many women walked away from Mr Craig. But then not many women had their own Mr Hunter Cole in their sights. Hunter's eyes were on her like laser beams as she sashayed her way over to him. Again, she was aware that the sexual tension was crackling away between them, she just hoped everyone was either too busy enjoying the party or too pissed to notice. Just as she reached him, Johnny and Fly took to the stage, where they'd found a drum kit from she wasn't sure but within moments, Fly was beating out the intro to one of their biggest hits. Johnny had his guitar slung around his neck, always handy that he could take over Sloth's role whenever he was in rehab. That would keep everyone busy for a bit. Hopefully she could ask Hunter about Trina. She watched him closely as she saw his eyes flicker away from her for a moment and around the room, clearly thinking the same thing she was about being too obvious. He pulled her to one side.

'God, this is sending me crazy, being in the same room as you and not being able to pick you up, carry you out of here and throw you straight onto my bed.'

'Don't start, you got me proper worked up before. I'm so fired up right now, I could go off like a rocket at any given moment. You look at me one more time like that with that whole smouldering look in your eyes then you might just see that happen.'

18

He laughed. 'You think I've been standing in a darkened corner for fun?' He glanced down at his crotch, she automatically followed his gaze where his tight trousers were leaving nothing to the imagination.

'Before you distract me again, I need your help with something.'

He leaned against the wall. 'Shoot.'

'It's probably nothing, but Trina and Dean haven't turned up. I can't get hold of her and I know she wouldn't miss this.'

He tried to keep his face neutral. He'd totally forgotten about Trina. Man, he was so off his game. 'Whaddya need me to do?'

'I just wondered if you could try and track her down?'

'Everything ok Mizz Valentina?'

She rolled her eyes at Hunter, bloody Tim was like her shadow. She turned round slowly, Plastering a smile on her face and positioning herself so she could hide Hunter's pole position problem.

'Fine, I was just speaking to Mr Cole about two of my guests who are missing.'

'All the VIPs are here,' he frowned.

'Yes, but my best friend isn't.'

'Leave it to me Mizz Valentina, Mr Cole doesn't know this city like I do. I'll find her in no time.'

Hunter stifled a smile, yep to Tim, he was just some dumb American, not some scally from The Dingle.

'Whatever works for you Timbo, I'll help anyway, teamwork.'

Tim grimaced at him. 'Fine, let's get on with it then.'

Brooke was fuming, the boy band guy she'd been flirting with had moved on to one of the bimbo looking girls by the bar. She'd been attempting to make both Logan and Max jealous, but Logan hadn't moved from the bar all night and had barely even registered that she was there and Max was so busy working the room and being at Magenta's freakin' beck and call that he was also oblivious to her. Although Brooke's ever eager beady eye had noticed that Magenta seemed to be focusing a lot of attention on the really hot hotel guy, Harley or Hunter or something sexy like that. She could see the attraction, he was giving Daniel Craig a run for his money in the hot body stakes. She'd love to know what they were talking about, probably he was in on whatever Magenta had planned for tomorrow, they looked thick as thieves. She and Magenta had posed together upstairs for pictures for the press, looking like the best buds that they were supposed to be. She'd even tweeted the picture #partygirls which had subsequently been retweeted a billion times.

She was so jealous of Magenta, she had everything and she still had hot guys falling at her feet. Brooke was only famous by association. She was fed up of being a hanger-on. She always thought she was destined to be something, she knew all those years ago working in the bar that that wasn't the life for her. She lived in a multi-million dollar mansion was married to a total hunk, who was loaded and yet she still couldn't be happy with that. Maybe if Logan showed her an ounce of affection she wouldn't feel so bitter.

'Hey girl,'

She turned with a frown on her face, to the voice that was speaking to her in the same annoying accent as Magenta's, but she quickly turned that frown into smile when she saw the face attached to the voice. 'Yes?' she purred.

'You're a hot bird, you shouldn't be sitting here on your own.'

Bird? What kinda language did they use here? She smiled sweetly at him.

'Wanna dance?'

She held her hand out to him so he could help her up off the chair she was perched on. 'With pleasure.'

He took her hand. 'Sound.'

'Sound?'

He smiled at her. 'It means great, trust me, when I'm finished with you, you'll be fluent in scouse.'

Jody was flitting in between the guests, catching up with some of the celebrities she hadn't seen since the last opening of an envelope. She sighed, she was being harsh, there were some proper bona fide celebs here tonight and the event was a big deal. She was just in a bad mood. She'd picked her outfit carefully. Max said her curves drove him wild, so she'd picked a Karen Millen dress in jade that accentuated all those curves perfectly. Her cleavage was on show and the dress fell to just above the knee, skimming her hips. She'd piled her long dark hair loosely up on top of her head, with loose strands dangling down, Max loved it like that, he liked to pull it out and watch it tumble over her shoulders. Max. Freakin'. Max. The man she adored and the man who ignored her, unless it was on his terms and she had his dick in her mouth or he was bending her over his desk. Unrequited love, it tortured her. She knew Max would never leave Magenta, they were the golden couple, the world loved them. She was so conflicted, Magenta was probably the only true friend she'd ever had and how did she repay that trust and friendship? By doing her husband. But Max, he was just intoxicating, she could never say no to him. For all the good it did her, he'd hardly even glanced at her all evening. She was trying to stay professional and be Magenta's uber efficient PA, tonight, when really all she wanted to do was sit at the bar and get totally drunk. Her cell beeped with a text, she retrieved it from her bag.

Lookin' smokin' in that dress, wanna grab ur sexy ass n bend u over

Max. One of life's true romantics, not even a kiss at the end of the text. She dropped the phone back in her bag and headed to the bar.

'Double Vodka and coke please. Go easy on the coke.'

Magenta knew something was wrong by the look on Hunter's face, that's when she knew Jase was still in there, she'd seen him look like that before, years ago.

'What?' her voice was barely above a whisper and she knew he and Tim wouldn't be able to hear her over Fly's loud drum beats and Johnny's voice booming out, ricocheting off the ceiling and bouncing off the walls.

'Maybe we should go somewhere more private, Mizz Valentina,' Tim suggested.

'We need to go somewhere quieter,' Hunter said.

She followed them out of The Den, the panic welling in the pit of her stomach she knew she'd been right not to ignore her gut feeling.

Out in the relatively calmer corridor she looked at Hunter, she searched his eyes again. 'Tell me.'

Tim cleared his throat. 'It would seem your friend is in hospital.'

'What?' Her hand flew to her chest in shock. She felt Hunter's hand on her bare shoulder and for the first time ever, didn't react to his touch.

'It's ok, we'll take you to her.'

Chapter Twenty One

FAZKERLEY HOSPITAL
11.40pm

Magenta looked totally out of place as she walked quickly along the hospital corridor, the staccato sound of her Louboutins sounding out of place and her five thousand pound red dress swaying behind her as she neared the ward Trina was in. It was almost midnight and visiting time was definitely over, but when you're

Magenta Valentina, doors open that would normally be closed for Joe Public. The ward sister was none the less a bit peeved that her ward was being disrupted. She greeted Magenta and told her that Mrs O'Hara had been moved into a private room for the night so as not to disturb or over excite the rest of the patients. She followed the Sister towards a closed door.

She felt Hunter's hand on her arm. 'We'll wait out here, give you and Trina time alone,' he flicked his head in Tim's direction. He'd been adamant that he couldn't let Magenta out of his sight and Hunter shouldn't escort her alone.

She smiled gratefully at him. 'Thank you.'

She pushed the door open and walked into the dimly lit small room.

'Treen?'

'Mags? Your party, why aren't you there?'

She sat down on the plastic chair next to the bed. 'You daft cow, why would I be there when you're here? What have you done to yourself?' In the low light she could see Trina's legs in plaster.

'I had an accident at work. I was helping some guy and I fell off one of the stacker stools, smashed both my knee caps in and broke both my legs.'

'Fuckin' hell, T.'

She rolled her eyes. 'Tell me about it, wouldn't bloody mind, but the customer I was helping just got off and left me there.'

'What an arse. So what happens now? How long will you be in plaster?'

'At least six weeks for the plaster, but I'm looking at another six weeks off work after that. I've only just been promoted. I can't afford to be off for that long. He's pretending not to show it, but Dean's out of his mind with worry.'

'Hey, stop it right there, forget about the money. You should be concentrating on getting better and resting.'

'It's not just that it's the school runs, it's the housework, the cooking. You know Dean, he could burn water, God love him.'

'Right, the money, I'll take care of and...'

'Mags no, I can't let you do that. You already gave me money before Christmas for the kids' toys, you can't do this again, I'm not a bleedin' registered charity.'

'No, you're my best friend and what kinda friend would I be if I walked out of here and didn't help when you know fine well I'm in a position to. All those years ago when Jase left me, did you turn your back on me? No. So I'm damn well not gonna leave you in the lurch.'

'That was different, I just took you out, got you pissed and let you cry when you needed to, hardly the same thing is it?'

'You are not gonna win this one Treen, I will sort out the money side of things and I want you to get someone in to help with the school runs and house work, I'm paying no arguments.'

Trina sighed. 'Look it's late, I'm drugged up to the eyeballs, I need to sleep. Can we argue about this tomorrow?' She yawned.

'Oh God, I'm sorry, I shouldn't have come here so late. Tomorrow is when we head off to the manor...this means you can't come doesn't it?'

Trina nodded slowly. 'I'm sorry queen, I hate letting you down and I was so excited about it...' her voice tailored off as she yawned again.

Mags stood up and stroked her friends' cheek. 'Don't worry chick, there'll be other times. I'll see you when I get back. In the meantime, get some sleep and don't worry about money,' her friend was already snoring lightly, she slipped quietly out of the room.

She saw Hunter and Tim waiting, but she headed over to the ward sister first. 'Thank you so much for letting me see her, I really appreciate it,' she opened her bag and took out a business card. 'Now, if you could just move her to a better room and here is my PA's card, please call her and she'll arrange a sizeable donation.' Magenta walked away, not being able to see the look of disbelief in the sisters' eyes. 'Bloody cheek,' she muttered to Magenta's retreating back.

They drove back to the hotel, Tim shoved in the back seat like a naughty school kid.

'How was your friend?' Hunter asked, trying to keep everything as formal as possible.

'Well, she's fine in herself, she's gonna be in plaster for a while and she's stressing about money, but that's the good thing about having Magenta Valentina as your best friend. I've told her not to worry about it.'

Hunter sighed inwardly. Thank God for Mags' sorting out that little issue, they really did make a good team.

'D'you know the arsehole that caused the accident just got off?'

'What a bastard,' he replied, staring dead ahead, not taking his eyes off the road as he drove.

'Yes, there are some very unscrupulous people around these days.' Tim added.

Shit, she'd forgotten about Tim in the back, just as well she hadn't said anything to drop Hunter in it, although what she'd be dropping him in, she still didn't have a flamin' clue. She yawned. 'God, I'm knackered now, d'you reckon anyone would notice if I didn't go back to The Den?'

Hunter turned to her briefly, his eyes twinkling with mischief. 'It's your party.'

'Yep and I actually feel like crying, if I want to. Obviously she can't come to the manor now. I'm gutted.'

'That's a shame,' Hunter replied, evenly.

She glanced over to him, his strong profile set in concentration as he drove. She narrowed her eyes slightly, there was something he wasn't telling her. Her brain was trying to make a connection and work it out, but she was too tired, jet lag was kicking in. She needed to rest, she'd need all her wits about her for the weekend ahead. It wasn't going to be the relaxing retreat they'd all think it'd be when she revealed her plans to them in the morning.

'Just take me to bed, Mr Cole,' she mumbled sleepily.

'Certainly ma'am,' as he glanced in his rear-view mirror he could see perfectly the look on Tim's face. He was getting far too suspicious, he might need to quieten him too.

Hunter had only been away from the hotel for two hours, but when he returned all hell seemed to be breaking loose as he wandered into the foyer. His attention was caught first by Johnny, fist pumping some guy and then embracing him in a big bear hug. He couldn't see who it was, his back was to him, but it was clear this was someone Johnny knew well. Hunter didn't like surprises, was this another addition to the ever growing amount of people he had to check out? He was then distracted by Brooke, leading some guy by the hand up the winding staircase to the next floor. Then Jody spilled out of the toilet door in a drunken heap.

Magenta was busy on her phone checking messages so she was oblivious to what was happening around her. He desperately wanted to see who the guy was with Johnny, his gut told him to be on his guard, he also wondered what the hell was going on with Brooke. Jody was a loose cannon, he was pretty sure PA's weren't supposed to spend as much of their time as pissed as she was. He knew from observing her over the last few weeks she was conflicted over her affair with Max. He was sure the drinking was her way of trying to cope with the guilt she felt over sleeping with her friend's husband. He needed to try and speak to her, sober.

Before he could decide which one of the three to go after, Magenta became aware of Jody sprawled on the floor. She ran over to her.

'Oh My God, what happened?' She crouched down next to her PA, stroking the hair away from her face. She could hear her mumbling incoherently. She tried to lift her into an upright position, but in her drunken state her limbs were not co-operating. 'Ja...' she caught herself just in time. 'Hunter, help me.'

He was by her side before she'd even finished her sentence. 'Shift over Mags.' Whereas she'd been struggling to even move Jody an inch, he picked her up with ease. 'C'mon, help me get her back to her room.' As he dragged Jody towards the lift he was beginning to think this was becoming a habit.

After safely depositing Jody into bed Hunter and Magenta were wandering back along the corridor.

'Some launch party this turned out to be, I haven't even been there for half the night.'

He shrugged as he walked along, his hands safely in his trouser pockets, he couldn't trust them to behave whenever he was in close to proximity of Mags. 'You didn't really look in the party mood...'

She nodded slowly. 'Yeah, you're right, it's all just a big farce and after Trina's accident...'

'Yeah, poor T. She's gonna be laid up for a while.'

There was an uneasy silence between them, for the first time she didn't feel as sure of him as she thought she did. He was the one that kept reminding her that he wasn't 'her Jase', anymore and for the first time she was starting to believe that. She was going to have to get to know him all over again. The foundations were there, they'd laid those years ago and it was obvious their feelings for each other had never gone away, but there was still so much that hadn't been said, so much she needed to know and so much he didn't want to tell her. She stopped walking. He carried on walking, then stopped when he realised she wasn't following him. 'You, ok?'

She took a step closer. 'Why won't you let me in? What's scaring you off telling me your big dark secret? I don't scare easily y'know.'

He tilted his head to one side and smiled. 'I know babe, one of the things I love about you, you got guts,' he took a step towards her, his hands suddenly finding themselves on her hips. 'After this weekend I can tell you everything you need to know, I'm not shutting you out because I can't let you get close to me, although when you know everything, you might not wanna even be within ten feet of me. I'm shutting you out because I have to, for now.'

'You do realise I'm serious about leaving Max don't you?'

He nodded. 'We'll cross that bridge when we get to it, right now, we just gotta get through this weekend.'

Despite the nervous ball that was welling up in her tummy, she smiled at him. 'Will you go back to your scouse accent when this is all over?'

'You got a real thing about my accent haven't you?'

'I just miss hearing you tease me in your soft, cheeky scouse tones.'

Before he could reply, they heard Max shouting her name. 'Pretend you've fainted.' As he spoke softly, he brought his leg up behind hers and gently brought it down against the back of her knees, causing her to look like she'd collapsed into his arms. He caught her in his arms, just as Max walked into sight.

'Ah, Mr Maxwell, there you are,' he walked towards him, supporting Mags as he went. 'Don't know what's up with the women tonight, but they are dropping like flies. Can't handle the drink.'

He off loaded Mags onto her husband. 'Reckon she'll be ok, she just needs to sleep it off.'

Max struggled to get hold of her. 'What do you expect me to do with her?'

Hunter had begun to walk away, but he stopped and turned slowly. 'Look after her, she's your wife.' He didn't wait for a response, he walked away, hating himself for leaving her with the person he suspected of wanting to kill her. He was going straight back to his room and check on the surveillance cameras he'd installed in her room. He could make it back up to her room in under a minute if there was an emergency. He didn't dwell on the fact that it could take less than a minute to do serious damage to someone.

Chapter Twenty Two

LIVER BIRD HOTEL – HUNTER'S ROOM

As soon as Hunter was back in his room he switched on his monitor to check on the surveillance cameras in Mags' room. He wanted to make sure she was ok. As he zoomed in he could see Max trying to kiss her, before his blood could even get to boiling point, Mags brushed him away, turned her back on him and went straight into the en-suite, closing the door behind her. He smiled to himself, that was his girl. Max stood for a moment, his hands on his hips, he looked at the closed door, then to the floor and then back to the door. He then stormed out of the suite.

Hunter picked him up a few minutes later in Jody's room, the poor girl was sprawled out on the bed. Surely Max, if he had any respect for her, would do the decent thing and let her sleep it off. He'd forgotten one thing though, Max was anything but decent.

He watched as Max shook her awake by the shoulder. She was mumbling incoherently. He couldn't hear what he was saying to her, his voice was low and he was whispering into her ear. Jody dragged herself up in an upright position and taking her by the hands Max pulled her up off the bed and slapped her backside as if to say 'you know it makes sense.' He then sat back on the bed, undoing his fly. He pushed her dress up around her hips and yanked her knickers off. He pulled her back onto his lap, lowering her onto his erection. Hunter winced as he saw the sharp intake of breath on Jody's face, clearly she wasn't ready for a quickie. She jiggled up and down as he pumped away at her, because she was facing away from him, Max couldn't see the colour on her face was almost matching her dress. Fortunately for her, Max didn't have a lot of stamina and within moments he'd pushed her off him and back onto the bed. Ever the gentlemen, he rearranged her dress, but just left her there as he vacated the room.

Hunter checked back on the surveillance camera in Mags' room, she was fast asleep, he'd just keep an eye on her till Max was safely fast asleep to make sure she was ok. As he watched her sleep his mind drifted back to the night they'd first started going steady. He'd always been aware of the gorgeous Maggie Vale, but he'd always felt pretty awkward and shy around girls,

20

he was tall and gangly with curly hair, not really what girls were looking for. Then he started playing rugby and things began looking up, his body started to change and his muscles began to fill out his tall frame. He noticed more of the girls in his year were coming to watch the rugby team play, he was pretty sure it was because of the other guys, but then he noticed he was getting the biggest cheers whenever he had the ball. It made his confidence sore. There was one girl in particular he noticed on the side lines, with her fiery red hair, you couldn't miss her. She always had a slightly bored look on her face, she intrigued him, the other girls were throwing themselves at him, he didn't want any of them, he wanted the girl with the mysterious look in her eyes.

His chance came mid-season, the school had organised a disco to raise money for a new kit, the boys were all growing and changing so much that they were beginning to burst out of their kits like the Incredible Hulk. Normally he wouldn't go near a school disco, but as vice-captain of the team he had to go. Seeing Maggie arrive with her friend Trina made it worth the ticket price alone. He suddenly realised why she always had that fed up look on her face, Trina was falling over herself to get Alex, the captain of the team to notice her. He smiled to himself, Trina was a pretty girl, but she was punching above her weight with Alex, the lads always teased him that he could be a poster boy for Just Seventeen. As Alex was taking away all her attention Trina was oblivious to her friend, who had obviously been dragged along to support her, or whatever it was that girls did when they fancied a guy. Not that she looked a damsel in distress, but she definitely needed rescuing, he just needed to build up the confidence to go up to her. He needed a good opening line.

Half an hour later, he was still watching her across the room. He'd made his mind up he was going to speak to her, but first he needed a piss, he'd had far too many Pepsi's in a short space of time, another reason why school discos were shit, no proper drink, just too many sugary drinks to get a load of teenagers hyper. Although if he knew the rugby lads, they'd have a stash of Hooch somewhere. The teachers hadn't cottoned on yet that it wasn't just lemonade. As he walked in the bogs he heard two of his team mates Gibbo and Robbo talking.

'I'd well give that Maggie one, she's fit.'

'I reckon she gives great blow jobs.'

He coughed, they half turned, still mid pee, to look over their shoulders. 'Sorry, lads, you're gonna have to go through me to get her, I'm afraid she's taken.'

'Ah, we got no chance against you.'

That was all the confidence he needed. He strode across the dance floor, sometimes the only way was the old fashioned way, no cheesy lines. He stood in front of her. 'Care to dance?'

That was when he fell in love, she looked up at him, smiled that beautiful smile of hers and looked at him with big wide green eyes. She nodded. 'Ta la.'

So, off they went, dancing to Blur's Country House and despite being more of an Oasis fan, he'd never felt happier. They hardly left the dance floor all night, he wasn't big on dancing, but right there and then he couldn't think of anywhere else he'd rather be than twirling this fit girl around in his arms, by the time the slow songs came on to signal the end of the disco, they automatically wrapped their arms around each other. To this day, he still loved the Donna Lewis track, 'I love you, always forever,' that had been 'their song'. Gibbo and Robbo had been right, they didn't have a chance against him, 'cos from that evening on, they'd been inseparable. He walked her home from the disco, Trina had already left with Dean, having given up on Alex who was last seen disappearing into the bogs with one of the sixth form girls. It seemed cupid was working overtime that night.

They walked slowly, stretching out the ten minute walk to Maggie's house out for as long as possible, without making her late home. He'd instinctively held her hand as they walked. He loved that she was so easy to talk to and they'd spent most of the walk laughing. That was until they reached the corner of her road. He stopped, pulling her into him, so she was practically propelled into his chest. She looked up at him, the moon casting a shadow across her face, but illuminating her eyes so they shone like emeralds. He had fallen for this girl, big time.

She smiled up at him. 'So, is this the bit where I invite you in for coffee? Only I think my six brothers would object to that.'

He laughed. 'I'm not a fan of coffee, I am a fan of kissing though.'

'Well, Jase, there's another thing we have in common.' With that she stood on tip toes, so her lips almost reached his. He could still remember those few seconds before their lips touched, the butterflies in his stomach, the sparkle in her eyes, just before she closed them, her long lashes brushing against the top of her cheeks. His hands slid down her back, pulling her to him, her lips found his and from the moment they started kissing he wasn't sure who was holding who up.

Hunter rubbed his stinging eyes, he was out of his day dream, he checked his watch, or night dream as it had gone two am. He could happily dream about Mags all night. His first kiss with her was ingrained in his memory, but so were the million or so that followed, they just got better and better. He glanced at all his cameras, everyone seemed to be asleep, with the exception of Brooke, she was MIA, last seen heading out of 'The Den' with some guy. He wasn't overly worried about her absence, he was pretty sure what she was up to. He'd give it another hour or so before he hit the sack himself, tomorrow was a big day. He reached out for his coffee cup, damn it was empty. Jase may not have liked coffee, but Hunter sure as hell did, it was his drug of choice to get him through long stints of surveillance.

Chapter Twenty Three

LIVER BIRD HOTEL - LIVERPOOL

Brooke strolled back into her hotel room just before breakfast, she thought Logan would still be asleep. She should've known better, he was already propped up in bed, laptop on. She sighed inwardly, she'd actually be quite happy to discover he was looking at porn at least that would mean he had some kinda sex drive. Knowing him, he'd think that session on the plane would last them till at least Easter. She'd even wondered if he was gay, but when he was on it, he was on it. He just seemed to have zero sex drive.

'Where have you been all night?'

She frowned, well she tried to but the Botox wouldn't let her. He didn't even look up from that stupid laptop. 'I've been networking.'

This had his attention. 'Meet anyone interesting?' He looked up.

She shrugged. 'No one of great influence.'

'You better get showered, we gotta meet in reception soon.'

She flicked her long blonde hair over her shoulder and sashayed into the bathroom. Any hot blooded man would've followed her. Maybe he was gay after all.

Talking about hot blooded men, her body was still pulsating from networking with the physio from that football club she was with last night. Being a physio meant he knew exactly how the human body worked and boy, did he know how to work hers. She let her dress fall to the floor, her knickers were somewhere in the hotel room of the physio guy, a little memento. She stepped out of the dress and into the steaming shower. It was one of those 'rainforest' type showers and within seconds her body was completely engulfed in hot water. As it hit her butt cheeks it made her wince slightly, it was still stinging from the spanking it took last night. Whoever said pain was close to pleasure was bang on the money. She tilted her head back and let the refreshing water cascade across her body, down through the valley in between her boobs. She was still smiling at the memory. First of all, it had been quite sensual, he'd massaged her body, using an oil that made her skin tingle, from head to toe. He really worked those pressure points, to work her into a frenzy, then when she thought she was ready for the main event, he'd told her to be patient. He'd instructed her to lie across his knees. Her bare skin against his causing a sweaty suction vacuum, she wasn't going anywhere. He'd parted his legs slightly so he could reach underneath and get to her clit with one hand and with the other he brought his hand down onto her ass. At first, it was gentle taps, a moan of pleasure escaping each time she felt his hand on her skin, but as he increased the pressure on her clit, the taps turned into full on spanks. At one point she was screaming with so much ecstasy that she thought hotel security were going to rock up to the room. Then just when she thought she was about to come, which she screamed out she was about to. He'd told her she couldn't come till he told her. He made her wait a full five minutes until he finally brought his hand down hard on her ass and said 'Come for me baby.' And almost like it was magic, she did. She'd never had an orgasm like it. It was the first of many last night, he took her in so many positions. When they'd finally finished, he sank back onto the bed, declaring. 'That was boss.'

She couldn't agree more, whatever, boss was. English guys were good in the sack.

Now soaping her body up, she was feeling herself getting horny again. She glanced up at the shower head, yep, that wasn't budging. They might be all high tech, these posh showers, but they were no good for any self-loving.

The reception area in the hotel was buzzing as Tim tried to do a role call to make sure everyone was where they should be. He was getting nowhere fast. These celebs were far too self-absorbed and too busy arguing amongst themselves. Hunter strolled over to him, his hands in his trousers pockets, it should've made him look like a scally, but instead it only enhanced the cool aura he gave off. It drove Tim crazy, the guy looked like some Hollywood film star. He was also insanely jealous of the attention Magenta gave him. Hunter certainly seemed to be golden boy where she was concerned.

'Yo, Timbo,' he greeted him.

'What?' he replied through gritted teeth.

'I'm worried about the weather, the clouds look like they are full of snow. If we don't get moving soon I don't think the choppers will be able to fly.'

'Trust me Mr Cole, we hardly get any snow here. We'll be fine. The clouds will pass and dump the snow further inland. You forget I know this city like the back of my hand.'

Hunter smiled. 'Whatever you say. I'll go and round up the troops.'

As he mingled through the group of celebs he did a quick head count. Only Johnny Kidd and

Savannah seemed to be missing, well, it's not like you could expect a rock star to be on time. Although in fairness, Fly was there, albeit slouched across one of the plush sofas with his Raybans on. Magenta was looking as gorgeous as ever, secret glances flickering between them. She was trying to calm Max down who was busy barking orders at Jody. That poor girl must be so confused, one minute he's ramming his dick into her, the next he's down her throat, yelling at her. Brooke sat poised perfectly on one of the plush chairs, examining her nails, trying to pull off the bored look, it might have worked except she was too busy watching what everyone was up to. He didn't like watchers, they tended to notice things they shouldn't. He'd have to keep a close eye on her, especially as he didn't trust her one iota. If Mags only knew half of what was going on. Logan was sitting opposite her, engrossed in his iPad, he really didn't think he had anything to worry about with him, but the insurance deal niggled away at him. Finally Johnny made his entrance, with Savannah by his side, there was someone behind him, but he was obstructed from view

'Sorry I'm late guys, Mags, I hope you don't mind someone else joining the party?' He moved to one side. 'My brother could do with a holiday.'

Hunter groaned inwardly, jeez, how many more unannounced guests? This was getting beyond a joke now. How the hell was he supposed to protect her with long lost relatives popping up? It was then he noticed the look on Max's face, blazing wasn't the word. He was glaring at Johnny who was grinning back, he couldn't see his eyes, as like Fly, he was wearing Raybans, soddin' rock stars. Mags, oblivious to the look on her husband's face stepped forward. 'Johnny, that's fine, the more the merrier. Wow, you brothers were certainly at the front of the good looks queue,' she held her hand out to Johnny's brother who had stepped in between Johnny and Savannah. 'I'm Magenta.'

He took her hand and shook it. 'I know, it's a real pleasure ma'am. I'm Shane, thanks for lettin' me crash in on your trip. Johnny said it'd be ok.'

She smiled 'Sure thing, it's not a problem.'

Hunter was still focused on Max, his eyes were on Shane a frown on his face. Mags may have been ok with Shane joining the party, but Max definitely wasn't. Unfortunately, now wasn't the time to find out why, they had helicopters to catch and despite what Tim said, he didn't like the look of that weather one little bit.

Max dragged Magenta to one side. 'What the hell are you playin' at, lettin' that jerk off come with us?'

She faltered for a moment, she wasn't expecting the venom in Max's voice. 'I, I didn't think it'd be a problem, I could hardly say no could I? Being put on the spot like that.'

He gritted his teeth at her, trying to keep his voice low. 'That's the problem Magenta, you don't think, unless it's about you. Well, newsflash, baby, the world doesn't revolve around you and your massive ego.'

She stepped closer to him. 'MY massive ego? Oh honey I think you got us confused there.' she laughed in his face, which only antagonized him even more.

'You listen to me, sweetheart and you listen good. I reckon you're due a wakeup call and when it comes, don't expect me to bail you out.'

She folded her arms slowly. 'Honey, if you're threatening me, then I suggest you watch your back, 'cos nobody else is watching out for it.'

'And to think I thought I was marrying an English rose all those years ago, turns out you're just like every other bitch out there, just with a prettier face.'

'You forget Maxie baby, I can hold my own, you don't scare me one little bit and if I'm a bitch to you, it's 'cos I need to be to protect myself. We all know the most important person in the world of Max Maxwell IS Max Maxwell, well maybe I think I'm worth more than what you're offering.'

He laughed. 'Yep baby, you're worth millions and I'm cashing in on every single dollar, I own you.'

Flicking her hair over her shoulder and raising her face to his in defiance, she said. 'You don't own me Max and pretty soon you're gonna get your own wake up call,' she planted a kiss on his cheek, but glared at him as she walked away. As she strode across the room she caught Shane's eye, she smiled her rock chick smile at him, which he returned. The smile stayed frozen on her face. There was something about him she didn't like. She hadn't been lying when she'd complimented him on his good looks. The Kidd brothers were certainly attractive, but Shane had a mean look in his eyes. Johnny was All-American rock star hot and sexy, Shane had this shifty look about him. It made her feel uneasy. Max she could handle, but the thought of finding herself in a room alone with Shane made her shiver and not in a good way. But like she'd just said to Max, what could she do about it. And there was a point, why had Max kicked off so much about Shane coming with them, what was it to him? This weekend just had to go as planned, it just had to. So much was riding on it.

Hunter wanted nothing more than to go over and check Mags was ok, but he knew he had to keep his distance in public, especially now as they were heading off for the weekend. Whoever hired him was in this room now, probably already aware of who he really was and what they'd paid him to do. He couldn't be seen to be cosying up to the target. Whatever she and Max had just been discussing was clearly heated and by the look on her face as she walked away he could tell Mags was angry. The annoying thing from his point of view was that Brooke was best placed to hear exactly what had been said, and by the sly smile on her face, it was obviously juicy. Man, he didn't trust any of them and as yet he had no real suspect.

His overriding gut feeling had always veered towards Max, but that was too neat, too obvious. Almost like, 'the butler did it.' It didn't sit right with him.

Two helicopters buzzed across the unnaturally looking snow filled skies covering the River Mersey, the water and the sky almost mirroring each other with the strange off grey colour that filled the sky just before a storm hit. Hunter glanced nervously out of the window, from the storm clouds, down to water below, which had waves higher than he'd ever seen on the river.

He checked the time on his watch. Fortunately they were due to land in six minutes. It was only a ten minute flight, would've only taken them half an hour at most in the limos, but hey, limos are so last year. The two helicopters were in tandem as they flew lower, the snow laden clouds forcing them to fly at a lower altitude. The Manor House was in the centre of the Wirral Peninsula, about a mile from a village called Thornton Hough. Hunter had the map open, the house was on the side of a hill and from what he could see, it was pretty secluded, the nearest buildings being in the small village. Secluded was always good if you were planning on bumping someone off, maybe not so good if you were planning on saving someone's life.

As the helicopter swooped down onto the lawn in front of the Manor House, he looked over at Mags. The clock had started, forty eight hours to save the life of the woman he loved, forty eight hours and the clock was running down. Game on.

Chapter Twenty Four

ARLEY MANOR HOUSE -WIRRAL

Magenta smiled as she walked up the path way to the Manor, enjoying the sound of the pebbles crunching underneath her DM's and laughing inwardly at Brooke trying to negotiate the pathway in her nude LK Bennett's. No style that girl, no style at all. Unlike the manor house, which was as full of Ye Olde English charm as you could get. Not quite Downton Abbey, it was smaller than that, but it certainly had a touch of quaint English charm. A double fronted Jacobean house, ivy framing the windows, lead in the window panes and an overly large oak front door. Standing in front of the facade it seemed it was a hit with Logan and Johnny, she could hear them both sounding impressed with the building.

'Y'see this is what I imagine when I think of England,' Johnny said.

'Reckon it's got a butler,' Logan added, sounding hopeful.

She turned to them. 'Normally it would do, but we've given the staff the weekend off, we've got Hunter, Tim and some of the staff Tim has brought with him. I kinda wanted a bit of exclusivity.'

Johnny nodded. 'Good call, you need people around you can trust when you wanna party.'

'Yep, but Johnny, that doesn't mean I wanna see videos of you in the airing cupboard shaggin' Savannah uploaded to Twitter.'

'What's an airing cupboard?'

Logan laughed. 'Love that that's your main concern.'

He shrugged. 'Think it's a given that there's gonna be some shagging goin' on this weekend.'

She grinned. 'That's what I'm hoping.'

'Ooh, dirty weekend with Mr M, hey?' Savannah joined in the conversation.

'Something like that.'

'C'mon kids, let's get inside, the snow is gonna start any minute.'

'Thank fuck for that, I'm freakin' freezin' my ass off standing here looking at this stupid building, it better be warm inside,' Brooke tried to stamp her foot, but she only ended up snapping her heel. 'Argh, I hate it here already.'

Logan took his wife by the elbow and ushered her inside, trying to placate her with promises that it'd be ok once they got inside.

Hunter and Tim, along with the three other members of staff that Tim had sent over earlier that day, by train, they weren't getting the thrill of being in a helicopter, dragged the many Louis Vuitton bags up the path.

'Hey, watch it, they're expensive,' a retreating Brooke shouted back.

'Does she want them a bit scuffed or, covered in snow, which they will be if we hang around here much longer,' Hunter muttered.

'You are obsessed with snow, I've told you it'll pass us by,' Tim said.

Hunter looked up at the clouds, he was no weatherman, but he was also not as stupid as Tim, snow was coming and he'd never seen clouds quite like that in this part of the country. He just shrugged his shoulders and carried on taking the bags inside. Pushing the heavy door open he stepped into the grand hallway, a vast space with a black and white chequered floor. Leading to a dark wood sweeping, curved staircase. Three chandeliers hung from the ceiling and huge gold framed mirrors hung on the walls. A grand piano sat nestled under the curve of the staircase.

'So, like, how does this work? Who gets first dibs on the rooms?' Johnny asked as they congregated in the hall.

'Mr Kidd, please, go into the drawing room where welcome cocktails will be served, we'll take care of your baggage in the pre assigned rooms. Naturally Ms Valentina and Mr Maxwell will be in the master suite, but I'm sure you'll all be more than happy with the grandness of your rooms. Stately homes is what us Brits do best.'

Johnny looked at Tim with slight disdain, he really didn't like this guy. 'I thought suckin' up was what you Brits did best.'

Magenta stifled a giggle. Max coughed, clearing his voice and turned to Tim. 'While we're on the subject of sucking up, you might wanna remember that it's Mr Maxwell and Ms Valentina, not the other way round, I always come first.'

'Ain't that the truth, honey,' Magenta smiled sweetly at her husband.

Hunter turned away so no one would see the smile on his face, he loved Mags' quick witted humour, she certainly put Max in his place. He busied himself fixing more 'welcome drinks.'

'Wow, this is one cool place, ain't never been in a place as grand as this. Johnny boy, mom would freak out at this.'

Hunter stopped mid pour, that voice, Shane's voice. He'd know it anywhere, well obviously he didn't when he first heard Shane, he was distracted sizing up his body language and working out what his addition meant to the group dynamic. But now, now that his hearing was the sense working over time, he knew exactly who Shane was, he'd spoken to him many times. He was the handler. Holy shit that would definitely mean Shane knew who he was and what he was really doing here. Things just got a hell of a lot harder. His mind ran over the scene back at the hotel when Shane made his grand entrance. Max's face, looking like thunder, Johnny looking like the cat that got the cream. What the hell was really going on here? Why did he suddenly feel like he was being played? He put the glasses down slowly. Focus, Jason. Ah crap, now he couldn't even get his own name right. Focus, Hunter, you are Hunter for a reason, whichever of these bastards hired him, he'd hunt them down and make them pay. Whatever games they were playing amongst themselves, he'd leave them to it. He turned round, two glasses in his hand, he handed one to Johnny and one to Shane, smiling at both of them. He raised an eyebrow at Shane, he returned the gesture. Well, if there was one thing he liked it was a challenge. He'd originally planned on a zero body count, but right now there were a least three people on his hit list, he was back in business, whoever heard of a hit man without a list. He smiled again slowly at Shane and walked away.

Chapter Twenty Five

Brooke and Logan were getting settled in their suite. She flung her Marc Jacobs bag on the queen sized four poster bed and placed her hands on her hips. 'Well, I suppose its ok,' she wrinkled up her nose. 'It smells a bit funky.'

'It smells of history, I was reading in the information booklet that royalty have stayed here,' Logan said.

She opened drawers and wardrobe doors as she carried out her inspection. 'I imagine any Royalty stayed in Queen Magenta's suite.'

'Ah, quit with the jealousy Brooke, she's supposed to be your best friend.'

'Mmm, supposedly.'

Logan frowned. 'What's that supposed to mean?'

She closed the wardrobe doors, spinning around to face him. 'Nothing you need to worry your pretty little head about, sweetie.'

'Look, this is Magenta's gig, so what she says goes for this weekend, ok?'

'God, you really are her little lap dog aren't you?'

'No, I'm her manager.'

'No. Max is her manager.'

'No. Max is her husband, he just likes to interfere in the running of her career. Mostly I let him, then overrule him when his back's turned. I find that's the best way to deal with his need to control everyone.'

She looked at him, her head tilted to one side. 'I thought you and Max were bosom buddies, why would you do things behind his back?'

A slow smile spread across his handsome face. 'We all do things behind people's backs, honey. It's human nature. It's whether we get caught or not that's the kicker.'

Her hands were back on her hips. 'What are you up to, Logan?'

He shrugged his shoulders. 'Me? Nothing, your conscience clear?'

A tension, almost as thick as the clouds outside, filled the room. Broken only by a knock at the door. Wordlessly he walked over and opened it.

Hunter stepped in. 'Hey, sorry to bother you, just wanted to make sure you were settling in ok and there's just some spare towels here. I'll leave them on the dresser for you to sort out,' he walked over to the antique french dresser placing the towels down.

'Thanks, man. We're just fine.'

22

'Great, shout out if there's anything you need,' he left the room, closing the door behind him and the whole heap of tension with it.

Fly's room was the next one along, he knocked on the door.

'Come on in.'

He pushed the door open, Fly was lying on the bed, a cowboy hat slipped from his head to partially cover his face, a cigarette hanging between his lips, his fingertips tapping a beat on his denim clad legs.

'Sorry to interrupt, just wanted to make sure you had everything you need?'

'Yeah, I'm fine, apart from this stinking jet lag.'

'Try and keep your watch on LA time, you might find that helps, just a little tip I picked up.'

'Cheers dude, hey, you don't know if there's gonna be any more women joining this little party do ya? I never go a weekend without getting laid, in fact, I reckon I probably get laid at least six times a week.'

Hunter laughed. 'Is Sunday your day of rest?'

Fly flicked the cowboy hat off his face. 'No man, ain't no rest for the wicked. Chicks just can't get enough of the Fly guy.'

'Sorry dude, but think your pickings will be limited this weekend.'

'Man, Johnny promised me some hot chicks if I came over here with him. Coulda brought a nice chick for me instead of his brother.'

Hunter saw an opening too good to miss. 'Yeah, that was a surprise, didn't know Johnny had a brother.'

'Yeah, the press likes to think there's bad blood between them 'cos Shane's not a good guy, Max wants them to play the 'brothers' thing down, thinks it's not good for Johnny's profile...' he paused. 'Ah, you don't need to know this, it's boring band politics. Either way though, Max sure as hell gotta be pissed that Shane's turned up. At least there's no paparazzi around to photograph them together.' Fly yawned.

'Get some sleep, want me to come and wake you before dinner?'

Fly nodded. 'Actually, could you send some hot British chicks instead?'

Hunter left, smiling to himself, he liked Fly, he hoped he wasn't behind the hit on Mags, he didn't think he was but there was definitely more to Broken Arrow than met the eye though. Secrets hidden from the public.

He carried on along the corridor and then up to the next set of stairs toward Mags' suite. He knocked on the door.

'YES.'

Max's voice came barking through the door. He pushed the door open. Max was standing in front of the window, yelling down his mobile phone.

'Whose monumental fuck up was this? I can't be seen in the same city as him, never mind the same God damn freakin' hotel. Get this sorted and get it sorted now.'

Max didn't even acknowledge Hunter who was in and out within seconds, having left towels on the French dresser.

He may have only been in the room for less than a minute, but he'd learnt a lot. Clearly that conversation was about Shane. What was the connection between the two of them?

Still pondering Max's conversation he headed to Jody's room where he found her with Mags, checking over some artwork of the costumes planned for the tour.

'Mmm, I'm not sure about that one, don't want to look too Gaga, I've got my own image,' Mags mused as she lifted a piece of paper up to her face for closer inspection. 'No way could Gaga carry that off, she hasn't got the boobs for it.'

'She's right,' Hunter grinned as he peered over her shoulder.

'Jeez,' she almost jumped out of her skin. 'You're like a stealth bomber sometimes, where did you spring from?'

'Just doing the rounds, checking everyone's settled in ok.'

Jody nodded. 'I love this place, so quaint and English.'

Magenta smiled. 'My mate's Nan used to live not far from here and we'd come over and visit her when we were kids, she had this huge big garden to play in, so we'd spend whole weekends here. When we drove past this place I was in awe of it, I'd always have this little day dream that one day I'd live here and be rescued from my dull and boring life and live happily ever after with my handsome prince,' Mags sighed.

'Well, I reckon you rescued yourself girl, you've never needed a handsome prince to bail you out, not that Max is on the shabby side of course,' Jody gave out an uneasy laugh. Over Jody's head, Hunter's eyes met hers for a brief second, both of them knowing that Max wasn't the handsome prince in the story. Hunter swallowed hard as he tore his eyes away from her. She didn't know it, but she did need rescuing.   He stepped towards the window, he needed a moment to clear his head. As he looked out of the window he could see the weird whiteness of the clouds as the snow began to fall. Big flakes of snow had already covered the lawn where the helicopters had landed less than an hour ago. This snow was definitely the 'sticking' kind and it was falling heavier by the minute. He turned back round.

'Wrap up warm girls, the snow looks like it's here for the weekend too. I'll get the heating turned up.'

Mags smiled. 'You really are the host with the most, you think of everything.'

'No, Magenta, you are the hostess with the mostest, I'm just here to make sure everything goes to plan and there's no hiccups.'

This time when her eyes met his, there was confusion in her emerald eyes, like she thought he'd just given her a coded message.

Jody, still engrossed in the costumes designs was oblivious to their secret looks bouncing off each other.

'Dinner will be at 7pm, pre-dinner drinks 6.30pm in the grand ball room,' he informed them and with that he quickly left. Being around Mags was driving him to distraction. One other thing he was looking forward to when this was all over was jacking in this undercover role of hotel management, he wasn't cut out to be in the hospitality business, he'd rather be on the other side of the bar. This whole situation was becoming one huge headache, but he hadn't become the best in his field by picking the easy jobs.

Like Fly, Johnny was also lazing on the bed, doing his best to ignore Savannah who was parading around the bedroom in a plunging silver La Perla bra and matching barely there thong. She swung her hips as she walked, her hair brushing past her shoulders like a golden halo.

'Don't know who you're tryin' to impress there darlin' you and I both know I don't do it for you.'

She turned, placing her hands on her slender hips. 'Sugar, you're a rock star course you do it for me.'

'Yeah, but you'd prefer me to be Magenta or even Brooke.'

She wrinkled up her perfect nose. 'Jeez, not Brooke, her tits are so fake, they do nothing for me. Real boobs are the best.'

He chuckled. 'Finally something we agree on. Look, you don't need to keep up the pretence when we're in private.'

She shrugged her shoulders. 'You never know who's watching, besides I'm not adverse to a bit of cock every now and then.'

'What you really mean is, you're not adverse to getting it on with me, so you can fuel your five minutes of fame with your 'one time when I shagged Johnny Kidd', stories.'

She took a step closer. 'Don't know what your problem is, so what I like to drink from the furry cup? Shouldn't bother you, you're still getting laid with me.'

'Your sexuality doesn't bother me, I'm just pissed at Max thinking he can run my life for me, pick which songs I release, tell me who I can date, I'm sick to fuck of it.'

'Max is ok, he knows this industry inside out.'

He laughed bitterly. 'Oh the voice of the clueless. Let's see if your still saying that when A. your career blows up after one song or B. He dumps your ass on some two bit indie record label.'

She frowned. 'If you hate it that much, why don't you dump *his* ass? You're Johnny Kidd, rock God, you don't need him.'

'Don't I know it, he's like a cockroach though, just when you think you've got rid of him he comes crawling back,' he rubbed his hand across his chiselled jawline. She sauntered over to him and began massaging his shoulders. 'Ooh, sugar, you're so tense.'

'Here's what I don't get, if you're into women, how can you turn it on for me? I wouldn't shag another guy for a billion bucks.'

She giggled. 'Ah Johnny, Johnny, Johnny,' she said his name in a seductive whisper. 'I appreciate beauty in all its forms, male or female, and you, my friend are beautiful. It's simple really,' as her hands worked the strained muscles of his neck he could feel himself growing hard. Jeez. This was a ridiculous situation. He didn't need to sleep with a lesbian, he could have any woman in the world, but unfortunately, this was the only one available to him at the moment. Now, if she bought a lesbian friend along, that'd be a much better story. Just as he was about to give into his sexual desires and pull her round onto his lap, there was a knock at the door.

He groaned as he fell back onto the bed. 'Saved by the bell.'

Hunter's eyes nearly popped out of his head when Savannah opened the door. Jeez, what a waste. Although he knew she was getting it on with Johnny too, so maybe not a waste, maybe just a huge sexual appetite.

'Err,' he dragged his eyes up to her face. He may be totally in love with Mags, but he was only human, couldn't really ignore a display like that when it was shoved in front of you. 'Just dropping in some extra towels and checking you're ok.'

'I'm more than ok,' she purred, also looking him up and down. He squeezed by her, man she was the flirtiest lesbian he'd ever met. Judging by Johnny lying on the bed, a bulge in his jeans pointing towards the ceiling, he obviously thought so too. He grinned. 'I'll leave you guys to it.'

Hunter, headed for the final room on his list, Shane's. When he got there, it was empty. Just Shane's battered suitcase on the bed. He was sorely tempted to have a look through, but without knowing where Shane was he couldn't take the risk. So he quickly planted the bug in the dresser, as he'd done with everyone else's room. He didn't have visual cameras in there, but at least he'd be able to hear what was going on. Now to get ready for dinner.

Chapter Twenty Six

Magenta sat at the dressing table in her suite, finishing off her make up before heading down stairs to the banqueting hall for dinner. She didn't know where Max was, he'd stormed off earlier, he was in a foul mood. She'd ask what the matter was, but she didn't really care. She leaned closer into the mirror as she slid her black kohl pencil across her eyelid. She knew Max was cheating, she just had to work out who it was with. Then she could exact her revenge. It wasn't because she was in love with him and she wanted to get her own back for breaking her heart, it was because she wanted to teach him a lesson. He needed to learn that it wasn't ok to treat women as his personal sex objects especially if you're married. She was going to hit him where it hurt, Maximum. Divorce wasn't enough, that would let him off the hook. She didn't need his money, in fact she didn't want a penny from him. She was going to sign her shares in Maximum over to Logan to give him control over the company, that would be where Max would learn the hard way that you don't mess with Magenta Valentina. Did he take her for a fool? Did he really think she'd sit back and let him walk all over her? If he did, he was sorely mistaken and he'd seriously mis-judged her. He may be laughing behind her back with his 'lover' thinking he was getting away with it, but what goes around comes around and she was almost ready to serve him with a rather large dish of getting her own back. She picked up her GHDs to curl her hair.

When Hunter came back into her life he'd said he was surprised she'd ended up with a guy like Max and in all fairness so was she, he was totally the anti of what she'd fallen for in Jase. In hindsight, that was probably why she'd settled for Max, she couldn't risk going through the pain of getting her heart broken again. She knew she was safe with Max, he couldn't break her heart because she'd never loved him. She'd only ever loved Jase and now that he'd re-emerged as the rather buff looking Hunter, she knew she'd never stopped loving him. Things had changed, she was different, he was certainly different. She wasn't the broken girl he'd walked out on, she'd toughened up, she was ballsy and gutsy. She was the type of woman who could look after herself, fight her own battles. But that didn't mean she didn't crave to be in the arms of someone she truly loved.

Would she have become Magenta Valentina, rock chick if he hadn't left? Probably not. After the charity single, her break through first single, 'I'll follow you' had come out of nowhere to hit the number one spot

23

and it had stayed there for a while, not long enough to becoming annoying, like 'Wet Wet Wet's', Love is all around. (A song that she had always hated.) But long enough for it to become her signature tune. Although she hadn't written it herself, the words fitted perfectly to the situation between herself and Jase. She'd recorded it in just one take. Her producer and Writer, Will Power, who was one of America's hottest producers told her there and then it would be a hit. She wasn't so sure, she thought it sounded a bit breathy as she sang, struggling to keep her emotions in check. It was that breathlessness that showed her vulnerability and made the song a hit. It became the 'break-up' song of that generation.

She pulled a dog-eared A5 notebook out of her bag, she carried this everywhere. Now she was writing her own songs, still with Will's help, she was always jotting down ideas and lyrics.

At the back of the notebook, hidden away was a picture. It was of her and Jase at Trina's 18th. She kept it so she could always summon up the emotion to sing 'I'll follow you.' It was her favourite photo of the two of them, they were leaning into each other, cheek to cheek, smiling happily for the camera, with an ever so slightly drunk look in their eyes. He had on a bright green collarless shirt with a pin stripped collarless jacket over it, all the rage in the mid-nineties. His Levi jeans completed the smart/casual look. His hair was in the usual 'curtain' style, which all the boys seemed to favour. She loved his hair like that. Whilst most of the other lads' hair hung straight in its centre part, his was slightly curly.

23

She could never keep her hands out of it. She was wearing a baby doll pink dress from Top Shop, the type of length you could only get away with when you're seventeen. She was wearing big chunky heels, circa baby Spice, 1996. She was sporting her new 'Rachel' from Friends hairdo.

She and Jase had been joined at the hip. He was always at her house, he didn't really see eye to eye with his own parents so the least amount of time he spent with them the better. They'd come home from school, watch Byker Grove or Grange Hill. Do a bit of homework (well, that's what her Mam thought they were doing in her bedroom.) Then they'd sit down to a plate of Scouse. Her Mam was never bothered about feeding him, she had her brothers to feed too, so one extra wasn't a big deal.

Sighing to herself she closed the book over, yep, she was pretty damn sure her life wouldn't have turned out like this if Jase hadn't got off. Where would the emotion and the heartbreak have come from to sing so passionately about it if she wasn't going through every single word herself? It could be argued that he did her a favour, doing one like that, but she was pretty sure she'd trade everything she had right now to have avoided hooking up with Max. Jase had only ever been the guy for her. How would things pan out now he was back? It was clear things weren't as straight forward as she would like them to be.

Giving her hair a final fluff with her fingers and twirling a ringlet round her finger she gave herself one last look. Time to go and put that Magenta Valentina smile on, play the doting wife and find out which one of her so called friends was screwing her husband.

Hunter took the stairs on the big wide staircase two at a time. As he rounded onto the second set of stairs he nearly fell over Shane.

'Jeez, man. What are you doin' creepin' around like that?'

'I was just trying to grab you for a moment,' Hunter eyed him warily.

'I'm here on vacation. I ain't here to check up on you. I know you'll get the job done. You're the best,' Shane side stepped him, patting him on the shoulder. 'I'm sure you'll leave here on Monday with your reputation intact.'

Hunter tread slowly up the remainder of the stairs, deep in thought as he listened to Shane, whistling away to himself on the way down. He didn't believe him one little bit. He was so engrossed in his own mind that he didn't see Mags standing at the top of the stairs, he arms folded as she scowled at him.

'Hunter Cole, you better start talking and you better start doing it now.'

Glancing around to check nobody was around, he grabbed her by the wrist and pulled her into one of the many spare rooms. He shut the door behind them, leaning against it. She stood facing him, her hands on her hips.

'Ah, man. D'you know how sexy you look, standing there like that?'

'I'm not meant to look sexy, I'm meant to look pissed off, angry, annoyed, she paused as she flicked her hair over her shoulder. 'You're not really a hotel manager are you?'

Dragging his eyes away from her he looked down at the floor, gathering his thoughts for a moment. Trying to get his steely look in his eyes, but knowing it wouldn't come. The only way he could look at her now was with pure love. Lifting his head slowly, he met her inquisitive gaze. He shook his head. 'No, I'm not a hotel manager,' he let a small smile escape. 'Gotta be honest, I was surprised that you believed I was. You think I'd settle for being bossed around by rich people?' A thought struck him, wasn't that what he was paid to do anyway? The people who hired him didn't want to get their hands dirty so he did it for them instead. Her voice pulled him away from that particular train of thought.

'Well, I didn't want to say anything in case I offended you, but I always imagined you'd have some kinda sporting career.'

Again, he smiled. She wasn't far wrong there either.

She couldn't help a smile wandering onto her face, despite being mad at him. 'Although, you do look pretty hot in the suit you wear.'

'It's the shoulders.'

'Stop distracting me and changing the subject. What the hell is going on?'

Mirroring her he put his hands on his hips. What to tell her? Not the truth, but he didn't relish the thought of lying to her either. The truth would put her in danger. 'I'm working undercover.'

'Undercover? What as a detective? A spy? Who do you work for? M15? FBI?'

He took a step closer. 'Sssh, undercover means not shouting your arse off.'

'Jeez, what the hell? Who are you following?'

'Mags, I'm so sorry, it's work. I can't tell you.'

'Or what? You'd have to kill me?'

His face clouded over. 'Don't even joke.'

'What? Am I in danger?'

Shit. She was getting too close to the truth. How could he have forgotten how smart she was? He shook his head. 'You are perfectly safe when I'm around. It's nothing you need to worry about.'

'How is Shane involved? Does Johnny know?'

'Babe, seriously. Don't go all Miss Marple on me asking questions. Like I said back at the hotel, the less you know the better. By Monday my report will be filed

23

and I can concentrate on you and our future...that's if that's what you want?'

Stepping into his arms she pulled him to her. 'Of course that's what I want, you know that. I just need to get rid of Max. Oh my God, you're not investigating Max are you?' He silenced her with a kiss.

Hunter stormed down the landing, Mags had left the room a few minutes earlier. No sooner had his lips found hers then they'd heard low voices outside the room. Mags had patted her hair and dress down and left the room. After a suitable amount of time had lapsed, he too vacated the room. He wasn't sure whose voices they'd heard on the landing. He was angry with himself, this was getting dangerous. Mags was finding out stuff she shouldn't really know. Yes, he was working undercover, but not the sort of undercover she'd assumed. Would it be safe to let her think she was investigating Max? The more she knew, the more danger she was in. He ran down the stairs quickly, his feet barely touching the stairs. He'd never felt so incompetent on a job, he was no nearer to finding out who wanted Mags dead. He'd pinned so much on imagining that she was going to walk out of here with him on Monday morning that he was forgetting one thing, he didn't actually believe in all that cosmic ordering shit.

He practically barged straight into Tim, not nice and still dim, as he entered the drawing room.

'Where have you been, we're supposed to be overseeing the pre-dinner drinks.'

Hunter looked past him, to where Fly was slouched on the sofa, messing with his phone.

'Well, you look rushed off your feet, there's only Fly here.'

Tim huffed. 'Yes, well. They itinerary stated pre-dinner drinks in the drawing room at 6.30pm prompt,' he glanced at his watch, it was seven forty five. 'We English pride ourselves in our pomp and ceremony. You Yanks wouldn't understand our attention to detail. The lateness of the pre-dinner drinks will cause untold damage to the foie gras.'

Hunter let him rant as he wandered over to Fly. 'Where is everyone?'

Fly shrugged, his eyes not leaving his phone and a look of confusion on his face. 'Ah man!'

'Everything ok, dude?'

Fly looked up, suddenly looking embarrassed. 'Shit. You've discovered my deep, dark, secret,' he handed over his phone.

For a second Hunter felt his adrenaline kick in, was he finally going to be given a break in this case? He burst into laughter as he viewed what was on the screen on Fly's phone. 'Candy Crush? Seriously?'

'What can I say man? I know it ain't very rock 'n' roll. Got hooked on the stupid game by one of Johnny's exes. Not sure which one, he's had so many. Man, this game should be called Candy crack and I should be in rehab, like Sloth.'

Hunter passed the phone back. 'Don't worry my friend. You're secret is safe with me.'

Fly swung his legs off the edge of the sofa and onto the floor, standing up. 'I gotta take a leak.'

As Fly left the room, Hunter sensed Tim by his side. 'Great, we've lost them all now. The banquet room was ready ages ago. Go and find them, Cole.'

'How does, 'go fuck yourself' sound?' Hunter turned on his heel before a red faced Tim could respond.

Still seething, Hunter bounded up the stairs. What did Tim what him to do? Put cattle bells around their necks? Actually that wasn't a bad idea, at least he'd know where they all were. He carried on up the stairs.

Chapter Twenty Seven

In another one of the many spare rooms in the Mansion, Max Maxwell currently only had one thing on his mind. It was one of the two things that were generally on his mind, money and sex and right now, it was the thing he'd been craving since he got here. One of Brooke's amazing blow jobs. Although he said they'd have to cool it while they were here, he figured the house was big enough for them to get lost in for five minutes or so. He was that frustrated, it would probably take less than five minutes. Being in such close proximity to Brooke every day and knowing what she could do with those full on lips of hers had been making his balls ache and on top of that, Jody was walking round in those short skirts she wore with a jacket, giving it the 'hot office' chick look. Now, if he could get them both in here...but he kinda liked that they didn't know about the other one. He groaned. Brooke was licking him like a giant lollipop, then taking him full in her mouth, every time he'd get into rhythm, she'd change tack, teasing him. God, that girl was good. They'd kept the room in darkness, only heightening how naughty their hook up was. He forgot for a moment where he was and let out a slightly louder moan than he meant too. A second after he'd let the moan out, the door handle turned...

Johnny was looking for Shane, he wanted to talk to him before dinner. Fill him in on his plan for Max. Not that he was really sure what the plan was. He wanted to shake Max up, just by having Shane here. He wanted to be free of Maximum records, or at least the hold Max had over him. He liked Logan being his manager, but he wasn't sure Maximum was the way to go. They were becoming too commercialised. Broken Arrow were a rock band, not something to tag onto 'Starmaker' whenever Max felt like it. He wanted his credibility back and more importantly he wanted his band back. He'd speak to Shane, together they'd work out a plan. He wandered along the long corridor, man these old English houses were big. He had no idea where his brother was. He supposed he better start checkin' the rooms out. He came to a solid oak door and turned the handle slowly.

Logan was pacing the floors, going up and down the stairs, iPad in hand, looking for an internet signal. The snow outside was causing havoc with the Wi-Fi signal and he couldn't seem to connect to his own provider. It was almost bringing him out into a cold sweat. He had to get back online, he had important stuff to do, stuff that if he passed the deadline, could cost him thousands. He was going in and out of rooms, checking them all for a stronger signal. He was having no luck so far. He reached the next door, sighing and hoping this room would work, he put his hand on the handle.

Jody strode purposely from the East Wing of the Mansion, towards the West Wing, she'd been on the other side of the mansion getting some work done. The internet connection was better on that side. She'd arranged an interview with HEAT magazine for early next week, she was going to try and get Johnny involved too. She was hoping she could bypass his agent and get Logan to agree, if he said no, she'd go straight to the top and to Max. He pretty much gave her everything she wanted, except the one thing she really wanted - him. He must know how utterly devoted she was to him. She would go to him at the click of his fingers, but then she desperately wanted to run away, hating herself for going behind Magenta's back. The hate was never enough for her to say no to Max though, he had her, hook, line and sinker. She shook her head as she walked. Now was not the time to think about Max.

She needed to find Magenta and give her a list of appointments for next week, she had to put her game face on, her, 'hot shot' PA face. Magenta hadn't been in her suite or downstairs in the banqueting hall. She began searching the rooms. All of them dark and empty, she shuddered slightly as she closed the door on one of the rooms, this house gave her the creeps. She couldn't say anything to Magenta, she'd had her heart set on this place, but it reminded Jody of something from one of those English murder mysteries her mom used to watch. What was it? Miss Marbles? Something like that. She reached for the handle on the next door.

Fly desperately needed a piss. He couldn't find the john in this freakin' house, too many doors, not enough toilets. He did a very un-rock star like jig as he went to open the next door, if there wasn't a john in that room, he was just gonna open a window and water the snow. He put his hand on the handle.

Magenta walked down the landing like she owned the place, which on paper she probably could. She had dreamed of staying here since she was a little girl and now, for the weekend, at least, she could pretend it was hers. She imagined coming here, unmasking Max and his lover, then, in front of everyone, declaring she was going to divorce him and then sign her shares over to Logan. She wanted it to be so public, so he couldn't wriggle out of it. She had the papers prepared and ready to go, she just needed to catch him in the act, which was why she'd begun checking the rooms when he'd gone AWOL. The problem was, that although this weekend had been her doing, she felt like there were other forces at work. Things she didn't know about. She felt unsettled at Hunter's revelation that he was working undercover. Who was he working for? Who was he after? She suddenly felt like her plan was a tiny side line in what was really taking place this weekend. She walked up the stairs, to the next floor and began her search of that corridor. She reached out for the handle of the first door.

Savannah was in urgent need of some girlie time, or at least a little pick me up to get her through dinner. She knew from the few conversations she'd had with Brooke that she might just be the answer she was looking for, fake boobs or not. Brooke was as bored here as she was. She was pretty sure she'd be up for spicing things up a bit. She thought she'd try her luck now while everyone else seemed to have disappeared. She was on the third floor, she wasn't sure which one was Brooke's room. If she wasn't interested, she could style it out, pretend she was already a bit tipsy and was just being over friendly. She reached for the door handle.

Hunter had received a tip off from, Rick his IT guy back in the States. His first real breakthrough. He needed to get his hands on someone's laptop, Rick wanted to hack into it. The sooner he got hold of it, the better. He was checking all the rooms, looking for it. He reached the next room and grabbed the handle.

Max squinted as the bright light from the hall spilled into the room, framing the person who was at the door. Brooke sprang away from him, leaving his dick to suddenly go limp. He knew whoever was at the door could see them, the light was like a spotlight on them, but with no lights on in the room, the person looking at them was in total darkness. They stood there for a second and then closed the door back over.

'Shit,' he muttered as he tried to pull his trousers up. The person had stood there so briefly and in Max's state of shock and surprise he'd been unable to ascertain if they'd been male or female. He caught some of his pubic hair in his zip in his haste to tuck himself back in. He swore again. 'Shit, shit, shit.'

He scrambled over to the door, swinging it open. He stepped out onto the landing, he looked from left to right, it was empty. He had no idea who'd just caught him out. He hoped it was just one of the staff, checking the rooms and in their embarrassment had quickly retreated. In his heart of hearts (if he had one), he knew this wasn't true. He'd well and truly been caught out and he didn't have a clue who it was. He stormed out of the room, without saying a word to Brooke.

Tim was losing the plot, the foie gras was overdone, he had an empty banqueting hall and a very angry chef. On top of that Hunter had gone missing after his foul mouthed tirade earlier. Just before he was about to scream, the banqueting doors opened, Hunter stepped through the door, a herd of celebrities following him. Tim's shoulders drooped in defeat, the guy was like the pied piper when it came to these people. He watched as Hunter stepped to one side, gesturing with one hand he said. 'Ladies and gentlemen, dinner is served.' Tim pulled Hunter to one side as the guests tucked into the starters. He spoke in hushed tones. 'I think you owe me an apology Mr Cole.'

'Whatever, I can't be doing with your brown nose act, it gets tiring.'

Tim took a step back in shock. 'Brown nosing? We call that being courteous over here in England, clearly you have no manners at all.' Feeling like Hunter was about to outsmart him again, he decided it was time to use his trump card. 'By the way, Cole. Who is Jason?' If he was expecting a reaction, Hunter hid it well. 'Don't know what you mean, mate,' he turned and walked away.

Calm on the outside, inside he was in turmoil. How on earth did Tim know about Jason? It begged the question, was Tim more involved in this than he'd given him credit for?

Chapter Twenty Eight

The guests were finally assembled around the long table in the great banqueting hall, which dated back to medieval times. There were hundreds of candles placed on the high window ledges, illuminating the room in an almost gothic way. Above the table were four large round cast iron chandeliers, again with candles used as lighting. Magenta was at the head of the table, Max, directly opposite at the other end and in between were the rest of the gang. Max was the last to be seated, he looked nervously around the table as he tried to work out who had walked in on him and Brooke.

Brooke was at the other end of the table, sitting next to Magenta, he groaned inwardly, that was just as accident waiting to happen especially as Brooke still looked as white as a ghost from the interruption. To Magenta's left was Shane, Max wasn't sure how he'd managed to wangle a seat next to her. On his other side was Savannah who was sandwiched in between the Kidd brothers. On Brooke's other side was Logan, he seemed very agitated, ringing alarm bells in Max's head. He kept calling over to Hunter, trying to get his internet connection working. Jeez, his business partner really was addicted to work, seemed he couldn't even stop for food. Fly was the other side of Logan and seated next to Max, leaving Jody on his left hand side and next to Johnny. Fly didn't look overly enthusiastic about sitting next to him, he seemed rather more concerned with Jody's ample cleavage which was right in his eye line. He had to admit, Jody looked stunning tonight, if Magenta was all glamour with her perfectly styled curls and expensive Valentino dress, Jody was more in fitting with her surroundings. Her long hair tumbled loosely over her shoulders, the dress she was wearing lifted her boobs up and enhanced them even further, she looked like a medieval wench in her long flowing maxi dress. Max was glad he was sitting down, otherwise all of the other diners would know what he wanted for starters. Getting rumbled clearly hadn't had an effect on his libido.

As the waiter filled his wine glass up he forced himself to drag his eyes away from Jody's tits and carry on looking around the table. Was anyone acting weird? Was anyone giving him a strange look? Fly was ignoring him, didn't seem interested in conversation he seemed far too interested in tapping his fingers on the table and staring at Jody's cleavage. That was pretty much the norm. He knew Fly wasn't his biggest fan. Who cared what some drummer thought of him? He didn't. Logan was still stressin' about his internet connection.

'Hey, Logan, my man. Let's have a night off from work hey? You deserve a night off. Enjoy yourself, top up on the wine, get drunk, it'll loosen you up.'

Logan put his iPad down on the table, glaring at Max. 'Whatever you say, Max.'

Hunter stepped in. 'Mr Hudson, I can take your iPad back to your suite it you like?' He'd already picked it up off the table. Before Logan could protest Max butted in. 'That's the idea, cold turkey my friend, wean you off your electronic gadgets. Poor Brooke, you're going to have to start putting touch screens on her nipples at this rate.' Max realised too late that he'd just opened himself up to ridicule or snide comments from whoever had found him and Brooke together. He steeled himself for the back lash, but nothing came, only a worried look in Brooke's eyes. Logan didn't say anything, he just downed his wine in one go and held the empty crystal glass out to the waiter to be re filled. Max winced, looked like Logan was on a mission. He'd rarely seen his buddy drunk, he was too in control for that, but boy, when he flipped that switch, it wasn't a pretty sight.

Switching his gaze to Brooke he could see she was glancing nervously between her husband and his glass, she was obviously thinking the same. She seemed very quiet and on edge. Understandable, she was probably also wondering who around the table had caught her with her mouth around his dick. He moved slightly in his seat, his erection digging in and making him uncomfortable. Man, what he'd give for Jody to be able to slip under the table and sort that problem out in her usual efficient way.

Turning his attention back to Magenta, aah, Magenta, his magnificent wife, the press loved to put as many complimentary words beginning with 'M' in front of their names as possible when they ran stories about them. They were the golden couple. 'Marvellous Max & Magenta'. Magnificent Magenta & Max'. Although he didn't like that one so much, he hated her name coming first. What would the press think if they knew the real state of their marriage? Less golden, more olden and rusty. He married her purely as a business venture, also he quite liked the fact that he'd rescued her career, from the ageing model she'd been to the global super star she'd become. That was all down to him and how powerful he was in this industry. But what do you do when the business venture goes sour? You rip up the contract and get rid of it as quickly as you can. He was under no illusion that Magenta loved him, he didn't think either of them had ever really felt anything for each other, they'd been swept along by the media buzz that surrounded them. That's what she got off on, the buzz. Besides, he was too self obsessed to love anyone but himself, you had to look out for number one, can't rely on other people to have your back.

Glancing over to Shane who was obviously loving being in between Magenta and Savannah and opposite Brooke, it was like the guy didn't know where to look next. He watched him as he practically drooled over his wife. He smirked to himself, Shane was no match for her. She was a strong woman that was one thing he hadn't counted on when he'd swooped in a saved her career. Once her confidence had returned and she'd mended her broken heart, over some guy from Liverpool, she was back fighting. There was a spark in her eye that hadn't been there when he met her and he knew it wasn't there because of him, it was performing that brought her back to life and kick started that 'scouse spirit' of hers, he wasn't even sure what 'scouse spirit' was, he just knew it made her stop being a walk over.

Next Max turned his attention to Savannah who was trying to ignore Shane and his lecherous looks and was attempting to make conversation with Brooke, who was more Savannah's type anyway. Putting Johnny and Savannah together was again just another business decision. He wasn't sure if the American market was quite ready for the lesbian version of Britney or Miley, still Savannah didn't seem to mind dabbling with the other side. Johnny might even turn her. Johnny on the other hand was clearly hating it. That boy had no business sense. Photos of him and Savannah were being tweeted faster than they could upload them and that sex video went viral, enhancing the brand, but he'd been wrong, only made them more in demand as a couple. He knew Savannah was happy to stick with the arrangement, her star was rising, she needed Johnny. He was less happy, he thought he was the star. Still, Max knew how to keep Johnny in line, although he was uncharacteristically nervous with Shane being in such close proximity. So, that left the delightful Jody. She seemed more subdued than usual. Although. When she was in the presence of both Max and Magenta, she tended to take a step back. She knew her place, although he liked to think it was because she couldn't trust herself around him. Fly was still tapping away and the incessant banging was starting to grate on his nerves. He turned to him. 'Stop with the noise with your fingers.'

Fly shrugged. 'I'm a drummer, it's what I do.'

'Yes, but not at the dinner table. Johnny's a singer but you don't see him singing away at dinner do you?'

'Yo, Johnny,' Fly shouted across the table. 'Give us a bit of the chorus of 'Livin' the dream'. He began banging the beat of the intro on the table with his hands.

Johnny started to sing 'You're my angel cake, Strawberries and cream, you and me baby we're livin' the dream.'

Magenta began singing the next line. 'We're Rock 'n' roll, we got heart 'n' soul, you and me baby, we're livin' the dream.'

Fly looked at Max and just grinned.

He lifted his glass to his lips, taking a long drink of his wine and giving the table one final glance as they all joined in with Johnny's singing.. He was none the wiser as to who the peeping Tom was, but he wasn't really worried. He was Max Maxwell, nobody could touch him. He smiled in satisfaction, sitting here like this, he really did feel like the king of his castle. Maybe it wasn't a bad idea of Magenta's to come here after all.

After dinner, in the drawing room Magenta was trying to chat to Brooke, who had been very quiet over dinner. She could usually be relied upon to stick a few sugar coated digs in, surprisingly she'd missed sparring with her. She handed her a Bacardi and coke.

'You ok, Brooke? You don't seem your usual vivacious self.'

Brooke smiled thinly, tossing her blonde hair over her shoulder as she lifted her chin upwards in a look of defiance. 'Fine.'

Magenta laughed. 'Now, that'd probably work on Logan, but, when a woman says she's fine, she's blatantly anything but.'

She wrinkled her nose up and paused slightly before she spoke. 'It's just Logan, he's a bit of a worry when he gets like this.' She glanced at her husband who was now wandering round with a bottle of JD in his hand, swigging from it and stopping to shout loudly into the ears of the people he passed.

For once, Magenta was genuinely concerned, she liked Logan. 'Want me to go and talk to him?'

She shook her head. 'Nah, it's not worth it, he won't listen and he'll only shout at you.'

'I didn't realise he had such a problem with drink.'

'He doesn't usually, he's pretty good at knowing when to stop and he's fine at home having a few beers, it's just when something's on his mind and he presses his self-destruct button that everything goes crazy.'

Magenta didn't know what to say, she and Brooke rarely 'talked' about stuff and this was way out of either of their comfort zones. She took a sip of her own drink to mask the awkward silence.

Jody was sitting in the corner of the drawing room, perched on the arm of a chair, she wasn't sure why she hadn't actually sat on the chair, she just thought that by sitting on the arm of it Max might be aware she was actually in the room. However, it wasn't Max's attention she was getting, it was Fly's. He'd come bounding over to her after dinner. She couldn't have missed his fixation with her boobs over dinner. Every time he spoke to her his eyes drifted downwards. She didn't mind, he was after all, Fly MacFly, international rock star. How many women across the world would love to have him pay them some attention? As she was feeling particularly unloved right now, she was happy to lap that attention up. His fingertips tapped lightly on the arm of the sofa, just by her leg, she glanced down, he looked up at her, grinning and moved his finger tips to her thigh, still tapping away.

'Do you ever stop drumming?' She giggled.

He shook his head. 'Always gotta be banging away at something.'

She arched an eyebrow. 'Charming.'

He laughed 'Ah, you know what I mean.'

'That's what worries me.'

He stood up. 'Shift over,' he angled his hip over towards her and moved her along the arm of the chair so he could lean against it with her, his long denim clad legs stretched out in front of him. For the first time since they'd been on this trip he was wearing a T-shirt. She couldn't help but look at his well-defined drummers arms. Thank God someone had put the heating on high in here, otherwise she might have gone the whole trip without seeing those bad boys up close and personal.

He grinned at her. 'Checking out the guns there?'

'I, err, I,' she stuttered. 'I, was just thinking how muscly your arms must have to be to err, bang on things.'

He laughed. 'Charming'

'It was just an observation.'

'You can observe me any time,' he flicked his hair out of his eyes. 'Can I make an observation?'

She nodded.

'Your tits would make a great set of bongos, could bang out a great beat on those.'

 She flung her head back as she laughed. 'Fly MacFly, is that the kinda chat up line that gets women falling into your bed?'

He grinned at her. 'It's not the lines, it's the laughter that gets 'em every time. Look at you, don't think I've seen you smile the whole time we've been in England and five minutes with me and you're laugh a minute.'

As he spoke she happened to catch Max's eye across the room. He had a strange look on his face, almost like he was jealous. She couldn't help but feel happy about that, she had to put up with him and Magenta being the golden couple and have it flaunted in her face every time she opened a magazine or clicked on the internet. Would it hurt so much if she shoved it back in his face? She smiled at Max, then broke eye contact with him, turning her attention back to Fly who obviously seemed more than happy to give her some much needed affection.

 'Well, that works for me.'

He slid back onto the chair, pulling her with him so she ended up in his lap. She giggled like a teenager with a crush as he tickled her.

 Max stormed over to Magenta who was in the middle of a conversation with Johnny.

'You need to keep your PA on a stronger lead, she's supposed to be acting like a professional. Look at her draped all over Fly.'

She followed his gaze. She smiled as she saw Jody giggling with the drummer. 'I don't have a problem with it, will do her good to have a bit of fun. She works hard.'

'She shouldn't be conducting a fling while she is supposed to be working.'

Johnny stepped forward toward Max. 'If Magenta doesn't have a problem with it, I don't see why you should.'

'Stay out of this Johnny, this has nothing to do with you.'

'It does when you come marching over here, interrupting a conversation I was having with Magenta. You're not in charge of everything you know.'

'Have you forgotten who you're talking to? I'm...'

'Yes, I know, you're Max fuckin' Maxwell, captain of the Universe. Well I got news for you Max. You ain't captain of my universe. I quit. Broken Arrow isn't your gig anymore.'

Max shook his head, a sly smile on his face. 'Johnny boy, you're forgetting you will always be indebted to me. Without my, let's say, intervention, you wouldn't be the rock star you are today.'

Logan stepped into the fray. 'He was always gonna make it, he was born a star.'

'Oh, we're not doubting he's talent, let's just say, he was lucky I stepped in when I did or his life may have turned out very differently.' Johnny's face was like thunder. 'This is over.'

Now Max openly laughed in his face. Magenta put a hand on his arm. 'Max, please, don't be like this.

'I would advise you to think very carefully, you know what'll happen if you break your contract.'

'You threatening me? In front of all these witnesses?'

He shrugged. 'Just stating a fact.'

Shane stepped forward. 'You leave my brother alone, or you'll regret it.'

'Ah, here we have baby brother stepping up to the plate, again. You're always there for Johnny aren't you Shane? Stupid blind loyalty.'

'That's enough Max. 'I ain't takin' your shit anymore,' he stormed out of the drawing room and out into the hallway, grabbing a coat as he opened the door. He was stopped in his tracks as he realised he had no chance of getting out. The snow was pressed up against the door at least waist deep. 'Ah shit.'

He heard Max's laugh behind him. 'Looks like you gotta put up with my shit a while longer John boy.'

A huge commotion followed when everyone realised they were snowed in. Tim was spluttering that he'd never seen snow like it, they never got snow like that in this part of the country.

Fly was worried the heating would go off.

Brooke worried they'd be stranded in this god forsaken place for longer than the weekend.

Logan worried that they'd run out of booze.

Johnny worried about being in the same house as Max for a moment longer than necessary.

Magenta worried about her plan not working.

Jody worried that the shit was about to hit the fan.

Savannah worried that she'd miss all the promo stuff she was scheduled to do next week.

Max worried that he wasn't going to be able to get laid again this weekend.

Hunter worried that he was still no closer to working out which one of the people currently standing in front of him, wanted Mags dead.

He watched as the all talked at once, he had to get out of there. His head felt like it was about to explode. He needed to take a step back from all of them, refocus and get to the bottom of this. He snuck out of the room.

Chapter Twenty Nine

Hunter locked the door to his room behind him and sat down at the dressing table, flipping his laptop open as he sat down. He quickly typed in all his passwords, he kept everything encrypted. Fortunately he was in one of the areas of the building that had good internet connection. He opened google, looking at the screen for a few seconds. The first thing he did was check the weather for the next few days to try and gauge how long they'd be snowed in for. He groaned when he saw it looked like snow was predicted to fall for the next twenty four hours. That would leave them in the Manor House till at least mid-week. Was that a good thing?? Did it mean he'd just bought himself some time and he wasn't on the clock? Or did it just put more pressure on him? Never deviate from the plan, that's how he worked. So therefore he still only had about thirty six hours to sort this mess out.

He typed in Shane Kidd into google. There was something off about the argument earlier, more than Johnny wanting out of his contract and Max had made some reference to Shane being loyal. It was niggling away at him. So far all that was coming up was a few pictures of him with Johnny, mostly before Broken Arrow made it big. Google seemed to have honed in on the word 'Kidd' and thrown up articles on the more famous Kidd brother. Stupid google, it always thought it knew best. He redefined his search and as he began to type in Shane again, google threw up 'Shania Twain', there google went again, trying to finish his sentences, it was worse than a woman for doing that. He sighed and continued typing, ignoring the lure of Shania. Shane Kidd Prison. That did it, finally google did its job. He read with interest the first entry.

SHANE KIDD RELEASED FROM PRISON

Shane Kidd, *younger and much troubled brother of Broken Arrow frontman, Johnny Kidd, was released from prison earlier today. He had been serving a sentence for drink driving. He crashed a jeep that he'd been driving in Malibu, his brother Johnny was the passenger. Both brothers were unhurt but Kidd junior had totalled the Porsche 911, and ploughed it straight into an oncoming cab. The driver of the cab was seriously injured.*

Although the cab driver made a full recovery, Kidd was charged with DUI and dangerous driving. At the time of the incident Broken Arrows manager, the world renowned Max Maxwell gave a statement. 'We count our lucky stars that nobody was killed in this accident and are extremely grateful that Johnny Kidd escaped unscathed. He is under the wing of Maximum and we look after our own. I'm sure Shane Kidd will step up to his responsibilities.'

It is not known if Shane will be reunited with his rock star brother, whose star has risen whilst his younger brother has been incarcerated.

Neither Johnny nor Maximum were available for comment.

'Well, fuck me sideways,' Hunter mouthed as he finished reading. It was clicking into place, he read Max's statement again, certain words stood up, 'escaped unscathed' and 'step up to his responsibilities'. Shane had been the scape goat. He hadn't been driving, Johnny had. The implications of Johnny Kidd causing an accident whilst drunk would have had ramifications across the globe and more importantly, would've lost Maximum a ton of money. It wouldn't have been Maximillion, it'd have been Maxilostmillions. He leaned back in his chair, letting it all sink in. Holy fuck, this was big. No wonder Johnny wanted to get away from Max, he was a constant reminder that Shane had taken the rap for him.

The other thought that kept popping up on the fringes of his mind was Max's annoyance at Shane being here and no one seeing them together. He knew Shane was the handler, did that mean it WAS Max behind the hit?

Before he even had time to digest that information, his phone rang. Checking the caller ID, he could see it was Rick.

'Hey man, please tell me you got some good news about the laptop.'

'Well, I don't know if it's good news or not, but I certainly got some juice.'

'Hit me with it.'

'Seems your guy likes to gamble, and we're not talking a bit of on line bingo, we're talking serious shit.'

'Go on.'

'He owes money all over the place, he's mortgaged his house to the hilt, he's taken money from the company, he's insured Magenta for millions. If anything happens to her, it'll pretty much wipe out the debts he owes. He's covered his ass well, nobody is aware of how deep he's into this. Not his wife, not Max.'

'Freakin' hell. Rick, I owe you big time my man. You have no idea how much this helps.'

'Hope you get things sorted dude.'

'Oh I will, don't ya worry about that.'

He ended the call. Freakin' Logan. He shook his head. The insurance document had always niggled at him since he'd discovered its existence. Bloody Logan? He hadn't been at the top of the list, ok he'd been fairly near but he'd never thought he was a serious contender. All the time he was attached to his laptop, iPad, Smartphone, it wasn't business it was gambling. No wonder Brooke couldn't hold his attention. He was bleeding Maximum dry and as smart as Max thought he was, he was totally unaware. Murder, the motives, in his experience were generally money or sex, sometimes both. In this case it was clearly money and greed. He took his gun out of his waistband, cocking it open to check the rounds, even though he knew exactly how many were in there. Son of a Bitch, there was a bullet in there with Logan's name on. Maybe even two, one for each bollock. He normally favoured the quick and simple execution style, but he was quite happy to remind Logan that he should've grown a pair of balls and dealt with the mess he'd gotten himself into like a man. He was also happy for him to die a slow painful death, that's what happens when you take a hit out on someone that the hit man happens to be in love with. He checked his watch, jeez, he'd only been in his room twenty minutes and he'd discovered more in that time than he had done the whole six weeks he'd been working on this. Suddenly things were becoming clear.

He shut his laptop down then pushed his chair back, tucking his gun back into his waistband. It was time to go and take care of the problem and he still had thirty six hours to spare, it hadn't come down to the wire. He'd saved Mags with plenty of time left over. That was why he was the best.

He unlocked the door, flinging it open, only to discover Mags standing there, in mid knock pose.

'Hey, that was quick.'

He glanced down the corridor. 'What are you doin' here?'

'Oh, that's nice. I just wanted to see you, I feel a bit on edge and you, well you know...'

He smiled at her, he did know. Everything felt right when they were together.

'Sorry, gorgeous. Just got a lot on my mind right now,' he pulled her into the room so they wouldn't be seen, in doing so, her body was propelled into his chest. Her arms automatically found their way around his broad shoulders, his did the same to her tiny waist.

'God, Mags, it's driving me crazy being so close to you but not being able to get close to you.'

'Me too, but don't worry, Max will be history before we leave here and I'll be free to be with you.'

'What's your plan, Mags, you can tell me. How can you be so sure it'll work?'

'Because I know my husband,' she looked up at him grinning. 'Anyway, it doesn't work like that. Like I'm gonna tell you my plan when you won't tell me what you're up to,'

'I have ways of making you talk Mizz Valentina,' his lips instinctively found hers as he kissed her lightly.

'Mmm, if this is torture, gimme all you got.'

He thought about his original intention to go after Logan, but hell, Mags was safest when she was him, busting Logan's balls could wait a bit. Just as he was about to manoeuvre her over to the bed there was an almighty scream ricocheting through the house.

Hunter was out of the door like a shot, Mags right behind him as he ran down the landing, towards the stairs and in the direction of the screaming. He reached the scene of the disturbance, the grand entrance hall, to see Brooke with her hands covering her face, Johnny and Fly crouched down next to someone lying on the floor. The front door was wide open, the snow was starting to melt into the hallway after being hit with the heat of the house, not defrosted enough to make a difference, they still couldn't get out. He couldn't make out who was on the floor, all he could see was a lot of blood seeping from the body, which had clearly been lying there for a while judging by how far the blood had spread across the black and white tiles of the floor. He stepped in between the two Broken Arrow boys, to be met by Tim's glassy eyes staring up at him, a spade wedge into his gut.

'Oh My God, what the hell...'

He stood in front of Mags to shield her from the sight she'd just seen. Max, Logan and Jody all came hurtling down the stairs. Max pushing everyone out of the way to get to centre of the drama.

'What's going on?' He demanded.

'Statin' the obv, here Maxi boy, but looks like we got a dead body on our hands,' Fly stated the obvious.

'I haven't got a dead body on my hands,' he spun round and pointed to Hunter. 'You, you sort this out, he was your colleague. How stupid to try and dig us out of the snow. I've heard of falling on your sword, but falling on your spade? Freakin' ridiculous. That's if he did slip on his spade. Where is Shane? This has his name written all over it.'

Johnny stepped over Tim's lifeless body and grabbed Max. Hunter pulled him back. 'Not the time man.'

Johnny shrugged him off. 'You'll keep,' he glared at Max.

'He's not worth it,' Fly shook his head at his band mate.

Hunter thought it was typical of Max to try and land this at someone else's door, and why not make Shane the scapegoat again? Hunter knew Shane wouldn't be involved in this, he didn't get his hands dirty. He glanced around the group as they all stood staring at the body. Logan had one arm around Brooke, the other around Mags, he had to keep himself in check. Seeing Logan in such close proximity to Mags was making his blood boil. Savannah and Jody were on the edge of the group, looking like they were trying not to look, their complexions had gone an off shade of grey. Their still appeared to be an odd stand-off between Max, Johnny and Fly. Someone had to take control of this situation and Max was right about one thing, it had to be him.

'Look, it seems to me that Tim thought he'd try and dig us out of here, the melted snow in the hall floor probably caused him to slip and he's landed on the spade, which, I aint no doctor, but looking at the way it's embed in his body, probably caused his death. It's just an accident, there's no need to apportion blame Mr Maxwell.'

'Yeah, the dude's right. It was an accident,' Fly backed Hunter up.

'Well, accidents need clearing up. Deal with it. This has taken up too much of my evening as it is,' Max walked away, grabbing Mags by the wrist and taking her with him. Logan and Brooke followed behind them with Jody and Savannah scarpering pretty quickly. Hunter looked at Johnny and Fly. 'Whaddya say guys, I know it's not your normal rock star role, but I can't move him on my own. We gotta pack snow around him, if we're stuck here till the middle of next week, it's not going to be pretty.'

'Where are we gonna put him?'

Hunter thought for a moment. 'I know it's a bit gross, but there is a store cupboard next to the pantry downstairs. Not very hygienic I know...'

'Reckon hygiene is the least of our worries.'

'I'll call the cops, let them know what's happened, that way we've done all we can and nobody can accuse us of trying to hide anything.'

'Thought you said it was an accident?' There was a nervousness in Johnny's voice. He flicked his hair out of his face and stood with his hands on his hips, almost in a stance of defiance. 'Chill, man. It was, but the cops will obviously want to rule out foul play, so we just need to do everything by the book.'

'Can we just get this over and done with, his eyes are freakin' me out,' Fly pulled a face.

'Sure, I just need your help to move him, I'll sort out keeping him chilled.'

'Brings a whole new meaning to the phrase 'chillin' out', hey?'

By the time Hunter and the boys had moved Tim's body and he'd spent a good hour or so packing snow tightly around his body, the house had fallen silent. He trudged wearily up to bed. With all the commotion that night, he'd forgotten he had the Logan problem to sort out. He was too tired for that now, he wanted to be on form when he dealt with that, couldn't have any sign of weakness showing. He didn't think Logan would fight back, but he couldn't assume it'd be an easy take out. He needed to sleep and be refreshed for tomorrow. Now that he knew Logan was behind the hit he knew Mags would be ok with Max and he also knew Logan wouldn't try anything, he'd paid him to do it for him. He flopped down on his bed, his body tired but his mind wired. What a mess. How could he ever have imagined, when he'd left that note for Mags all those years ago in the Adelphi, that this would be how he'd come back into her life. He'd hoped he'd only have to be in the States until he turned eighteen, which would've only have been a few months. He should've told her what was going on, they could've run away together and been together for the last eighteen years. He rubbed his eyes with his fingers. Who was he kidding, if they'd have run away, they'd have never lasted two minutes. So he'd taken the cowards way and left a Dear John letter because he couldn't bear to see her cry and he didn't want her to see his heart break, he was supposed to be a tough guy. When he'd walked out on her that night, he truly thought that within six months, a year at most he'd be back for her. Eighteen years later, he was finally making good on his promise. He was back for his little scouse Liver bird and nothing was going to get in his way now. She was the only woman who had ever gotten him, he loved her then and he loved her now. He just hoped that when this was all over, she'd get who Hunter was and still want to be with him. He yawned, sleep was calling. He rolled onto his front, pulling a pillow close to him. Normally he didn't mind sleeping alone, in fact he preferred it, but now he knew Mags was so close by, this bed felt huge. He finally fell into a fitful sleep, dreams of watching seventeen year old Jase, with his curly boy band curtains chasing after Max and Logan, whilst Mags was tied to a chair.   In his dreams, he was trying to join in, to save Mags, but he couldn't escape from the room he was in, he was shouting at Jase, telling him to protect Mags. He woke up, still shouting Jase's name.

Chapter Thirty

The mood was quite subdued the following morning when the guests assembled around the banqueting hall for breakfast. Mags had pulled Hunter to one side as she entered the hall. 'What did you do to Tim?' She whispered.

'Me? Nothing! I was with you.'

'You stupid git, I meant what did you do with the body.'

He grinned. 'Ah, I thought you were doing a Max and accusing people of murder.'

'Don't be soft, like you could hurt a fly.'

'What? Who's hurting me?' Fly appeared behind her.

She laughed. 'That was good timing. Not talkin' about you rock star, talkin' about the actual insect.'

'S'ok then. Is there food in there? Couldn't eat last night but I'm freakin' starvin' now.'

Hunter gestured over to the table. 'Go straight through, full English on its way any second.'

'Man, I love those.'

Hunter watched as Fly happily wandered over to the food. 'Well, he seems to be over last night's ordeal. He and Johnny helped me move the body.'

'Where is it?'

'You really don't wanna know.'

'Yes, I do. What if he pops out of a cupboard or I open a door and he falls out of it.'

'We're not in the middle of Cluedo you know.'

'I was always better at Monopoly.'

'You are one crazy bird, always have been, always will be.'

She lowered her voice. 'I suspect, Mr Cole, that is one of the reasons why you love me.'

'One of the many.'

'One of the many, what?' Max boomed, he appeared out of nowhere.

'PG Tips, one of the many teas we have on offer this morning.' Hunter didn't miss a beat as he replied to him. He saw the look of relief in Mags eyes.

'You and your freakin' English tea. Don't know why you can't just drink coffee like the rest of us normal people.'

Hunter winked at her and smiled as she followed her grumbling husband to the table. They were the last to take their seats.

Before she sat down, Magenta addressed her guests. 'Listen guys, I just wanted to say. I know what happened last night was awful. A terrible, terrible accident and obviously being snowed in makes it worse. I would like to thank Mr Cole for dealing with it in a professional manner and I hope it doesn't take the shine off this weekend. Tonight, in this very hall I have arranged the party to end all parties and I feel it should go ahead. Mr Smith did a lot to organise this weekend. So, I think it's only fair to carry on as planned. Everyone ok with that?'

'Getting drunk? Sounds good to me,' Johnny answered before anyone could speak. Hunter stood in the corner of the hall, a small smile on his face. Professional, Mags had just called him, she got that right. Which reminded him, Logan Hudson had an appointment with a 9mm calibre. He pushed himself off the wall and wandered out of the room. He was going to use the time they were having breakfast to do some snooping.

Because of the snow, the bins in the store room hadn't been emptied. This wasn't a very glamorous part of his profession, but it was usually the part that gave Hunter the most leads. It was amazing what people threw out. It was like they thought if it was in the bin it was gone forever. Not so when there were people like him about. He knew Logan was the guy who hired him, but that didn't mean he was going to sit on his arse. He wanted to make sure he hadn't missed anything. He rummaged through the bins which contained the rubbish that had been collected from the suites upstairs. So far there was nothing exciting. Marlborough packets, Fly's. He tipped them upside down to check nothing had been hidden in the packet. There was an empty condom packet, he assumed that was Max's. A lipstick case, he took the top off, the lip stick was worn down. He turned the case round, it was called ravishing rouge, obviously belonging to one of the girls. Then he struck lucky. He moved some tissue out of the way, the tissue was hard, something was wrapped up in it. He slowly moved the tissue to one side, to reveal what it had been hiding. A pregnancy testing kit, a positive one at that.

He sank to the floor, holding the test by a corner of the tissue. 'Bloody hell,' he muttered as the enormousness of this flooded his brain. Firstly, whoever had taken this test had brought it into the house with them. No one had left since they'd arrived and now they were snowed in, that was impossible. Secondly, he had no idea who it belonged to. He thought back to the night before, all the girls had been drinking. Unless the person hadn't known last night, he recalled something from a far corner of his brain. Weren't pregnancy tests supposed to be taken in the morning for a more accurate result? In which case, it may only have been done within the last few hours. So, that gave him Brooke, jeez, that'd be fun. Who's the daddy? Jody, with Max's baby. Savannah, with Johnny's? He knew they were sleeping together. And Mags with...his baby? It had been six weeks since they slept together. He knew she hadn't slept with Max in the meantime. Six weeks? Wasn't that usually when women found out? He was clutching at straws. He knew about a lot of things, but pregnancy wasn't one of them. Shit. Mags and his baby?

There was a one in four chance of her being the pregnant one. He'd been in this situation before, last time hoping it was negative, this time hoping this positive test belonged to Mags. He suddenly remembered where his brain was recalling this pregnancy stuff from. It was way back, when he was still Jase. His mind transported him back to Trina's kitchen.

It was just after double Geography when Mags had collared him and told him her period was late. They'd always been really careful, although there was that one time in the back of his brother's Fiesta when they couldn't really see what they were doing in the dark and she'd said as long as he pulled out in time, it'd be ok. He thought he'd pulled out before the vital moment.

He'd felt sick all afternoon. They'd arranged to go to Trina's after school as her Dad would still be at work at the docks and her Ma would be at her job, cleaning in the local primary school. Trina was supposed to start tea for her family. So, he found himself sitting at Trina's Ma's kitchen table, Mags to one side to him, Trina to the other. She pushed a rectangular shaped blue box across the table to Mags. He didn't question where Treen had got the pregnancy testing kit from and he didn't question why there was only one inside the box, when on the package it clearly stated it contained two. Mags took the test out and looked at them both nervously. 'You gonna do it now, babe?' She nodded slowly.

'No, wait you can't. You need to wait till the morning, your wee will be stronger then so the test will be more accurate. If you do it now, it might give you a false negative or a false positive.'

Mags began to cry. 'I can't wait till tomorrow morning. I'm in bits as it is. Oh Jase, what if it's positive. Me Ma will kill me, then she'll kill you. This is off its head.'

'Babe, it'll be ok. Whatever the outcome is, we'll deal with it one way or another.'

'One way or another? So if it's positive, you want me to have an abortion?'

He shook his head. 'You're putting words into my mouth, I meant positive or negative, we'll deal with it.'

'Well, if it's negative there isn't much to deal with is there? We will have just had a lucky escape.'

Trina reached across the table, taking her friends hand. 'It'll be ok, queen. I promise.'

'I hope you're right, T.'

He'd spent a very sleepless night on the bottom bunk in his bedroom at home, his brother Craig on the top bunk, snoring away. He wanted nothing more than to be with Mags, to hold her in his arms and comfort her. He imagined she'd be getting about the same amount of sleep as he was. Then, in the morning, when she did the test, he wanted to be there with her. He felt like such a shit, she shouldn't have to go through this on her own. He promised himself that if it was negative, he'd never put her in this position again, he'd wear two johnnies if he had to. If it was positive, well, that was another story.

1995 was pre-mobile phones that weren't the size of a brick and he certainly wasn't going to use the house phone to see if his girlfriend had taken her pregnancy test yet. So he waited for her on the corner of her street. He could tell by the look on her face what the result of the test was. He had never felt more relieved in his life as they walked together holding hands. Neither of them were ready to be parents yet.

As Hunter recalled those long forgotten memories, he realised it was Trina who had informed him of the laws on taking a pregnancy test in the morning. Now, here he was years later, possibly in the same predicament, so much for double bagging it with the condoms, but this time it was different. This time he was more than ready for Mags to be carrying his child. He heard footsteps coming down the corridor, he quickly shoved the test in his pocket.

In the commotion of the dead body in the hall last night, Max had totally forgotten the evening's earlier mishap when he'd been caught with little Max on show. Absolutely nobody had mentioned it, given him a knowing look or made a loaded comment. He was pretty sure now that whoever had seen him and Brooke getting down to it was one of the staff. He even hoped it might have been the dead guy, two birds, one stone so to speak. He stood up from the banqueting table and headed over to pour himself some fresh coffee, whistling to himself as he did so. Brooke sidled up alongside him. 'How can you be so calm?' she whispered.

'Hey, start acting suspiciously and people will notice, just be your usual self Brooke and get bitchin' nobody will have a clue then that you might have been up to things you shouldn't.'

She pulled a face at him, knowing there was no way she could get into an argument with him right now, not with their spouses just a few feet away. He just grinned at her, standing so close to her, but giving her a downwards look, she knew the smile on his face was because all he was looking at was her cleavage, which even for her standards was massively on show. Before she could come at him with a smart comment his attention was taken by someone on his other side.

'Ah Jody, good morning, you're looking very ravishing, I must say.'

Brooke noticed how the poor girl could barely speak in the presence of the great Max Maxwell, she'd blushed from head to toe. Savannah appeared behind Jody, almost pushing her out of the way as she grabbed a coffee cup.

'And here she is, my newest, brightest star. This girl is gonna go a long way under my guidance.'

Savannah smiled sweetly. 'Whatever you say boss.'

Magenta watched her husband with interest. She knew he'd be in his element being surrounded by three beautiful women. She had different thoughts running through her head. She was reminded of the Witches of Eastwick or the witches in Macbeth. She saw those three women differently than her husband did, that's for sure.

'Makes you sick doesn't it?' Johnny leaned in to her.

'Oh yes,' she replied. But not for the reasons Johnny thought. It made her sick that she'd ever been taken in by Max in the first place and even worse that she'd married the gobshite.

'You're too good for him Magenta,' Johnny smiled at her.

'So are you my friend, maybe we'll both get our wish this weekend,' she stood up and walked out of the hall. Johnny stared after her, not quite sure how to take her parting words. He looked back to Max who was now laughing loudly, enjoying being the centre of attention. He smiled to himself, Magenta obviously had the measure of him and if there was one thing he'd discovered about her in all the years he'd known her, she didn't suffer fools and right here in this house, he was looking at the biggest fool of them all. Suddenly he was glad he came, he had a feeling there was about to be something big going down and he had front row seats. Go, Team Magenta.

Chapter Thirty One

       Hunter was in the pantry checking on Tim's body. He was putting more snow around the body, the heat from the kitchen was melting the original snow. He obviously hadn't thought this through when he put the body in here. The last thing he wanted was for it to start decomposing on him, that wouldn't be a pretty sight. He sighed loudly as he packed the snow over his face.

'Hey man, you buildin' a snow man there?'

He looked up to see Fly, who'd stuck his head around the door. 'Might not be a bad idea, at least it'd keep him chilled. I could just go and plonk him in the garden and build around him.

What you doin' down here anyway?'

He stepped into the room. 'I'm bored, so I thought I'd get some food.'

Hunter looked over to a store room off the pantry. 'You don't fancy doin' me a favour do you?'

'What?' Fly asked slowly, eyeing the body up.

'We gotta move him, it's too warm in here. I figure if we move him into the store room, I can open the window in there and then there's less chance of the snow melting. Can't lift him on my own he's a dead weight.'

Fly pulled a face at Hunter's lame attempt at humour. 'You called the cops?'

Hunter nodded. 'Yep, rang this morning, given a statement over the phone but they'll still wanna re-interview us all when they get up here and examine the body.'

'You tell 'em it's currently resembling Frosty the snowman?'

He nodded. 'Yeah, wanna be above board about the whole thing, it was an accident after all.

No reason to withhold information.'

Fly stepped forward. 'Come on then, let's get this over with. There were a lot of things I thought I'd be doing on this vacation, but playing hide the dead body wasn't one of them.'

'Cheers dude, I appreciate your help.'

Despite both men having well developed muscles, Fly with his drummer arms and Hunter with his forever working out arms, they still struggled to move Tim.

'God, you weren't wrong, he is a dead weight,' Fly puffed.

After a few minutes they managed to successfully manoeuvre him into the store room and Hunter patted him down again with the snow that had fallen from his body.

'If you move him again, gimme a shout,'

'Thanks, man, but I reckon we're good now.'

'I wasn't offering to help move him again, I just didn't wanna open a door in this freakin' place and he fell out.'

Hunter laughed. 'You sound like Mags, she said something similar.'

'Mags?'

His stopped mid laugh. 'Err, Magenta, don't know why I called her that...'

'I've noticed you two seem pretty close.'

Hunter shrugged. 'We just work well together. We get each other's sense of humour I guess.'

Fly nodded slowly. 'You just look like you've got chemistry that's all.'

Hunter paused before he answered, he couldn't give anything away. 'It's her Liverpool background. Liverpudlian people are notoriously friendly. She just makes you feel at ease, you must get that?' he spun the conversation back on Fly.

'Yeah, I guess you're right, she is like that. Probably why she tolerates Max, God knows he doesn't deserve her.'

'He seems like a bit of a prick.'

'A bit? Try a whole lot of a prick and that's not a compliment to the size of his dick.'

'They're the ultimate power couple though, aren't they? America loves them.'

'Yeah, well, I reckon she's better off out of it. She doesn't need him. It's about time that girl followed her heart.'

Hunter stared at Fly, he was confused, this wasn't a chat he expected to have with him.

Something dawned on him. 'You? You wanna be with her?'

Fly flung his head back laughing. 'Hell no, Jeez man, do you not read the papers?'

'I never believe what I read in the papers.'

'Well, when it comes to me, you should. In fact I'm probably worse than they say. I mean yeah, I'd do Magenta, who wouldn't but I ain't into any relationship thing.' he screwed his face up when he said the word relationship as if it was the worst swear word he could think of. 'I'm just saying, I notice things,' he winked at Hunter. 'Catch ya later dude.'

His bizarre conversation with Fly left Hunter unsettled, what did he mean by, 'I notice things' what had he seen? He shook his head, he couldn't give that any more brain time, he had to go and confront Logan. He slowly walked up the stairs, he knew Brooke wouldn't be with him, she was in the lounge with Savannah doing something with their nails. He put his hand to his hip, ready to pull his gun, he didn't want to pull it too soon in case he bumped into someone on the landing. He stood outside the closed door leading to Logan's room. He looked from one end of the corridor to the other, clear. He pulled the gun out, cocked it and kicked the door open.

Brooke was enjoying her pampering session with Savannah, it was about time someone lavished attention on her. She was annoyed at Max for his lack of concern over the interrupting incident. Yes, she had her eyes on the prize and wanted to be the new improved Mrs Max Maxwell but she wanted to do it on her terms. She didn't want someone 'outing ' them. Her hand was laid out over a cushion as Savannah painted her nails with 'dangerous damson'.

'That colour will go great with the black leather cat suit I'm wearing tonight.'

Savannah nodded. 'You wearin' that lipstick too sugar? That'll really set it off.'

'Yeah, it's my favourite.'

Savannah sprayed quick dry onto Brooke's nails. 'What's the colour?'

'Ravishing rouge.'

'It certainly is,' Savannah raised an eyebrow, her tone loaded with intent. 'Can I try some?' Brooke went to reach for her purse.

'No, no, no. Your nails!'

'Oh my God, I'm such a ditz sometimes.'

'Let me take care of it.'

Brooke shifted over slightly, fully expecting Savannah to reach across to get her purse. Instead she kneeled in front of her, placed one palm on her knee, with the other hand she lifted her hair off her shoulder and let it hang loosely down Brooke's back. She moved in closer, her eyes flickering across her face, she ran her tongue over her lips slowly before she landed them on Brooke's lips. She let the kiss linger then pulled away.

'So, whaddya think? Is this colour me?'

Brooke nodded slowly as she looked at her lipstick imprinted on Savannah's lips. Although she'd done girl on girl stuff before, nothing felt as intimate as those few moments, which was ridiculous when she thought about some of the positions she'd got in with Lara. Their antics had been purely for show, never for effect. This, despite looking fairly innocent felt anything but.

'Mmmm, definitely ravishing,' Savannah winked as she moved away from her. 'I was thinking, it must get kinda boring hangin' around waiting for that husband of yours to get off whatever technical device he's currently attached to.'

Finding her voice, Brooke replied. 'You could say that.'

Why don't you join me and the Broken Arrow boys tonight for our own private party? Fly is desperate for some action and I'd be happy to help you out of that cat suit of yours, I know they can be tricky to get off when they've been stuck to your body for a few hours.' Brooke gulped, Jeez, given the choice she'd prefer a nice hard dick, but boy, did Savannah know how to press her buttons, her nipples were harder than anything Max had ever been able to achieve. And if Johnny and Fly were involved tonight too, well, she could get the best of both worlds. She grinned at Savannah. 'You're on.'

'Let's have a little drink to get us going hey?' Savannah stood up and walked over to the fully stocked bar in the corner of the lounge.

29

'Think you've already got me going.'

Savannah turned, smiling an all American smile at her, as her blonde hair swung over her shoulder. 'I'm an expert.'

Logan was startled by the person barging their way into his room, so much so that he dropped the gun he was holding under his chin. He froze as he saw Hunter coming at him with a gun. Before he could recover his composure and retrieve his gun from the floor, Hunter, with his gun still trained on him reached down and picked up Logan's gun.

'What the fuck?'

Logan was caught totally off guard, he'd been expecting to blow his own head off, not have the hotel guy come in and do it for him. He stared in disbelief at Hunter. He was also feeling a little nauseous, two seconds later and he would've shot himself, which was what he wanted.

Wasn't it?

'Logan, I'll say it again, in English this time. What the fuck?'

Logan just shook his head, he'd lost total control of his voice. He'd built himself up to pulling the trigger and ending the hell he was in, now he was still in that hell and he didn't know whether to feel relieved or not. He focused on the only thing he could do. 'Your gun?' Hunter still had it trained on him.

'It's for protection. I needed to ask you something and I kinda thought I'd need back up. Wanna tell me the story behind your gun?'

'I always carry one with me, it used to be my dad's.'

Hunter rolled his eyes. 'I don't want its life history, I wanna know why you were about to blow your brains out. Or what little brains you have left after almost bankrupting Maximum.'

By the startled look on Logan's face he knew he'd hit the spot.

'How do you know about that? Who the hell are you? Who do you work for?' He sounded more panicked with each question.

'I'm freelance, I work for myself.'

'Doing what?'

'Taking care of things for people.'

Logan swallowed hard. 'You're here to get rid of me?'

Hunter shrugged as he stepped closer, the gun still aiming point blank at Logan. 'Well, if I was, you'd have beaten me too it. No, I'm here to question you, to see if there is someone you want rid of.'

'I don't know what you're talking about.'

'Magenta.'

Logan frowned. 'What's Magenta got to do with this?'

'Hmm, let's see, you run the company into the ground, you take out a massive insurance policy on her and I'm thinking this is where I come in, I dispose of her neatly for you. You collect on the insurance and Max never needs to know you nearly crippled his company.' He shook his head.

'No, I would never hurt Magenta. Yes I've ruined the company but that's why you caught me in here with the gun. I was about to end my life...'

'Yeah, I figured that's what you were doing when I saw you with a gun under your chin, didn't think it was a party popper. So what? You were taking the cowards' way out? I'm no fan of Max but you'd have been leaving him in the shit big time if you baled on him now.'

'It's just got too much, the debts, the gambling, living a lie every day.'

'So, answer my question about the insurance. Why take it out on Magenta if you didn't intend to collect on the pay out?'

He sighed. 'It's all a cover up. It was to buy some time with the people I owe money to and I did intend to collect the money.'

Hunter pulled a confused looking face.

'It's a set up. I confided in Magenta a while ago. I can't talk to Brooke, she's away with the fairies. Magenta discovered a while ago that I was up shit creek with the gambling debts so she came up with a plan. We were to take a new insurance policy out on her and towards the end of the tour, when cancelling the last few dates wouldn't wipe out too much money, she'd have a little accident.'

Hunter took a step closer.

'No,' Logan shook his head. 'Not like that. Nothing serious. Just enough for her to be unable to perform, we could collect the insurance money and pay off my debts and get the company back on the straight and narrow.'

'But you just said you'd never hurt her.'

'Why d'you think I had a freakin' gun in my hand? I can't go through with it. We're committing fraud, she could go to jail all because of me.'

'There must be something in it for her too.'

He nodded. I was gonna sign all my shares over to her, I'd still be running the company but she'd be like my guarantor if you like. So I don't gamble my company away again.'

'So she'd be a silent partner?'

'I guess so.'

'She already got shares?'

He nodded. 'Yeah, it was a wedding present from Max. She's only got a few though.'

'If you added those shares to yours what would happen.'

A look of clarity dawned on Logan's face. 'She'd be the main shareholder.'

'Does Max know any of this?'

He shook his head. 'Not a clue.'

Hunter stifled a smile. So that's what she was up to. Stealing Max's company from right under his nose. God that girl had some balls. That'd teach Max never to mess with a scouser.

'What they hell are you doing coming barging in here with a gun anyway?'

Hunter raised an eyebrow, clearly he was over his own little gun tooting moment and forgotten he was on a highway to hell. What to tell him? Did he trust him? The guy was obviously messed up but seemed to be telling the truth. However, he told people things on a need to know basis and Logan didn't need to know about this. 'I'm Magenta's undercover body guard.'

'You're what?'

'Undercover bodyguard. She's been getting some threats from crazy fans. I'm just here to make her feel secure.'

Logan narrowed his eyes. 'I'm her freakin' manager. I haven't authorised for extra body guards and what's this about threats?'

'You didn't hire me. Jody did. The letters came via her PA. I'm on Magenta's payroll. But listen you gotta keep this to yourself. Jody doesn't want Magenta to panic or the press to get hold of the story. That'll just fan the flames of the crazy assed fan.'

'This is all just fucked up.'

Hunter nodded. 'That, we can agree on. Listen, you all good now? You ain't gonna blow your head off only I gotta go and check in with Magenta.'

Logan nodded. 'Probably just as well you turned up when you did. I probably would've regretted it.'

'Yeah, I'm sure it's the kinda thing you do and then two seconds later you're like, damn why did I do that?' Hunter replied sarcastically.

'Whatever. Look, I'm good now, you don't need to babysit me.'

Hunter shrugged. 'Fine with me. Want me to look after that gun for you anyway?'

Logan handed it over. It was only once Hunter had left the room that he realised he hadn't really answered the question of why he'd burst in brandishing a gun. If he was protecting Magenta from a crazed fan, why had he come into here pointing a gun at him? He'd have to speak to Jody. Something wasn't right.

Hunter was deep in thought as he stomped along the corridor. So, it wasn't Logan after all. He was quickly running out of time and not just because of the time constraints of the hit but people were starting to know too much. Mags knew he wasn't really a hotel manager. Logan thought he was a body guard. Jeez this was a mess. If he scratched Logan off the list, that left Max, which was looking unlikely. Johnny who had more beef with Max and had nothing to gain by wanting Mags dead. Brooke was looking more and more an obvious choice, with Mags out the way she could have Max and if she knew about Logan's debts then she'd be even more desperate to get away. Fly seemed like he'd never hurt a fly. He smiled at the pun. Which left Jody and Savannah, neither of whom seemed to have anything to gain. Savannah was only here by her association with Johnny and Jody was Magenta's PA, if anything happened to her, she'd have no job. He closed his eyes for a second as he ground to a halt. Clear your mind, Hunter. He told himself. Concentrate. The answer is staring you in the face.

He opened his eyes to see Mags appearing at the top of the stairs. Mags, she was the answer. It was the question he was having trouble with.

Chapter Thirty Two

Magenta stood at the top of the staircase, watching Hunter as he stood along the corridor, eyes closed, the frustration clear on his handsome, rugged face. She watched as she saw him take a deep breath as if to relax his state of mind and a few seconds later he opened his eyes, which automatically found their way to her. She smiled at him as she began to walk towards him, her heart beat quickening with each step. The smile on her face was matched by the one on his and all evidence of the strain on his face a few moments ago had all but disappeared. She was literally a few steps away from being in his arms when Savannah appeared further along the landing. So instead of having a brief few moments with Hunter she carried on walking, smiling politely as he stood to one side to let her through and she disappeared off into her suite.

She lay down on the bed, stretching out. Damn, Savannah, denying her a moment on Hunter's lips. He was the man she was meant to spend her life with. Not Max. She needed her association with Max over and done with and she needed it doing now, she couldn't wait any longer and she certainly couldn't wait another six months to the end of her tour when she accidentally had a little accident. She'd need to speak to Logan and tell him the plan had changed. She'd make sure he was ok though, she'd sign her shares over to him instead and hope to God that he'd learnt his lesson and wouldn't gamble them away. Still, she didn't have time to babysit him, she had her own plans.

She retrieved her phone from her pocket, she had a few bars of signal. She flicked onto Twitter. She hadn't updated anything for days. She quickly scanned down her feed, nothing massively interesting. Her fingers flew across her keyboard as she tweeted @RealMagentaValentina Keep your eyes peeled, something huge about to happen #staytuned. She was amazed that Hunter didn't have a Facebook or Twitter account. She hadn't asked him right out but she'd searched for him and even used his old name. Everybody had some kind of internet profile these days, well everyone except Hunter. She supposed it fitted in with the mysterious person he'd become, he seemed intensely private which was at odds with the Jason she used to know. He'd been so open. Although she could tell Hunter was struggling to keep her at arm's length, not physically, they couldn't keep their hands off each other any chance they got, not even emotionally, he was letting her see glimpses of the real him. No, it was whatever had brought him back into her life, whatever it was he felt she needed protecting from. She smiled to herself. Like she needed protecting. She wasn't the naïve seventeen year old he used to know any more. She let her phone drop onto the bed as she thought back to a simpler time, pre mobiles when your private thoughts were written in a diary, not on Facebook or Twitter. A simpler time when the only thing that mattered to her was love.

She closed her eyes and could see as clear as if it was yesterday she and Jase, heading out to town to sneak into the Krazy House. A city centre nightclub that blasted out rock music till the early hours. She was wearing faux leather pants from Paddy's market, a velvet crop top and a denim jacket over it. Her DM's finishing the look. Seventeen was when she'd really discovered her inner rock chick and she'd never let go of it from then. Jase looked as cool as ever in his jeans and tight fitting black t-shirt, his floppy curls making him look even sexier. She was nervous as she walked up the cobbled street, hand in hand with Jase towards the club. Her fake ID clutched in her other hand. Two girls in front of her in the queue, who actually looked older than her, were turned away by the bouncers. She gripped onto Jase's hand, he just squeezed it back reassuringly. As it was, the bouncers didn't even ask for her ID. They just smiled at her and let her through. The butterflies in her tummy disappeared.

'Thank God you're so tall, we got away with it.'

He grinned at her. 'I think it's because you're so beautiful that we got away with it.'

Her blushing cheeks was her reply. Still holding her hand he pulled her into the throng of people in the club, the floorboards vibrating with the bass. Her boots stuck to the floor from the stickiness of spilt beer. She didn't care. She could feel the music flood through her body and with Jase by her side, enveloping her in his love she couldn't have been happier.

She sighed at the memory. Yep simpler times, when getting into a nightclub was the be all and end all, when slow dancing to G'n'R's 'Don't Cry' signalled the end of a great night, when kissing along Hanover Street as they stumbled along to the bus stop was the only way to travel. Yep, being in love was the only thing that mattered. It was the only thing that mattered then and it was the only thing that mattered now.

She was so over being a 'power couple', she was so over being Max's puppet. Although she'd always managed to hold her own with him, it was getting tiring. Did she really want to spend the rest of her life like this? Like hell she did. Tonight was the night it was over, tonight she would take her life back and be free. Free to love the man she'd never let out of her heart. She stood up and wandered over to the window, pushing the heavy velvet curtain back so she could see out of the glass. The only fly in the ointment was the snow. After tonight she really didn't want to be holed up in the mansion, as lovely as it was, any longer than she had to.

She hadn't factored in being snowed in. It wouldn't affect her actual plan, it'd just mean dealing with the fall out sooner rather than the later. On the plus side, Hunter was here and he had her back. If the snow was an unexpected pain in the arse in regards to her planning, then Hunter was a turn up for the books. At least the snow seemed to have stopped falling for now. She glanced at her watch, just gone 4pm. She'd go and run a bubble bath and have a nice relaxing soak before she got ready for the party.

A while later Logan was sitting at the bar in the main lounge. He'd poured himself a neat whiskey and downed it in one, now he was nursing the second glass. He'd needed the first one for shock. Had he seriously thought blowing his head off was the only solution he could come up with? He should trust Magenta, she wouldn't let him down. He just needed to be patient, it was a long game they were playing. Trouble was, the longer the game went on, the more antsy he became. He wanted it over, but as he was starting to appreciate, it was the situation he wanted over, not his own life. He just had to hope that the people who he owed money to would be ok with waiting till the end of the tour. They weren't too pleased when he'd broached the 'repayment' plan to them, but as he pointed out, if Magenta had an accident too early in the tour then the money would be lost in refunded ticket costs, insurance premiums and lawyers' costs. The list was endless. They seemed to accept this, although all be it very grudgingly. Having Magenta in his court was saving his bacon.

He took a sip of his drink, concentrating on the warm liquid burning the back of his throat slightly as it slid down. By the summer this would be over with. He'd be a free man and he'd never gamble again. He needed to get his life back on track, starting with his marriage. He was well aware he'd been a shit husband recently, Brooke deserved better. He knew she wasn't happy, he couldn't blame her, it was all his own fault. If you don't care for something you love, it withers away and dies. It was time he revived their love. He'd be open and honest, tell her about the gambling. If he was serious about stopping he needed her on side, he needed her to help him. It'd be all too easy to log back onto the gambling sites he used if Brooke wasn't in the picture. He'd get this weekend out of the way and then when they were back in New York he'd sit down with his wife and have a serious talk with her. Before he could brood any more Fly wandered into the lounge, heading straight to the bar. 'Hey Logan. My man.' he greeted his boss as he pushed himself up on his tip toes to lean across the bar, grabbing two bottles of JD.

'This bar is eight foot long, I'm sure it would've been easier to just go round it and get your liquor.'

'But this way is so much more fun, feels like I'm using someone else's drink.'

Logan raised an eyebrow. 'You are.'

It was then Fly really looked at Logan. 'Wow, you ok? You look like shit.'

'Thanks for the compliment. Think I'm coming down with something.'

'The whiskey will help.'

Logan nodded. 'Yep, purely medicinal,' he narrowed his eyes at Fly. 'Why two bottles of rum?' The drummer started laughing. 'You sound like a freakin' shampoo commercial.' he altered his voice to sound like he was doing a voice over. 'Why take two bottles of rum into the shower?' He carried on laughing at his joke.

'Freakin' looped you are MacFly, freakin' looped.'

'Just having a little pre-dinner party with Johnny and Savannah if you know what I mean.'

Logan sighed, knowing all too well what that meant. 'Just do me a favour, no taking any photos, I don't wanna see you pair of cockstars all over Twitter.'

Fly was still laughing as he walked out of the lounge, swinging a bottle of rum in each hand. As Logan watched him go, he was fleetingly reminded of Jack Sparrow, where has all the rum gone indeed? He turned back to his drink. At least some people were having fun on this trip.

Brooke stood outside the big oak door that led into Johnny's room, she lifted her hand to knock but then thought better of it. She placed her hand on the knob, turning it and sauntered into the bedroom, letting everything swing from her hips to her long blonde sleek pony tail. She was surprised to find only Johnny, who was sitting on the window seat and Fly already on the bed. She wondered where Savannah was. She stood at the foot of the bed, one hand on her hip, the other hip angled towards the floor, all the better to display her figure in the skin tight black cat suit she was wearing.

'Where's Savannah?' She had been expecting some girl on girl action after their kiss earlier and then she assumed they'd get down to it with the boys.

'She ducked out for a bit,' Fly pushed himself up off the bed. 'No reason why we shouldn't get this party started without her, though.'

She nodded as a slow sexy smile spread across her face. Was her fantasy about to become reality? Fly held her attention as she watched his eyes follow the zip of her cat suit, from the peak of her cleavage down to her crotch. She half expected it to unzip it's self just by the sheer magnetism in Fly's eyes. She almost jumped as she felt the zip move lower. She'd been so focused on Fly, she hadn't noticed Johnny sneak up on her and move the zip, tantalisingly slow at first as Fly's eyes followed Johnny's hand snake down her body. Once the zip was undone, revealing her breasts, she had no need to wear a bra, those man-made bad boys didn't budge, they were just there in all their splendour to show off when she felt like it. Right now, she'd never felt more like it in her whole entire life. Johnny stood behind her, pushing the cat suit down her body, her skin was already sticky, both from the suit and from how turned on she was right now. As she felt the suit disappearing further down her body she beckoned Fly over with her finger. She placed her hands on his shoulders so she could steady herself as she stepped out of her sky high heels. She purposely pushed her bare ass out towards Johnny as she manoeuvred out of her shoes. It obviously had the desired effect as she felt his hands over her butt cheeks.

She stalked across over to the bed and lay down on her back, naked on the bed. The boys didn't need asking, they were by her side in seconds, Johnny on the left side of the bed, Fly to the right. Fly pulled a little bag of powder from his jeans pocket. 'Whaddya say we add some icing to those fabulous tits?' He winked at Brooke.

'Ah man, you know I ain't into that shit.' Johnny pulled a face.

Brooke giggled. 'Johnny, don't be good, c'mon live a little.'

'What I'm about to do to the bosses wife is anything but good.'

'Don't disappoint a girl already.'

He grinned. 'Not good for him, I mean.'

Fly sprinkled the contents of the bag over Brooke's tits, whose nipples were already pointing skywards. The guys dropped to their knees, simultaneously taking a ripe nipple in their mouths and licking her clean of coke.

Brooke arched her back in pleasure, this was only the beginning and it was already one of the best experiences ever. She felt their lips trail down the sides of her body, resting around by her inner thighs. She looked down to see Fly's dirty blonde hair and Johnny's raven hair bobbing up and down as they ravished her with kisses. This was definitely a Kodak moment. She giggled again at the situation.

Fly looked up. 'What's so funny?'

'This is, do you know how many women across the globe are in bed now, jerking off to you two and here I am in bed, with both of you. Don't reckon it gets much better than this.'

Fly moved further up the bed, closer to her. He caught some coke that hadn't been licked up and scooped it up with his finger. He ran it over her lips, her tongue greedily lapping it up.

'Oh, I assure you, Brooke, baby, it gets far better.'

'Well, you might wanna lose your clothes, not much I can do when you're both fully dressed is there?'

Johnny yanked at his clothes, pulling them off. Fly was only seconds behind as he flung his T shirt and jeans to the floor. The boxer shorts followed just as quickly.

For a second Brooke was speechless. It wasn't every day you found yourself lying naked in between two rock star Adonis's. She took a moment to take in the view. Fly stood to her right, his cock standing just as tall. Just as he'd surveyed her body before, she did the same to his, taking in the tattoos, the nipple piercing the drummers arms and a cock that could be used to whack a beat out on a drum kit too. He grinned as her saw her eyes light up at the size of it.

'If it's makin' you smile now, baby. Just wait till I'm done with you.'

She switched her attention to Johnny. God she felt like she was in a chocolate shop, or the Kurt Geiger shoe shop. Johnny was just as statuesque as Fly, apart from their different hair colouring they were almost mirror body images of each other. Hmmm, decisions decisions.

Chapter Thirty Three

Hunter emerged from the kitchen, having checked that the kitchen staff were ready with the meal and also to give Tim a once over, making sure he hadn't leaked all over the floor. So far it was looking ok. Well as best as a corpse could look. He was running on nervous energy and adrenalin. He was going to keep a close eye on the girls, see who was drinking, surely whichever one of them was pregnant would lay off the booze? He knew it was all going to kick off tonight, but he didn't know exactly what the outcome would be. All he knew was, he was going to be stuck to Mags like glue. He could feel the tension in the manor increasing throughout the day, it'd be a melting pot if it wasn't so cold. The hall was in semi darkness, being lit by low lighting. You'd jump at your own shadow, it was all very Addams Family. He heard heels coming down the stairs. He hid in the shadow of the staircase as he watched Mags descend the stairs, each step carefully measured as she negotiated the stairs in her killer heels. She was wearing a figure hugging purple dress, on Brooke it'd look like trash but on Mags it looked sensational. Her long red hair hung poker straight down her back, the usual natural curl to it not in evidence tonight. In short, she looked dressed to kill. He carried on watching, she had a steely look of determination across her face and as she reached the door to the grand hall she took a deep breath, smoothed her dress down, held her head up high and walked through the door in the only way Magenta Valentina knew how to, with attitude. He stepped out of the shadows and followed her, doing his own final checks, the most important one being his gun. He had a hunch he'd be needing it tonight.

Magenta was last to enter the banqueting hall, as she had intended. She was impressed with the decoration. She wasn't expecting much, what with them being stuck in a snow globe but the staff from the Liver

Bird who had come over with them had done a great job. It helped that a lot of the stuff had been sent on before they'd actually arrived. Magenta knew what she wanted. Like the previous night, candles were the main source of light, but this time swathes of purple and silver fabric adorned the walls, fluttering in the slight draft that was only natural in rooms the size of this in old houses. The banqueting table was also decked with silver candelabras and arrangements of purple gerberas, tulips and even purple roses which were entwined with silver leaves. It looked stunning. She was so taken with the room that she momentarily forgot to acknowledge her guests who were all seated around the table. She smiled at them. 'My apologies, I'm forgetting my manners. I'm just so impressed by the decoration in here, I've forgotten to say hello,' she stood at the head of the table. Hunter appeared from nowhere, or maybe he'd been there all along and she'd been oblivious to him too. Her mouth twitched slightly as she tried to suppress a smile. He pulled the chair out behind her, ready to let her sit down. She watched as he walked over to the drinks table. He was out of his usual suit and shirt attire and was dressed down in jeans that emphasised his arse and his thigh muscles straining through the denim. He wore a plain white t-shirt with a checked Burberry shirt over it, left unbuttoned. He looked hot, she also noticed he had cowboy boots on and with his day old stubble he was definitely rocking the rough and ready look.

'Magenta? Magenta?'

She pulled her eyes away from Hunter's delectable derrière and turned her attention to Brooke, who sat to her right. She reached out placing a hand on hers. 'Sorry, darling. What where you saying? I was still admiring the décor.'

Hunter was now walking back to the table with bottles of wine, she could tell by the bemused look in his face that he'd gotten her loaded reply to Brooke.

'Well, I was just agreeing with you sweetie, the colours you've chosen works so well with the style of this room and the colour is so you.'

Magenta nodded. 'Well, purple is supposed to be a regal colour and I am the queen of rock am I not?'

'Hell yeah!' Fly boomed from the other side of the table.

Magenta smiled as she surveyed the table. Max, uncharacteristically quiet next to her on the other side.

'Hey Magenta, thought this was the party to end all parties, looks like it's just a replay of last night's dinner,' Johnny shouted over.

She tilted her head to one side, smiling at him. 'Johnny, darling. Have I ever let you down? Have faith. But you are right, we need to get this party started,' she turned her attention to Hunter. 'Mr Cole, would you mind sticking the iPod on?'

He gave a nod of his head as he wandered over to the docking station in the corner. 'Now that's what I'm talkin' about,' Johnny cheered as the intro to one of Broken Arrow's stadium anthems, 'Getaway' filled the room. Fly was already tapping the table along with his drum beat coming from the iPod.

Magenta lifted up her purple champagne flute. 'Well, my lovely friends, it's time to propose a toast,' she waited until everyone had raised their flutes. 'Welcome to my divorce party, it's gonna be one hell of a night.'

The sounds of shocked gasps and smashing crystal were drowned out as Johnny's voice, coming from the iPod, hit the chorus. 'I've made my plan, I'm making a getaway and hell yeah baby, I'm gonna make you pay.'

Magenta smiled slowly. 'Perfect timing Mr Kidd,' she retrieved an envelope from her evening bag, still holding court as there appeared to be a satellite delay in the room whilst everyone digested Magenta's statement.

Predictably Max spoke, or rather shouted first. 'What the hell are you on about woman? You can't divorce me! I'm Ma...'

She butted in. 'Oh give it a rest Max, we all know who you are, you tell us often enough,' her tone implied boredom. Johnny caught her eye as he stifled a giggle. He was the only one who seemed to be smiling. Everyone else have various states of shock and disbelief on their face. She tried not to look at Hunter, she needed to keep her cool stay in control.

'On what grounds?' Max boomed.

'Here are the divorce papers, read it yourself. However for the benefit of our guests, let me tell you a little story about a man named Max, he thought he was the most powerful man on the planet, but most of us know that's

Simon Cowell,' she enjoyed the apoplectic look on his face as his eyes scanned the divorce documents and his ears heard her verbal attack. 'So, Max, who is the villain of this story by the way, just in case you were in any doubt, was constantly straining to be the top of his game, but not quite getting there. Yes he was successful but the whole world knows that 'Starmaker' ain't no X Factor. Anyway, Maxie decides to further his popularity and become a dominant force in the music world, he needs a wife and not just any wife,' she paused as she took a slow drink of her champagne. She didn't need to rush, she had them all on the edge of their seats, literally. Every one of them was now leaning forward across the table. As she set her glass down, she shook her head. 'No, our Max Maxwell needed a particular wife, he needed someone that was already popular, loved by millions, someone who would look great on his arm. Enter stage right, Ms Magenta Valentina, the perfect English rose to go with his American charm. What a couple we made. The press loved us instantly, Max's popularity soared so you'd think that'd be the happy ending?' she shook her head again. 'Dead wrong there,' she saw Max wince again and this time she knew it was because she'd gone scouse on him. 'Y'see, for there to be happiness in the first place the two people involved in the marriage would have to at least like each other, and should really love each other. That's where the Valentina/Maxwell marriage failed on both counts. We were the worst arranged marriage on the planet. As soon as I married him I knew I'd made a mistake. Why didn't I divorce him sooner? I hear you ask,' she grinned. 'Well, as I'm sure you're aware, he's Max Maxwell, he only lets you go on his terms and I know he had no intention of divorcing me,' she leaned in towards the table. 'Let's get one thing straight before we go any further. I signed a pre-nup, I neither want nor need his money so before your minds start wandering, this isn't to do with any financial gain on my part,' she leaned back in her chair. 'Where was I? Oh that's right, yes, so, why did I wait until now to file for divorce? Well finally, I found my way out. Maxie dear, can't keep it in his pants and I had evidence of an affair,' she paused again to let that one sink in. She watched as accusing looks flew around the table. 'Now, I have to hold my hands up and say I wasn't entirely sure who it was with, but I had enough to start divorce proceedings, the usual stuff, hotel rooms booked for two when I wasn't with him and the receipt for a meal for two that judging by the oysters on the menu and champagne wasn't a business dinner. Then there was the lipstick returned to me from the Plaza which I'd left behind after my recent stay there with Mr Maxwell. Hmmm, that'd be the recent stay when I'd actually been in Liverpool? I'm talented, but even I can't be in two places at once,' again she took a moment to see the penny drop in certain people's eyes,' so, I devised a plan, I was going to invite you all here so I could discover who Max's bit on the side is and then that would be everything I needed to file for adultery, naming both the guilty parties and thank them for setting me free. Let me tell you, I'm not bitter, I'm just glad to finally be out of such a loveless marriage.'

'Just hang on a minute, what the hell are we here for then, 'cos I can tell you one thing, I certainly haven't been shaggin' ole Max,' Fly butted in.

'As if babes, he's like way old, and he ain't my type,' Savannah added.

Johnny raised an eyebrow at Savannah's comment.

'Just hold it there, you guys were invited along as witnesses, I didn't think you'd mind and Savannah, I know Max wanted you along on this trip but I think it's fairly common knowledge that your more into ladies?'

Savannah blushed slightly. 'Well, yeah that's true, but Max thinks it'll harm my career if I come out, that's why I've been hanging with Johnny, not that it's been a bummer.'

'Yeah we know, we got the video nasty on twitter,' Fly rolled his eyes as he spoke.

It interested Magenta that the only people who seemed comfortable talking right now were the Broken Arrow boys and Savannah, the people who didn't have anything to hide or weren't affected by the outcome. She looked over at Jody who hadn't spoken all evening and was staring at her plate. She imagined she was very uncomfortable in this situation and Hunter, well, he was now leaning against the bar, arms folded, taking it all in. 'Come on guys, let me get back to my story, we're just getting to the good bit. So thanks to my husband's ever wandering dick and its welcoming committee. I could contact my lawyer and get the documents sorted.'

'You'll never prove this,' Max stood up from his chair, waving the papers at her. 'You could name anyone you like in these papers, it'll never stick.'

Magenta shrugged. 'Well let's ask her shall we,' she reached into her clutch bag, pulling out a lipstick. 'What do you think Brooke? Ravishing Rouge, just your colour?'

Brooke, who had been trying to look unaffected by the whole conversation now found herself in the spot light. 'I err...I err...oh crap.'

'Brooke, don't say anything,' Max snapped at her.

'Let her speak Max,' Logan said.

Magenta shot a look at Logan who was sitting very calmly at the end of the table. It seemed

Max was taken aback by Logan's directness. 'Logan, I really think...'

Logan stood up, his chair scrapping across the tiled floor. 'Max, I really don't give a damn what you think, I want to hear what my wife has to say. Brooke?'

All eyes were back on Brooke. Magenta felt a wave of guilt wash over her, Logan. Shit, she should have spoken to him first. It was all well and good outing Max for being a bastard and Brooke for being a tart, but she hadn't factored Logan in on this story, well she had, he'd be ok in the end. She'd seen to that, which happened to be the next big reveal she had for Max, but before that she still had to deal with Brooke.

'Yeah, Brooke, spill. You're amongst friends,' Magenta added.

Brooke narrowed her eyes. 'It was you wasn't it? You saw us the other night. What were you doing? Checking the rooms to keep tabs on your husband?'

Magenta shrugged. 'Something like that.'

'Brooke, will you shut the hell up, she can't prove anything.'

'Err, excuse me Mr Hotshot, think she's just admitted it and we can all back Magenta's story up,' Johnny was now reclining in his chair, cowboy booted feet propped up on the table, clearly enjoying the discomfort on Max's face.

Max sighed. 'Yet again, dumbass do I need to remind you that I can ruin you like that,' he snapped his fingers. 'No other record company will touch you once I'm done with you.'

'Hmm, funny you should mention record companies,' Magenta said.

Max looked back to his wife. 'Magenta, what have you done?'

She stood up, walking slowly round the table towards Logan, talking as she walked. 'Well, I'm sure you'll recall me mentioning before that this wasn't about money for me and to that effect, I have signed over the shares I had in Maximum,' she placed her hands on Logan's shoulders. 'To Logan. Max darling, meet your new boss.'

Johnny nearly fell off his chair laughing. 'Magenta, baby, this is one hell of a party.'

'Woohoo, Max is a goner,' Fly cheered.

'Magenta, this isn't what we talked about...I don't understand,' Logan looked confused. 'I know, circumstances have changed. You now have control of the company. I figured you were the wronged man in all of this,' she looked back up to her husband. 'Max, you need to learn there are consequences to your actions, I figured signing the shares over to Logan was my attempt at an apology on your behalf,' she smiled her million dollar smile at him. She knew Max would never let Logan have control over the company, he'd sooner walk away and that was the only option he had left.

Max was raging. 'You can't freakin' do this, you crazy woman. You are not divorcing me,' he spun round pointing at Logan. 'And YOU are not having my company.'

'I think you'll find I can and I already have,' Magenta smiled.

'Over my dead body,' he shouted back, storming out of the banqueting hall.

Chapter Thirty Four

There was a moments silence in the banquet hall as the information filtered through to everyone, then everything seemed to go crazy at once. Logan pushed his chair back and headed straight for the bar, grabbing a bottle of vodka from the side and plonking himself down next to where Hunter was still leaning against the bar. Brooke looked like she wasn't sure whether to go after Max or follow her husband. Magenta obviously wasn't waiting for her to make her mind up and she headed straight to Logan. She placed a hand on his arm when she reached him, 'Logan, I'm sorry,' she spoke in hushed tones so the others who were talking away about the revelations wouldn't hear her, Hunter's close proximity didn't concern her, it was only stuff she'd be telling him later anyway. 'I should have spoken to you first, but I only found out yesterday about Brooke and I didn't want to lose my element of surprise. I know it was selfish but I hope that by signing the company over to you, you can forgive me.'

He looked at her for a few moments before he spoke, his head tilted to one side. 'Jeez Magenta, I don't know what to think. My wife and my best friend. What a fuckin' cliché,' he shook his head and let out a false laugh. 'They musta pissed themselves laughing behind our backs.'

She nodded. 'That's why I did what I did, the company for you, freedom for me. Now you'll have control of the company and with Max's shares you can pay off your debts,' she reached out for a bottle of Bourbon and poured herself a shot, downing it in one. She then lined up another.

'You've got balls Magenta, I'll give you that.'

She shook her head. 'It ain't balls, it isn't even my inner goddess, I'm just a scouse bird.'

She saw the expression on Hunter's face as she looked over Logan's head, he winked and gave her a smile. With that she downed the next shot, turned and walked away.

Hunter put his hand on Logan's shoulder. 'You doin' ok mate?' He cringed as soon as he said it, his scouseness was coming out now too, he was sounding less American by the second.

He'd need to rein that in. Fortunately, Logan was too self-absorbed to notice.

'Kinda thinkin' blowing my head off might've been a good idea.'

'That's never the answer.'

Logan tried to laugh. 'I'm jokin' anyway at least my money worries are over. Now all I gotta do is kick Max's butt.'

Shane wandered into the room, in all the excitement, nobody realised he was missing at dinner. 'Sounds like I missed out on something big. Saw Max before, he wasn't looking too pleased. What did I miss?'

'Everything,' Johnny told his brother, sounding like a kid on Christmas morning. As far as he was concerned, Max losing Maximum was the best thing ever. Magenta sure as hell was one smart cookie. It was tough on Logan, but Brooke was always a slapper and always would be. 'Where you been anyways?'

'Sleeping off too much booze.'

Fly walked over. 'Man, you need to be in the band, you just slept through your hangover!'

From his position at the bar, Hunter was perfectly placed to watch the fallout from the bomb Magenta had just dropped. He hadn't managed to stop a small smile spreading across his face when he'd seen Max's reaction to Mags' meddling. Not that anyone had noticed, they were too focused on the Max and Magenta show. She had totally proven the theory that you never mess with a scouser and she'd managed to resolve Logan's gambling debts at the same time. So, over Logan's head, he was watching the rest of the room. The Broken Arrow boys seemed the most jovial about the revelations, Johnny was now free from Max's blackmail, so to see him fall from grace like that must have felt good. Brooke was still sitting at the table, looking totally deflated. Savannah was at her side, obviously trying to comfort her as she stroked Brooke's hair. Mags was with Jody, their heads bent together in deep conversation. He rubbed a hand over his chin, all this did was confuse him even more. Now Mags had well and truly put the cat among the pigeons, surely that made the target on her head even bigger. He had to resolve this situation and he had to do it quickly, every minute it went on he just knew she was in more and more danger. He wasn't letting her out of his sight tonight.

'Magenta, I'm your PA and your friend, you should've kept me in the loop,' Jody's shaky voice could've been down to anger, but she knew it wasn't anger, it was shock. How could Max do this?

'Look, I'm sorry. I had to keep everyone in the dark until I knew who he was shagging. For one crazy moment I even suspected you.'

Jody laughed nervously. 'Oh come on, as if Max even notices I'm there.'

Magenta frowned. 'You say that like you wish he did.'

'You're twisting my words.'

'Hmm, whatever,' she waved her hand to one side as if to brush the comment away. 'While the divorce is coming through and I finish off the tour I need to take some time out and figure out what I wanna do next.'

Jody had to put her PA head on, it was the only way to get through this conversation. 'Max isn't going to let you walk away, despite what you think. You two are the golden couple, he won't let that little money spinner go easy.'

Mags snorted. 'Ever the old romantic. I am not spending my life married to someone I couldn't give a flying fuck about. I've finally found my way out and I will fight him every step of the way if I have to. He's not wriggling out of this one.'

'Y'know Max, he always comes up smelling of roses.'

'Well not this time, it's time he learnt that shit sticks.'

Jody shook her head. 'Well, looks like it's gonna get interesting around here,' she picked up her glass, downing the contents in one go.

'You're damn right,' Magenta stood up. 'I suppose I better go and check on him, hopefully he's had time to let it sink in.'

As Magenta strode away, Jody visibly deflated. She was in the centre of this debacle and Magenta didn't even have a clue. As for Max, she always knew he was a bastard, she just didn't realise how cold hearted he was.

Brooke tried to intercept Magenta as she stalked across the banqueting hall, but she held her hand, palm up, towards her. 'I'm not listening to anything you have to say.'

'But, I need to explain,' she protested.

Magenta came to an abrupt halt, placed her hands on her hips and raised her head up, so she could look right down her nose at her former frenemy, now just an enemy. 'Then I suggest you begin with your husband,' she turned to walk away, but Brooke grabbed her by the elbow, spinning her back round to face her. 'Listen miss high n' mighty, thinking you're all that. You'd be nothing without Max, you're gonna regret throwing him away.'

Magenta laughed. 'Oh I think not, beside you'll be there to get my cast offs, I was brought up to pass my used items to the less fortunate.'

'You bitch, you frigid bitch, can't even keep your man satisfied in bed. No wonder he went looking elsewhere.'

'Oh and there you were, legs wide open, just waiting for him. Bet he didn't even have to ask did he? What did you do? Go into his office in your trampy short skirts and offer your services?'

Brooke's cheeks coloured, Magenta knew she wasn't far off the mark. She gave a satisfied smile. 'Thought so, you little tramp.'

'That's it,' Brooke launched herself at Magenta, taking her by surprise and making her lose her balance on her Louboutins. She reached out to steady herself, but all she found was Brooke's arm. The two women tumbled to the floor. Brooke began clawing and scratching away at Magenta's face, who in retaliation grabbed Brooke's hair extensions, pulling them as hard as she could.

'Cat fight,' Fly yelled. 'Go girls.'

Hunter, who had been watching the interaction between the two women from the other side of the hall was now towering above them, attempting to pull them apart. Both women were really going for it and were managing to brush him off. In the end there was only one thing to do.

'Stop, she's pregnant.'

Chapter Thirty Five

Magenta was perched on the edge of the sink unit in one of the bathrooms, Hunter stood in front of her, tending to the scratches on her face. She winced as he dabbed her eyebrow with cotton wool.   'Ouch,' she screwed up her face.

'Sorry, I'm trying to be gentle.'

'Normally I'm desperate for you to touch me, but right now it freakin' hurts,' she reached up to her hair in an attempt to fix it after the mess Brooke had made of it. 'What?' she snapped as she saw a slow smile spread across Hunter's rugged face.

'Was just thinkin', you have never looked so sexy.'

She rolled her eyes. 'Oh shut up, you sarky git,' she tried to sound cross, but she never could be with him.

He dabbed the cotton wool in the warm water and lifted his hand towards her cheek. She grabbed his wrist, making his arm stop in mid-air. 'How did you know?'

He paused for a second whilst he moved his arm down and placed his hand on the unit, her hand rested on top of his. 'I found a pregnancy test in the bin the other day, I knew I had a one in four chance of getting it right, but when you and Brooke were kicking off at each other, the odds narrowed. I took a chance and my hunch was right.'

'One of four chance? So you thought it might have been me?'

'It was a possibility.'

'You do know, if that pregnancy test had been mine, well the baby would've been yours?'

He nodded slowly, now probably wasn't the time to tell her he'd had her under surveillance for the last six weeks and he knew she hadn't been anywhere near Max.

'How would you have handled it, y'know, if we were having a baby?'

He gave her a wry smile. 'Probably better than I did all those years ago.'

'Ah, we were just stupid kids then,' she shrugged.

'Not that stupid, there were some things we were deadly serious about,' he leaned closer to her, his lips lightly touching the scratches, kissing them better. This time, she didn't wince. Instead, her head instinctively tilted backwards and her legs automatically parted to let him stand between them. His kisses trailed along her throat and his hands moving along the silky fabric that covered her thighs. She sat upright, pushing him away.

'Hold on a moment.'

'What?' he looked confused.

'The first time we get to, y'know, do it, for the first time in six weeks and I ain't doing it with my arse in the sink. I'm not some girl from Bootle, y'know.'

He started laughing. 'That's ok, I'd thought you'd gone off me. What do you suggest then?'

She looked at her Gucci watch, the diamonds picking up the reflection from the shining marble in the bathroom as she flicked her wrist. 'Hmm, I reckon we got at least another twenty minutes before anyone notices we're missing. Let's go to my suite.' She hopped off the sink unit and took him by the hand. This time it was him who seemed reluctant and it was her turn to question him.

'You gone off me now?'

He shook his head. 'No, it's just, there's something I need to tell you, something I'm not comfortable keeping from you any more.'

'Look, babe, we got twenty minutes? What do you want to do? Have a nice cosy chat or get rid of this frustration building up between us?'

'Well, when you put it that way...'

He followed her out of the room as they quickly ran down the corridor towards her suite, there would be plenty of time to talk later. Right now, she was right, he felt like he was ready to spontaneously combust his body was coiled with lust.

The two bodies fumbled with each other's clothes as they clashed together with urgency, shirt buttons ripped off, the zip of a dress yanked down such was their desire for each other. Weeks of pent up sexual tension and missed opportunities culminating in this moment. Now as they crashed through the suite door they didn't even make it to the bedroom, they fell clumsily over the coffee table knocking over a bottle of Whisky as they landed on the sofa.

'Sshh', she giggled drunkenly, placing a finger on his lips.

'Don't worry, everyone's too busy downstairs to miss us,' his mouth came down on hers again, his hands hungrily pushing up her skirt. Her breasts were exposed now that her dress had slipped off her shoulders. He rolled his tongue over an already erect nipple, as his hands disappeared further up her skirt. His cock throbbed as he felt the dampness of her knickers, the foreplay had been the weeks leading to this moment. She wriggled out of them as he undid the zip on his jeans, she lifted her hips and wrapped her legs around his waist, pulling him into her. Her hands grasped his firm buttocks pushing him even further. He grabbed the back of the sofa to gain a quicker rhythm. This was hot, fast, urgent sex. Their bodies building up to a crescendo, both of them needing this release. They were slick with sweat. This wasn't about a marathon, it was a sprint to the finish. They went limp with exhaustion and he collapsed on top of her, nuzzling her neck.

'I wanna do that again, properly.'

'There was nothing improper about that.'

He lifted his head so he could look into her eyes. 'I wanna take my time, feel every inch of you, kiss you all over...'

She sighed. 'Time is something we don't have, we'll be missed.'

He stood up, pulling her with him. 'We can make some excuse, c'mon you know we need to do this.'

She nodded. 'I know.'

'No point standing here chatting is there? We're wasting time,' he led her by the hand towards the bedroom.

Pushing open the door a scream stuck in her throat as her hand flew to her mouth.

'Shit.'

On the bed, naked, on blood-stained sheets was a body, a quite clearly dead body.

'That's my husband,' she gasped.

She opened her mouth again to scream but before any sound came out, Hunter placed a hand across her mouth and moved in front of her. 'Ssh,' he reached down, pulling a gun from his boot. 'Stay behind me.'

'What the...?' Hidden guns, what the hell was going on? Magenta felt a chill go down her spine. She moved with him, shielded behind his athletic physique. She couldn't always see what he was doing, probably because she was too scared to look, but it was obvious he was looking for Max's killer. At least that's what she thought was happening. Right now she couldn't be sure of anything. He stepped slowly, but sure footed around the suite, checking behind the curtains, in the walk in wardrobe, the bathroom, under the bed and then finally back into the lounge area were moments earlier they'd been caught up in the throes of passion. However, that now felt like a lifetime ago. She felt like a brick was wedged in her stomach, every time she glanced over her shoulder at Max she wanted to throw up. Satisfied that the room was clear, he walked back over to the body.

'I think we can safely say, whoever shot Max is no longer in close proximity.'

'How can you be so sure?'

Hunter placed two fingers against Max's throat. 'For starters, he's cold and secondly, we would've heard the gun shot from the lounge area.'

'Unless they used a silencer?'

He raised an eyebrow. 'Wow, you're good. I suppose so, but it's usually only assassins who use silencers.'

'Is that possible? Could someone have put a hit on him?'

He couldn't help but laugh.

'What? It's possible, right?' She frowned.

Oh the irony. 'I don't think a hit man killed him. You know everyone here.'

She shrugged. 'There is someone who spooks me out,' she lowered her voice. 'I don't trust Shane AND he's been in prison.'

'There's more to Shane's imprisonment than meets the eye, but I don't think he's a contract killer,' trust me, there is only one of them around here.

'Oh My God, what the hell are we doing just standing here chatting next to Max's dead body? We need to call the police.'

'No point, we're still snowed in, they can't get here yet. We need to solve this one ourselves.'

'And how the hell do you propose we do that? Where the hell do we start?'

'Well, the cops can't get in, which means nobody can get out...'

'Which means whoever shot Max is in the house.'

'Told you, you were good.'

'What are we going to do with him? We can't leave him here oh but then we can't move him either, we'd be tampering with the evidence.'

'Sure you weren't a cop in a former life?'

'Don't you remember we used to watch The Bill in me Ma's every week?'

'Clearly you paid more attention than I did,' he paused. Was now the time to tell her who he really was?

'Right now, I don't know anything, apart from you being the only person I trust right now.'

And there was his answer.

'We'll do this together, I've got your back.'

'Who says I need my back watching? Maybe I need to watch yours,' she tried to smile but seeing the serious look in his eyes, the smile froze on her face.

'What?'

He rubbed a hand across his face. Ok, maybe now was the time. 'Mags, I need to tell you something.'

The brick in her stomach now felt like it was doing somersaults. 'It's bad, isn't it?'

'Depends on your point of view.'

Before he could carry on any further there was the distant sound of shouting coming from somewhere in the house. He grabbed her hand, his gun in the other. 'Come on and remember, stay close,' he burst through the door, running down the corridor. She was glad she hadn't put her Louboutins back on, there was no way she'd be able to stay upright, never mind keep up with him. They carried on towards the raised voices, down the stairs. He only slowed down as he got closer, his gun raised in preparation. He walked slowly into the banqueting hall where the noise was coming from. Peeking over his shoulder, Magenta gasped in shock for the second time that night.

Fly was lying spread eagled on the banqueting table, clad only in his denim jeans, but decorated in strawberries and cream. Johnny was tied up on a chair, Savannah strode between them, cracking a whip, which was obviously the gun shot sound they'd heard. She was swinging a bottle of Bollinger from her other hand, alternatively drizzling it over Fly's chest and then turning her attention back to Johnny.

'Bloody hell,' Magenta said.

'Hey, Magenta, baby doll,' Fly slurred in a drunken haze. 'Come and join us.'

'She's busy,' Hunter pushed her out of the room, closing the door behind him. He looked at Mags, with a bemused look on his face. 'Well, don't reckon we'll get much joy out of them tonight.'

'I suppose that gives them an alibi then.'

He shook his head. 'We have no idea what time Max was killed. His body was cold,' he paused as he saw her wince. So the guy was a jerk, but he was still Mags' husband. Legally at least. 'What I meant was, it could be a good few hours that he's been lying there for,' he glanced at his watch. 'It's at least three hours since you saw him last...'

'That doesn't mean I was the last to see him,' she got on the defensive.

'I didn't say that, I was just trying to point out that we have no time of death and we have no idea who the last person to come into contact with him was...'

'His killer you mean?'

He nodded slowly, pushing his unruly curls out of his face with both hands, leaving them behind his head as he contemplated the situation.

'So, what do we do now?'

'I guess we're body sitting.'

'What?' Mags asked.

'Well, we can't just leave him up there on his own.'

'Yes we bloody well can, he's hardly likely to be after some company is he?' She tried to sound in control of the situation.

'What if the killer comes back? Tries to hide their tracks or move the body?'

'Seriously, you've been watching too many films,' she put her hands on her hips. 'Your imagination is clearly running away with you.'

'You don't know the half of it,' he paused again, dropping his hands to his on waist, almost mimicking her stance. 'We need to talk.'

'Why do those four words feel like they are loaded with stuff I don't want to hear?'

'Come'ead girl.'

Now she really did feel sick to her stomach, lapsing into scouse was a bad sign.

Chapter Thirty Six

Back in the suite, in the lounge area and as far away from Max's body as she could get Magenta curled up on the window seat. She kept eyeing the closed door to the bedroom, knowing what was on the other side. Her eyes were drawn to the sofa, how could she and Hunter have been getting down to it on there, with no idea what was waiting for them in there? Her eyes were back on the bedroom door. She shuddered, what did she expect to happen? Max to walk through the door, zombie style? Still nothing surprised her any more after this weekend. She was literally on the edge of her seat as Hunter began his 'we need to talk chat'. Well, she thought he was about to start, he was too busy feeling around the frames of paintings, checking under the desk and behind cushions.

'What on earth are you doing?'

'Checking for bugs.'

'Hunter, now is not the time to check for creepy crawlies, you working for Rentokill too?'

He stopped and threw her a look. 'Not those kinda bugs, listening devices.'

'Like in Spooks?'

'Yes, babe, like in Spooks,' again he threw her a look.

'Right, Hunter Cole. You are going to tell me right now what's going on. Why are you looking for bugs? You've been acting shady ever since we bumped into each other again.'

'Yeah, well, about that. We didn't actually bump into each other.'

'Yes we did, I was in the bar at the hotel and you were there too.'

He wandered over to the drinks cabinet. 'I think you're gonna need a drink for this. Vodka?'

'I'm easy, but whatever it is, you better make it a double.'

He didn't say it, but he was pretty sure a triple would be better. He poured the drink, with one for himself and took it over to her. He perched on the back of the sofa so he could face her as she sat on the window seat. He stretched his long legs out in front of him he downed the Southern Comfort he'd poured for himself and then plonked the empty glass down on the table next to the sofa. He didn't want to drink, he needed his wits about him, that one was for Dutch courage.

'Well?'

'We didn't just bump into each other.'

'So you've said and again, I beg to differ.'

'I knew you'd be there.'

'You knew? But hardly anyone knew I was going to be there,' she smiled slowly. 'It doesn't matter how you find out. The point is, we've found each other again.'

'It's not that easy.'

'Don't be soft. Of course it is, well it was till someone killed Max...we probably have to keep the fact that we're together under wraps. It'll look suspicious.'

'Mags, I bloody well love you, but will you please just shut up and let me speak? Trust me, you might not be so keen after I've told you this, in fact you might even regret letting me...'

She stood up, in front of him and placed her finger on his lips. 'Letting you back into my life?

My heart? My bed? You never left it in the first place.'

He put his hand over her finger, removing it from his lips. 'Please, Mags. You need to hear this. Sit down.'

She sat back slowly on the window seat, drinking the vodka as she moved. 'Go on then, spit it out.'

'You wanna know what happened to Jason Lomax?'

She tilted her face in his direction. Now he had her attention. 'Hell yeah.'

'I wasn't lying when I told you he was long gone. He went into Army and never came out.'

She frowned. 'You're confusing me. Jason is right in front of me, just using a different name.'

'Jason signed up for the Army, Hunter came out. I had to reinvent myself when I came out,' he reached over, grabbing the bottle of Smirnoff and passed it to her. 'Probably gonna need this, it's a long story.'

Taking the bottle from him and unscrewing the top she replied. 'Looks like I'm sitting comfortably. Crack on with it then.'

'They say the Army is an education and it's true. I learnt more there than I did at school and I don't think any uni would've prepared me for my chosen career path. I went into the Army, then moved quickly to the Marines as I was a rising star, my career in the forces looked rosy, but I ended up coming out with a whole new persona. I kept my head down and got on with being a soldier, my dual nationality meant I had every right to be a member of the US forces, but that didn't sit well with some of my colleagues, especially my Sergeant, Sergeant Travis. It was well known there was a bit of beef between us. Anyway, one night I'd headed into town, I had a night off and I was gonna grab a few beers and get some down time away from work. I pulled into the car lot of a run-down bar. Before I could even get inside I noticed something was happening just around the corner, I could hear muffled noises. At first I thought it was just people getting it on, but as I got nearer I could her a woman asking for help as the guy she was with tried to smother her cries with his hand. Obviously, I wasn't gonna ignore that, so I went off to investigate. I found Travis with his jeans around his ankles, pushing this woman up against the wall and she was trying to push him away. I grabbed him off her and we got into a fight. A bad fight, he was giving as good as he got, but I was stronger. Too strong. By the time some of the Army guys arrived to see what all the fuss was about, Travis was dead on the floor. I was arrested, with no chance of getting off. I was as good as dead too. The girl I'd helped had run off, so I had no witness to corroborate my story.'

'But…but you're here, did the girl come forward?'

He shook his head. 'I was rescued, for want of a better word. I had an excellent service record and not only that but I was in the top 1% of sharp shooters in the forces, I was shit hot at what I did. By the time this all happened it was 2002, six months after the September 11 attacks. A top secret government committee had been formed to combat terrorism on home soil. They wanted a sniper to take out targets, quickly and efficiently. So as I sat in the holding cell, thinking I had no way out, no way to prove it was an accident, these two guys in suits came in and I walked out of that cell as Hunter Cole.'

'What the fuck?' Was all she could say.

He smiled. 'Indeed. What the fuck was what was going through my head as I met my contact, with all my new documentation in the name of Hunter Cole, which was the moniker I'd decided to use when the guys in suits said I had to change my name, as far as the Armed forces were concerned, a guy called Jason Lomax was about to start a life sentence in jail. The suits had pulled strings to give me a lighter sentence, well, the other me. Some homeless guy who is now doing life for my crime as opposed to the death sentence that would have been handed to me. My English accent was long gone, one of the first things I'd lost during my time in the Marines in an effort to fit in. I grew my hair slightly longer, losing the military crew cut and grew a goatee. I also had a swagger and a confidence that Jason never had. As Hunter Cole I felt invincible and I had every reason to, I was being trained up to be an even better sniper than I already was in the next part of the fight against terrorism. I was to become a trained assassin. Now the task force has been disbanded, I'm freelance, I go where the work is.'

Mags dropped the bottle, miraculously it didn't smash, the carpet was so thick it gave the bottle a soft landing. Of all the things she imagined he was going to tell her, trained assassin was not one of them. As she began to process her thoughts, things jumped out at her, the gun, the secrecy, the whole Spooks things, his suspiciousness of Max. Max! 'You? You shot Max? You let us find him, knowing he was already dead?'

He shook his head quickly. 'Babe, you're jumping to conclusions. I wasn't sent here to kill Max.'

34

The air was suddenly thick with tension and not just the normal sexual tension usually between them. She looked at him, his eyes suddenly unable to meet hers.

'But you were sent here to kill someone?' He nodded slowly.

'Who?' Her voice was barely above a whisper.

His eyes finally found hers and she knew what was about to come out of his mouth.

'You.'

She tried to inch away from him, aware that he'd only have to take one step forward and he would be able to grab her, but her back was up against the window, she turned her head to look out. In the darkness she couldn't gauge how far the drop would be, the snow outside would break her fall, right? She turned back towards him, fear making her skin prickle. He'd already taken the step forward and was now right in front of her. She looked into his eyes, she'd been so easily taken in by him, tricked, she'd let herself fall in love with him all over again and all that time he'd been waiting for an opportunity to kill her.

'Mags, babe,' his voice was gravelly as he spoke. 'If I wanted to kill you, I'd have done it by now, believe me I've had plenty of opportunity.'

'Please, just tell me what the hell is going on,' she pleaded, unable to keep the fear out of her voice.

He reached out, his fingers tracing her jawline. For the first time ever, she flinched under his touch. 'Babe, don't be scared. I would never, ever hurt you. Yes, I was sent here to kill you but that was never my plan. My own agenda was to find out who ordered the hit and kill them instead.'

'So, you did kill Max?'

He shook his head. 'I don't know yet who is behind it all. I'm not saying it wasn't Max, could be that someone got there first but we can't assume that we're out of the woods yet. I have to take the threat against you as just as real as ever. I've been trying to protect you, not kill you.' 'Who could want me dead? Why didn't you tell me this before? I can protect myself you know?'

'I am the best at what I do, I have never failed at a mission yet, in order to fail at this one I need to be even smarter to work out who wants you dead. If you knew someone was trying to kill you then you'd interact with everyone differently. I needed you to be yourself, I couldn't risk suspicions being aroused that I wasn't going to fulfil my contract. Someone in this house is expecting you to leave here in a box and my job is to make sure it's them not you.'

Her hand came up to her face. 'I don't believe you. Nobody would seriously want me dead, not even Max, hell, he didn't know I was about to divorce him and he would've fought tooth and nail to stop me...but he wouldn't have had me killed. As for everyone else, they are too self obsessed with their own lives to give a damn about what I'm up to. You're wrong.'

'Mags, listen to me. Someone hired me to kill you.'

34

She tried to push him away. 'So you keep saying but I don't believe you. I think you killed Max and you've concocted this ridiculous story to deflect the suspicion from you.'

'Why would I kill Max?'

She shrugged. 'I don't know? To be with me?'

'You were going to divorce him, he wasn't going to be in the way of you and me getting back together.'

'Yes, but you didn't know I was serving him his divorce papers tonight.'

'At which point, Max was very much alive.'

She stared at him, at a loss for words as to where to take this next. He had totally bamboozled her.

'Look, why on earth would I make this up?' He sighed.

'So you can play the big hero, my knight in shining armour, saving my life.'

He flung his arms out in exasperation. 'Didn't you listen to any of that story? I was in jail, I'm a wanted man, or at least the real Jason is and I've killed people. What part of that makes me sound like a hero? Trust me if I was making something up I'd invent a story that painted me in a better light.'

She screwed her nose up as she watched him rant, she hated to admit it, but he had a point. Still, she wasn't buying this. 'Ok, so tell me, how on earth does a lad from The Dingle end up in an American jail and then become a professional hit-man? That's just crazy.'

He raised an eyebrow. 'So, tell me, how does a girl from The Dingle become a model, world famous singer and then marry a now dead American music mogul? 'Cos that's just the craziest story I ever heard.'

She folded her arms and glared at him, again, he had a point. 'Do you know what is crazy, Jason?' She saw him flinch at the mention of his real name. 'How the hell we got to this point. We were two young and stupid kids and that's where we should leave us. Whatever crazy arsed situation we now find ourselves in, once we've dealt with it, we're done. I can't deal with this and I can't deal with you.'

'I'm not leaving you, not until I know who is out to get you.'

She stood up, pushing past him. 'All I know is, since you arrived back on the scene, there has been more dead bodies than I've had the misfortune to see. If you are behind all this, then just get it over and done with. I don't know what I've done to make you want revenge. You left me remember? But just finish it, I'm bored of it all.'

'Bloody hell Mags, will you just bloody well listen. For the billionth time, I am not trying to kill you, I don't want revenge, I want you and if you can't see that then you're not the girl I remember.'

She spun round to face him, her eyes flashing. 'You're damn right I'm not the girl you remember, the girl you dumped and waited nearly twenty years to come back for. I don't need you Hunter Cole, the guy I loved, well looks like he's never coming back either. I was wrong to think he was still in there,' she began to walk away, he grabbed her wrist.

'Don't say that, I love you that means I am who you think I am.'

'Oh whatever, you're just doin' my head in now, I need some space,' she broke free of his grasp.

'Mags, whatever you're feeling right now, please, just stay here with me. It's too dangerous for you to be on your own. Ok, so you hate me right now, that's fine, but please let me do what I came here to do and keep you safe.'

She stomped over to the other side of the room and to the book case, she removed a book, revealing a hidden safe, she punched in the code, opened to door and took out a revolver.

'I can look after myself,' she headed over to the door of the suite. 'I suggest you carry on body sitting Max or whatever it is you need to do.'

He watched her leave, damn that head strong, fiery, scouseness that he loved so much. It was going to get her killed if she wasn't careful.

Chapter Thirty Seven

Magenta stormed along the landing, not entirely sure where she was storming off to and also slightly regretting walking out on Hunter, if what he'd just told her was true, she could be in danger. She waved the gun randomly in the air, where on earth was she supposed to put this anyway, it's not like her Valentino dress came with a matching gun holster. She sighed, there was just too much going on in her head to process. Her big reveal at dinner, finding out Brooke was pregnant, finally getting her hands on Hunter and then discovering Max's body and that was before she discovered someone wanted her dead. She plonked herself down on the top step off the sweeping staircase. Stupid that in a house this size she suddenly felt lost and didn't know where to go or who to trust. She put the gun down next to her, what was she thinking with her big show of defiance to Hunter? She'd never used a gun in her life and knowing her, she'd only end up shooting herself in the foot or something equally stupid. Her thoughts were distracted by a door opening somewhere downstairs, from her vantage point at the top of the stairs she had a bird's eye view of anything that was going on in the grand hall way with the luxury of being hidden from view by the low lighting. She looked through the banisters to see what was going on.

Jody was coming through one of the doors, looking like Shane was either propping her up or she was leaning into him. They staggered a few steps and then came to an abrupt stop as Shane pulled her into him. He was kissing her, his hands stuck firmly to her backside.

Magenta couldn't be sure if Jody was wriggling with pleasure or trying to get away from him. She felt uncomfortable watching this, she didn't trust Shane one little bit and she certainly didn't want Jody to get hurt. She began to stand up, her conscience wouldn't let her leave Jody in this situation. Before she could make a move another door opened. This time Johnny appeared. She was relieved to see that Johnny's presence distracted Shane who turned round to face his brother. On letting go of Jody, she slunk off. Magenta couldn't see where, she just seemed to disappear into the shadows. Magenta smiled to herself, disappeared off into the shadows, where did she think she was, some ancient gothic castle? Although she could see everything that was going on, their voices didn't carry up the stairs. Whatever they were talking about seemed very animated as Johnny shoved Shane he retaliated straight away by shoving his brother right back. Again, this altercation was interrupted as Fly and Savannah wandered out into the hall way, Fly still half-dressed and Savannah still brandishing the whip. Jeez, those Broken Arrow boys really knew how to party, seemed it wasn't just Sloth who partied hard. Savannah seemed to round the boys up and herded them back into the banqueting hall.

Magenta had no idea what that had been all about. Jody and Shane? Last night Fly had been all over her. What was she up to? And what had the two brothers been arguing about? As much as she felt uneasy around Shane, she'd only ever seen him come to Johnny's defence, especially where Max was concerned. She didn't care what Hunter said, the only person she thought was capable of killing Max was Shane. So Max wasn't the most likeable person, but she supposed you didn't get to own your own company by being a nice guy. He'd made a lot of enemies on the way up but she couldn't imagine anyone would want him dead. Brooke wouldn't want the possible father of her child dead. Logan had control of the company now, so where was his motive? Jody always seemed to have a pretty good relationship with Max, one of the few people who could let his bad temper go over her head. Johnny and Fly obviously didn't want to work with him anymore but now Logan was the sole owner of Maximum that issue had disappeared. Savannah wasn't even on the radar. Max had invited her this weekend so if she was planning to kill him she probably wouldn't have time to plan the murder. Which left Shane. Shane who had turned up out of the blue, Shane who knew Max was blackmailing his brother, Shane who had a criminal record and Shane who had the shiftiest eyes she'd ever seen. Yep, she was convinced it was him, she just needed to convince Hunter. She frowned slightly, something was bothering her, she had the same funny feeling in the pit of her stomach, the one she'd had on the way back from the hospital after visiting Trina. The feeling that Hunter wasn't quite telling her everything. Hunter who not only owned a gun, and by his own admission was a trained assassin. What if he had killed Max? He'd denied it and she believed him, at least she thought she did. But that feeling wouldn't go away. What was she missing? What had she over looked? She could really do with Poirot's little grey cells, or Miss Marple popping in, even Jessica Fletcher would do. Seems she was going to have to solve this mystery on her own.

'You're not on your own.'

'Jeez Hunter. Firstly, don't creep up on a girl, especially when you only told her half an hour ago that someone wants to kill her and secondly, get out of my thoughts.'

He sat down next to her, moving the gun from the floor and shoving it into his waistband.

'Firstly, sorry, I didn't mean to scare you and secondly, I don't have magic powers, if I could get into women's heads I wouldn't have to kill people for a living, I'm sure I'd make more money knowing what women were thinking.' She frowned at him.

'You spoke out loud, you wally,' he shoved his shoulder up against hers in an attempt to make her smile. It worked, slightly, one side of her lip curled up into a small smile.

'I'm supposed to be mad at you.'

He shrugged his shoulders. 'What can I say? You never could resist my irresistible charm.'

'Trust me, I'm having no trouble resisting it right now with all this going on around me. My head is wrecked. I can't work out who I can trust any more or if I've ever been able to trust anyone. How the hell do we sort this mess out?'

'Well, you obviously trust me if you're including me on helping you sort it out, or is that the Royal 'We'?'

'Help me if you want, I'm more than capable of fighting my own battles.'

'I know you are, I'm just not sure how good you are at fighting off a gun,' he knew he'd gone too far when he saw her face cloud over. 'Sorry, didn't mean to be so blunt. I'm not used to taking other people's feelings into account. What I meant was, I want to help and I want to protect you. I know you think you don't need it but the fact of the matter is someone wants you dead and until we can work out who that person is I'm your best weapon. So use me and abuse me.'

She dropped her head onto her knees for a second then lifted her head back up, placing her hands on either side of her cheeks. 'This is totally off its head.'

'Spoken like a true scouser, couldn't have put it better myself.'

'So, if we're going to get out of this in one piece, I assume you have a plan?'

He shrugged his big shoulders and ran his hand through his hair at the same time as he pushed away some curls that had fallen over his eyes. 'I'd say a haircut would be top of the list, but I reckon we have to deal with a few urgent matters first.'

She nodded, her eyes narrowing in concern. 'Like two dead bodies? What on earth are we going to do with Max? We can't leave him there. It could be days before we get out of here. God knows, I never loved him, disliked him most of the time but I never would've wished this on him.'

'You've got a good heart Mags, far too good for him. Don't worry about his body, I'll take care of it.'

She sighed. 'So, what are we supposed to do tonight? Looks like everyone's pissed or high so we'd get no sense out of them tonight but we can't leave Max, what if someone finds him? But I sure as hell don't want to sleep in the suite tonight, that's if I can sleep at all.'

He pulled her close. 'We'll lock the suite up, if anyone wants to get in that much they'll have to break the door down and I'll set up a wire trigger inside the room so if anyone does go in, we'll catch them. Sleep in my room tonight. I want you close by anyway, you'll sleep ok 'cos I'll be there to make sure you're safe.'

Her head was resting against his chest, the warmth from his body, comforting on her cheek and the sound of his beating heart calmed her soul. It'd be ok, as long as they stuck together it'd be ok, just like the old days with Trina and Dean. A thought stuck her, the feeling she couldn't quite shake off fleeted into her brain long enough to give her a moment of clarity. She tilted her head to look up at him, surprised to see he was already looking at her and their eyes were inches from each other. 'Trina,' was the only word she uttered, but that one word filled his green eyes with so much that she didn't want to see. Suddenly the penny dropped and she realised what her conscious mind had been trying to bury. She would've pulled away from him if she wasn't struck still with the emotions flooding her body. 'It was you?'

He nodded slowly. 'Babe, I am so sorry. Treen was never meant to be involved in this and then when you invited her to come over here for the weekend I knew I had to do something. She knew me as Jason, she'd blow my cover.'

'You could've told her, filled her in on what was going on. She would've been on your side, she wouldn't want any harm to come to me. Instead you smash her bloody knee caps and give her untold financial stress. She's my best friend!'

'Don't you think I know that? Did you really think I wanted to do that to her? I couldn't let her come here and tell her what was really going on. What if she slipped up or found out too much and the wrong person found out she knew you were supposed to be dead by

35

the end of this weekend? Believe me, broken knee caps would've been the least of her worries. She'd have been signing her own death warrant. The only way to keep you both safe was to get her out of the picture. It was one of the hardest things I've had to do, she's a good person, she didn't deserve what I did to her, but trust me,' he took her face in his hands so he could look her directly in the eye. 'It was the only way. Hate me if you want but the alternative would've been much worse,' he lowered his eyes and his nose brushed against the tip of hers. 'I love you Mags, I would do anything to keep you safe, do you think Trina could've lived with herself if anything happened to you and she'd been involved?'

She shook her head, placing her hands on top of his, which were still on her cheek. Tears were clouding her view, it finally sunk into her head how serious this all was and it wasn't the death of her would be ex-husband that did it, it was what had happened to her best friend.

'Guess shit just got real,' she tried to joke, instead it came out as a sob.

'As real as it's ever gonna get, but I got your back baby,' he smiled slowly. 'Listen to us, we've clearly spent far too much time on the other side of the pond, we're sound like some dodgy American cop show.'

This time she did manage to smile as he wiped away her tears. 'You got that right.'

'When this is all over how about we spend some quality time in our home town?'

'Sound, nice one.'

He pulled her up. 'C'ome on, you gotta get some sleep. Big day tomorrow.'

Chapter Thirty Eight

Hunter had gathered the bleary and hung-over party guests into the farm style kitchen, he wanted to get some coffee down them before he needed to grill them about Max. It was a sorry looking bunch that were seated around the big pine table in the kitchen. If the world's media could see them now. Savannah was the only sprightly looking one. Brooke looked like death warmed up, quite apt in the circumstances. She had refused the coffee, said she was struggling to keep things down in the morning. Fly asked if the black coffee came in an intravenous drip. Johnny was unusually quiet and just sat starring into his cup, well as much as you can stare when you're wearing Raybans indoors. Shane sat just as quietly next to his brother, nursing the same hangover. Jody was rocking the smudged make up and last night's outfit look. Whatever she'd been up to last night, looked like she'd never made it back to her own room. Logan looked as rough as hell, his perma Californian tan looked to have stayed State side. He was fifty shades of off grey. Which left Mags, her best poker face on, knowing that the shit was about to hit, but not letting on to anyone.

'C'mon man, what did you drag us outta bed at this sorry assed time for?'

Deciding it was best to cut to the chase, he didn't pussy foot around. 'I'm afraid we stumbled across another body last night in one of the bedrooms.'

'We? Who?' Johnny took his shades off, his bloodshot eyes on Hunter.

'Magenta and I, last night, we found...'

'Max,' Brooke mumbled.

'Holy shit, where is Max?' Fly asked.

'Dead, shot dead.'

Hunter glanced over to Mags as she spoke, but only briefly, he turned his attention back to the others. There would only be a split second to assess the looks on their faces at this news. Unfortunately, the look of shock on their faces could also be confused with guilty. Right now they all looked shocked and guilty in equal measures.

'What the fuck? Was it you?' Logan asked, directing his question to Magenta.

She laughed bitterly. 'What? The wronged wife. Don't forget, I'd told him I was divorcing him. Why did I have any reason to kill him?'

'Magenta would never shoot anyone,' Jody came to her friends defence.

Before Hunter could speak everyone began talking at once.

'Shot?'

'Who shot him?'

'Why would anyone want to kill Max?'

'Freakin' hell, we've all got a freakin' motive.'

'Glad the bastard's dead, I'll shake the hand of the person who killed him.'

'This place is getting like a morgue.'

'Look, everybody calm down,' Hunter spoke above the noise. 'Come into the drawing room, it's nice and warm in there. The fire is on and we can talk this through properly in there.'

'Talk it through? Who died and put you in charge?' Fly frowned. 'Oops, bad choice of words. It's pretty obvious what went down last night. One of us bumped off Max. So what you're suggesting is we have a nice little chat in the drawing room to see who shot Max in the bedroom with the revolver? Was this your plan all along Magenta? Are we part of a murder mystery weekend?'

Hunter spoke before Mags had a chance too. 'This is serious Fly, this isn't a game. The stakes are too high.'

'Ok, Mr hot shot, why are you being the main man? The guy in charge? What are you hiding? I'm pretty sure you ain't just a hotel manager.'

Hunter took a deep breath before he spoke, Jeez, Fly was one smart cookie, smarter than he gave him credit for. 'I'm ex-army. Hotel management was the first job opportunity after I quit the forces. I've seen things only you guys could imagine in your worst nightmares, so I reckon I'm over qualified to deal with a situation like this.'

'Wow, man, the Army, you serve in Iraq? Got a buddy over there, it's tough,' Johnny defused the tension that was building between Fly and Hunter.

He nodded. 'You got that right, some of the toughest terrain on the planet, gives you massive problems and that's before you start the day job,' he was aware they were drifting off course.

'Anyway, Fly is right, someone here did kill Max.'

'How can you be so sure it was one of us?' Brooke asked.

'Jeez, you're a dumb blonde,' Fly rolled his eyes at her. 'We've been snowed in for days, if we can't get out, nobody can get in.'

'Lay off her Fly, she's pregnant,' Logan chastised him. Brooke threw him a grateful look.

'We need to get to the bottom of this, the police won't be able to get here till the earliest, tomorrow and as far as they know, they're only investigating Tim's death,' Hunter said.

'But that was an accident,' Magenta butted in.

'I know, but they'll still have some routine questions to ask,' he looked around the table again. 'We'll go into the drawing room and talk this out. You lot head through. I'll bring in some more coffee.'

As they scraped the chairs back and headed out. Fly shouted over 'Yeah, I'm gonna need that coffee Irish.'

Hunter snuck into the pantry by the side of the kitchen, unobserved by the two people who had hung back in the kitchen. He couldn't see who was talking to Shane, the corner of the kitchen obstructed the view, but that was ok, all he needed was his ears.

'Shane, we got to call this off, there are too many dead bodies cropping up all over the place. We can't risk another one. One you can pass off as an accident, two looks like murder and if Max's wife gets bumped off as well its three strikes and we're out.'

'There's no we in this, I only met you this weekend.'

'I'll take you down with me, so you best get this stopped pretty damn quick. The plan is on hold. Magenta leaves this place with the rest of us as soon as this freakin' snow melts.'

'I'll deal with it. Now be quiet, walls have ears.'

They disappeared out of view and into the hallway. Hunter smiled, Shane was right, walls do have ears and now not only did he know who shot Max he know also knew who had hired the hit on Magenta. Now it was show time.

Chapter Thirty Nine

Hunter brought the tray of coffee into the drawing room, letting everyone take a cup as he moved around the room.

'How jolly civilised is this, feeling very British right now, serving coffee in the dining room whilst we unmask a murderer. Tally ho,' Fly tried a very unsuccessful English accent.

'Fly, will you stop arsing about, look around, you're sitting amongst a killer or maybe all this joking is to deflect attention from you? Did you kill my husband?' Magenta arched an eyebrow at him.

'Soon to be ex-husband as you keep reminding us and while we're on that subject, what did Max say about giving you a divorce when he stormed out, 'over my dead body', there's your motive right there.'

Hunter put the tray down and stood in front of the fire place, forcing everyone to move position slightly to look at him. 'Before we start throwing accusations around, let's go round the room one at a time and see where we all were last night and who might have a motive.'

'I don't see the point in this, the police are only going to ask us all this when they get here,' Logan sighed.

'Got something to hide there?' Savannah asked.

Logan just shrugged. 'Just seems pointless to me.'

'Brooke, let's start with you.'

She rolled her eyes. 'I just knew you were going start with me. Firstly it couldn't've been me I was with Johnny and Fly, then Savannah upstairs.'

'No babe, that was before dinner, there's no way we would got down to it if I knew you were pregnant, that's a bit gross. We didn't find out you were having a baby till you had your cat fight with Mags,' Fly corrected her

'Fly, there is nothing wrong with pregnant lady, that's when women are at their most beautiful and sensual,' Savannah placed a hand on Brooke's knee and smiled in support. Brooke scowled at Fly. 'D'you know what? You are being a total jerk right now. So I got confused, you weren't that easy to remember anyway. Johnny is a much better performer than you and Savannah puts you in the shade.'

Too late, Brooke realised she'd just said too much. Logan stood up. 'Freakin' hell Brooke, is there anyone in this room you haven't slept with?'

'Well, I haven't slept with Magenta, or Jody or Hunter...' she trailed off when she realised Logan hadn't wanted a reply to his question.

'We are over Brooke, I don't care if this baby is mine or not, but we are so over.'

'Oh the baby is yours, Logan.'

Brooke and Logan turned their heads to Magenta. 'What? How do you know who the father of my baby is?'

'I thought Max would've told you that he was firing blanks? It was quite a sore point actually. The all-powerful Max Maxwell could never build on his empire. He'd spent millions on tests to try and make him fertile, but money can't buy you everything.'

Brooke stared at her open mouthed. 'He would've said.'

Magenta nodded slowly. 'You'd think so, but he was quite embarrassed by it, felt it made him less of a man. He sued the arse out of a magazine that threatened to run the story.'

'I suppose that blows a hole in my theory for why Brooke would kill Max then?' They turned back round to face Hunter.

'What theory?' Brooke almost growled.

'Well, that you killed Max because he wouldn't stand by you if the baby was his. Sounds to me like he'd have been over the moon if he'd hit the back of the net.'

'I didn't kill Max. I wanted to marry him,' shit, she really was saying too much again.

'News to me,' Logan narrowed his eyes at her.

'I'm sorry, Logan but it was always Max. I married you to stay close to him. If it wasn't for her,' she glared at Magenta. 'He would've been mine.'

Logan stood with his hands on his hips, staring at the floor. 'I really don't know what to say to you any more.'

Hunter put a hand on his shoulder. 'Bet you could kill Max right now, hey?'

'Don't be silly. He's already dead. I didn't kill him, I've only just found all this out right now,' Hunter nodded. 'Yes, but you were probably worried that he'd try and take the company back from you and how would you sort out your gambling debts then?'

'Gambling debts? What gambling debts?' Brooke asked.

Logan gave a bitter laugh. 'Yeah, don't think you'll get much of a pay-out in the divorce Brooke, once I've paid off my gambling debts all I'll have left is Maximum,' he turned to Hunter. 'Which is legally mine. There is no way Max could've got it back from me. Magenta made sure those contracts were water tight.'

Magenta nodded. 'Sure did, wanted to make my leaving gift to Max something he'd never forget.'

Hunter moved from the fireplace to the other side of the drawing room, to where Johnny and Fly were slouched on a sofa, Shane was in the corner in an upright reading chair. 'So, if we haven't got anywhere with the Hudson's, let's try Broken Arrow.'

Fly held his hands up. 'Hey man, this has got nothing to do with me.'

'It was more Johnny and Shane I wanted to speak to. It was clear to all of us that Max had something of a hold over you. Something so serious that it prevented you leaving Maximum of your own free will and tied you to Savannah when you didn't want to be.'

Fly laughed. 'Hell, who doesn't wanna be tied to Savannah, the things she did with that whip last night, still got the marks to prove it.'

'And there's my alibi. I was tied up last night and yes it was by Savannah.'

'We're not sure of the time of death yet, so opportunity can't really be questioned yet. Let's stick with motive. You and Shane are close, right?' Johnny nodded slowly glancing nervously at his brother.

'But we never see you together in the press. In fact Max encouraged you to distance yourself from him and his criminal record.'

Again Johnny nodded slowly.

'But, let's just play devil's advocate here, what if Shane had taken the rap for someone and he hadn't been driving the car at the time of the accident?'

Fly went to stand up but Johnny put his hand out to stop him.

'You're right. It was me driving the car that night, I put the guy in hospital. The band was just taking off, just signed a massive record deal. Going to prison wasn't part of the contract. Fortunately, as Max saw it, Shane was with me in the car. He convinced Shane that the best thing to do to protect my career was to say he'd been behind the wheel. He'd get a short prison sentence but be set up financially for life, he'd be on Max's payroll. If I ever wanted to leave Maximum then Max would leak the story and I'd be ruined.'

'So, by telling Max you were quitting the company, there was the real possibility that he could reveal the truth to the media?'

Johnny shrugged. 'I was past caring, fed up of keeping this secret from my closest buddies, Fly only found out recently.'

'But, if you killed Max, he'd never be able to say anything?'

'I told you, I was tied up last night.'

Mags remembered the argument she witnessed last night between Johnny and Shane. 'I saw you two arguing last night, what was that about?' She asked Johnny.

He frowned. 'Don't remember arguing.'

'I saw you, Shane was in the hallway with Jody, then you came out and you pushed each other.'

'Oh that, it was nothing. Just told Shane to lay off Jody that's all. She was in a bit of a state.'

Fly decided it was time to deflect attention from his band mate. 'So, Hunter, if you reckon you've got this all figured out. What about Magenta? Or do you think she's not capable of murder?'

'Anyone is capable of anything when they're pushed too far.'

'Go on then, ask her or are you afraid of the answer?'

'I know it wasn't her, she was with me last night and we discovered the body.'

'Thought we weren't focusing on alibis? Like I said before, what if Max refused to divorce her?'

Magenta stepped in. 'He had no grounds to refuse me the divorce, he'd committed adultery.'

'Sounds like you were up to the same thing last night,' Brooke butted in.

'I'd already served him the divorce papers.'

Brooke laughed. 'Oh I love that, you ditch your husband then jump into bed with the next available hot guy.'

Magenta blushed. 'It's more complicated than that...'

Savannah jumped in, trying to stop another fight developing. 'What about me? Where's my motive and opportunity?'

37

Hunter frowned. 'You're the dark horse, Max invited you at the last minute. I can't work out any reason you'd want him dead, he was championing your career, your star is rising. Other than making you keep your sexuality secret, I couldn't think of a reason. You strike me as the ambitious type, the kind who would be happy to keep her private life in the closet whilst you're flaunting yourself around the world on the arm on a hot rock star. Am I right?'

She nodded. 'So, that makes me the one you least suspect and we don't have a butler, so by the law of averages, doesn't that make me the killer?'

Hunter smiled. 'You've been watching too many movies.'

'So, I guess it's my turn now then isn't it?' Jody asked.

'Hunter, Jody would never do anything to Max. In fact, she's probably the only one, with the exception of Brooke that actually liked Max.'

'It's funny that you mention Jody,' he turned back round to Magenta. 'Sorry you're only just about to find this out and it will probably hurt you more than anything you've learnt this weekend, but...'

'No wait,' Jody butted in. 'Let me tell her, I don't know how you know all of this, but this needs to come from me.'

'Jody, what on earth are you going on about?' Hunter took a step back, to let the two women talk.

'Max and I...'

It dawned on Magenta, just by the guilty look on Jody's face. 'You slept with Max?'

 She nodded slowly.

 'Just the once? How many times? Surely it was a mistake?'

Jody hung her head in shame. 'I hate myself for this Magenta, you are my only friend and I did this to you. It's been years, three years.'

Magenta stood up. 'You've been shagging my husband for three years?' She shouted.

 'But, but I knew you didn't love him.'

 'I know I didn't love him, that's not what hurts, what hurts is that you did this to our friendship. Do you think I cared about what he was up to with Brooke? I was made up, it gave me the opportunity to leave him. But you, you knew how lonely I was, you were the only person I trusted.'

 'I am so sorry, I never meant to hurt you.'

 Her heart was breaking and again not because of Max, she'd finally seen him for what he was, but because of what she'd lost in Magenta, her respect, her love and her friendship, those things were irreplaceable and she had no chance of getting them back.

 'But you did intend on shooting Max though? Am I right?'

Both women turned towards Hunter.

 'What?' Magenta exploded.

Jody's silence pretty much confirmed her guilt.

Magenta turned to her. 'You didn't?'

  'She did, but she didn't quite finish the job,' as Hunter spoke the door to the drawing room opened and in walked a very alive and kicking Max Maxwell.

Chapter Forty

THE PREVIOUS NIGHT

Max was angrier than he'd ever been in his life. Who the hell did Magenta think she was? Divorce? She was one crazy woman if she thought he'd ever agree to that. Sitting on the sofa in his suite he loosened his tie and poured a large measure of scotch into a crystal tumbler, knocking it back in one go. He'd never divorce her. The brand was too big, too important, it'd be catastrophic, like if David & Victoria Beckham broke up or Barack and Michelle. Unthinkable. He shook his head. No, it was never going to happen, she'd be nothing without him. Actually, he knew it was the other way round, if she left him and Maximum along with Broken Arrow he'd be the one who had nothing. Not that it sounded like he had much left. Logan now had control of the company and Brooke being pregnant was throwing a spanner in the works, clearly she thought the kid was his. It seemed in the space of one evening his life had imploded.

What did he tackle first? Getting his wife back? Getting his company back? Getting rid of Brooke? Pouring another glass he stood up, pacing the suite, nursing the glass in his hand. He hadn't become the powerful man he was without learning how to prioritise. What was most important? The company, obviously. That's what made him rich. Most men would say their wife, but she'd never made him happy and he wasn't stupid enough to know that she'd never been happy either. Maybe he should let her divorce him, on his terms of course. He could start a new company, Logan was becoming an albatross around his neck a dead weight, he'd be better off without him. Yeah, he could start with Savannah and he had a whole conveyor belt of acts to take with him from 'Starmaker' the industry was all about throw away pop right now, not some middle aged singer or a has been rock band. He had a whole load of quick buck singers at his disposal. That's exactly what he'd do and he'd ruin Logan and Maximum whilst he did it. Magenta would end up on the scrap heap that would be the best revenge. That's why he loved being him, ten minutes ago he thought he was finished, now by following his thought process through he knew he'd be the triumphant winner and all those bastards downstairs who thought they'd won would be laughing on the other side of their faces when he rose from the ashes, every bit like the magnificent Phoenix, in fact that's what he'd call his new company.

He'd get onto his lawyers as soon as he was out of this hell hole. He knew his instinct was right about coming here, he never should've got on the jet over to

England. New rule, always listen to your gut, it's never wrong. He heard the click of the door open, he turned round. 'Jody,' man he'd forgotten about her in all of this, she was so easy to forget. Man she looked pissed. 'I was just thinking about you.'

She narrowed her eyes at him. 'I'm sure you were Max.'

'Look, honey, I'm sorry you got caught up in all this Brooke thing. You know how full on she can be. It was just easier to play along. Didn't want her running along to Logan and causing trouble.'

'Anything for an easy life, hey?'

'Come on baby, you know it's always been you, has been for years. Brooke was just a quick fix while you were out of the country.'

She stepped closer to him. 'I've lied and cheated the person I count as my closest friend because of you and not only that, I've cheated myself, I was so stupid, so blind. I thought you...' she couldn't finish the sentence, the words were caught in her throat.

'You thought I loved you? Course I do, who wouldn't love those magnificent tits?'

She tried to recover her composure. 'It's all a joke to you isn't it? You have no idea what I've sacrificed for you.'

He held his hand out to her. 'Baby, come over here, I've got a plan and it very much involves you. I'm going to give Magenta the divorce she wants, I'm going to let Logan have the company 'cos I'm starting a new one and you'll be by my side and together we'll watch those two fall from grace as we become the new king and queen of the music industry. We'll get our revenge.'

She regarded him slowly as she watched that multi-billion dollar smile spread across his face, if there was one thing you could say about Max it was that he was never down and out for long. She desperately wanted to tell him that America didn't have a king and queen so as usual he was talking bullshit and as for revenge, there was only one person who she was gunning for. Instead, she stepped forward, letting him take her hand in his and falling into his embrace. If she was going to fight Max, then the only way was to use her weapons of mass destruction. Almost on cue, he bent down to kiss the top of her cleavage which were spilling over the top of her dress.

'Did I tell you how stunning you look tonight? Easily the most amazing woman in the room.'

She let his words wash over her, how lovely it would be if he actually meant it, but she knew he never would. She however, had taken a leaf out of the Magenta Valentina book of life and grown some balls. 'Max,' she croaked huskily. 'It's been too long, I need you.'

He stopped kissing her left boob and his head jerked up. 'So you're with me? You're on board?'

She nodded. 'But first, I gotta get on board you,' she used both her hands to push him towards the bedroom.

'Man, I knew I married the wrong woman,' he grinned. 'Come on then tiger, reverse cowgirl?'

She shook her head. 'Not tonight baby, I'm gonna ride you like a cowboy, I wanna see the look on your face,' when I blow your brains out she finished silently.

Hunter was waiting patiently in the room opposite, the door slightly ajar so it gave him a view across the landing and straight over to the door of Magenta's suite. He couldn't be entirely sure what was going on in there and he couldn't be sure of the outcome. The plan was dangerous, but less dangerous than what he actually thought was going on in there. He'd have to stay put until someone left the room and then he'd have to wait a moment or two before he went in. He looked at his watch, twenty minutes had passed since he followed Jody out of the banqueting suite and up here. He couldn't wait too much longer, he ran the risk of Magenta coming to find him. She wouldn't be distracted by the Broken Arrow boys for too long and she certainly wouldn't want to be in Brooke's company, plus she was going to need cleaning up when she realised her face was bruised. He literally had that short window of time until the adrenaline in Mags' body wore off and the clock was ticking fast. He breathed a sigh of relief when he saw Jody open the door opposite, look both ways down the hall and high tail it out of there as fast as she could. He slipped out of the door and over to Magenta's suite, holding his breath as he hoped his plan had worked.

He found Max unconscious on the bed. He went over to him, gave him a slap around the cheeks. Max spluttered back to life, gasping noisily his eyes flashing with the look of someone who'd just seen their whole life flash before them.

'Ssh, it's ok, you'll be alright.'   'She....shot...me....' he spluttered.

'Don't talk. You were shot with blanks, fortunately not at close range so it's not fatal. I swapped the bullets for blanks, you'll survive. I saved your life, but now you gotta do me a favour. Ok?'

Trying to open his mouth to speak Hunter cut him off. 'Don't speak, you need to recover and we need to be quick, so just nod or shake your head and listen to what I tell you to do.'

Max gave one nod, it was all he could muster.

'Ok, point number one. Do you want Magenta dead?' Max shook his head.

'Good, that means it was worth me saving your life and I don't have to re shoot you.'

A panicked look appeared on Max's face.

'Relax, I'm not going to kill you. Point two. Do you want me to stop Magenta from being killed?'

Max again gave one nod. 'What...the…'

'Please don't speak, time really is of essence. Right this is what I need you to do in order for me to make sure Magenta is safe. Play dead. In an hour or so I'll be coming in here with her, she'll see the blood, you look pretty pale anyway, she'll assume you're dead. Then you are to stay locked in here till eleven am tomorrow morning when you will come into the drawing room. Then, I'll be able to tell you everything. But, if you value your life and you value Magenta's you need to do as I say,' Hunter pulled out a gun. 'Otherwise you'll find out I'm a better shot than Miss Stanley.'

Chapter Forty One

The silence in the drawing room was deathly quiet as Max stood next to Hunter, the previous night's shenanigans now revealed.

'But, but, I shot you, you were dead,' Jody whispered.

'First rule in murder Miss Stanley, always, always check your weapon is loaded with bullets,' Hunter said.

'Why would you do this, why would you make us think Max was dead? Why would you put poor Magenta through this?' Brooke whimpered.

'How did you know she was going to do Max in?' Fly asked. 'Like you said before, we all had a motive.'

Hunter shrugged. 'Firstly I found the gun in her room, I'm pretty sure that was just for her own protection, but you never know what someone might do when they are pushed to the edge and I think Max pushed her over the edge that night. Not only did she find out about Brooke, but Max totally ignored her, as he'd been doing all the time he's been here, unless it was for a drunken shag. As Jody has said many a time, nobody sees her, she's invisible. It was time for her to be seen and not be forgotten and killing Max was as sure as hell gonna make that happen. That right Jody?'

In her slumped heap in the corner she nodded slowly.

'So, that's why you put blanks in the bullets? You were that sure she'd kill him?' Johnny asked.

'Honestly? Until I followed her to Max's suite, knowing she'd got the gun from her room I wasn't sure of anything.'

'So, err, forgive me for like being the dumb blonde, but why didn't you stop her before she shot him? A blank coulda still killed him if she'd shot him close range,' Savannah interjected.

'Whoa, how d'you know so much?' Johnny turned his attention to Savannah.

'My brothers are massive Kung Fu fans and I remember all the stuff from when Brandon Lee was shot with a blank.'

'Yeah but I think a bullet did get loaded in there by mistake, almost like an accidental Russian Roulette,' Shane added.

'Can we just stick with this drama? You're confusing me,' Fly said.

'Savannah, you're right, it could've all gone wrong, but I had to take that chance, I had to make you all think Max was dead.'

Johnny narrowed his eyes. 'Why? What's really going on here? You sure you're just ex forces?'

Hunter nodded. 'Yep, ex-marine corp. I was what you call a high flier, the army invested a lot of money and training in me, I was the best sniper in the country, until I was dishonourably discharged,' little white lie there, he didn't need to go into the full story.

Fly was on the edge of his seat. 'Wow, cool man, what did you do?'

He glanced at Magenta, knowing she was the only one who needed to know his full story. 'That's a story for another day, promise I'll tell you over a beer one day. Anyway, when I was kicked out I had to make a living and the only thing I knew how to do well was shoot.'

'So what did you do? Become a gun for hire?' Fly laughed.

'Yep.'

'Quit with the bullshit, man.'

'I am deadly serious. I am an assassin and a bloody good one. Never failed a mission yet.'

'That on your business card?' Johnny laughed nervously.

'I don't work with business cards. My calling card is the bullet wound I leave in my target.'

Brooke swallowed hard. 'So, Max was your target, but Jody got there first and she stole your thunder. Is that it?'

Hunter laughed. 'Couldn't be further from the truth,' he paused, looking round the room, never before had he had such a captive audience and he knew right now someone was bricking it. 'I was hired to kill someone else,' he paused for dramatic effect and noticed Mags glanced nervously around the room. 'Magenta.'

As he said he name a whole host of 'Shits', 'Holy cow,' 'What the fuck' filled the room. He took their moment of outburst as a chance to gauge their reactions. Some looked suitably shocked, some looked dumbstruck, some looked bewildered, but very difficult to tell who's shocked look was actually a 'shit, I've been found out look.'

'Who would want Magenta dead?' Savannah asked.

'Who indeed?' He looked around the room again. 'That's why I needed you to believe Max was dead, I was hoping one of you would let your guard down, thinking maybe Max had been shot instead of Magenta and one of you did.'

Before he could carry on Fly interrupted. 'But why didn't you want to kill Magenta,' he quickly turned to her. 'No offence babe,' he was back to looking at Hunter. 'You said you'd never failed a mission, so why weren't you following orders and putting a bullet in her?'

'Quite a demanding question there Mr MacFly, anything you'd like to tell me?'

Fly shook his head. 'Not at all, I just reckon once you met Magenta you were more interested in jumping her bones.'

'Wouldn't put it quite as crudely as that, but you're not far wrong. You see when she said before it was complicated, it's more than complicated. Magenta and I knew each other a long time, first love if you like,' he stopped for a moment. 'First love that never really went away,' he looked over to her and smiled. 'There was no way on this earth that I had a bullet with her name on it, but I knew if I didn't take the job, someone else would and then she'd surely be dead. So I took the job but my intention was to find out who wanted her dead and stop them.'

'You're gonna kill whoever hired you?' Johnny asked.

'I would if I had to, to protect the woman I love, but I'm hoping it won't come to that.'

'So what's the plan? Someone just gonna fess up? Or d'you know who it is?' Fly asked.

'Fortunately I know who it is. At first I thought I'd try and work it out, I thought It'd be easy enough especially as in the beginning everything kept pointing back to Max, but that seemed too obvious.'

'And obvious is wrong?' Savannah asked.

'No, it was just there were too many strands to tie together, Max and Brooke, Max and Jody, Max and Logan, Max and Broken Arrow and obviously Max and Magenta. Max is the common denominator in all of those things, and he wants to control them all. If Max wanted Magenta dead, he couldn't control her, or try to control her any more.

'But you can't control Magenta, she's the most feisty woman I know,' Johnny said, sounding confused.

Hunter nodded. 'Yeah I know, me too. What I mean is, controlling her career. Also she's worth more to him alive than dead.'

'Obviously, she's his wife,' Savannah rolled her eyes.

'Money wise, Savannah,' Magenta put in quickly. 'You have a lot to learn about this business.'

'So, despite all roads leading to Max, I was pretty sure it wasn't him.'

'Who the hell is it then?'

Hunter moved aside to let Max sit down, who for once in his life seemed to have nothing to say, he was totally dumbstruck by the whole situation.

'Anyone need a top up before we carry on?' He asked.

'Freakin' hell Hunter. Just tell us will you,' Fly threw his hands in the air in desperation.

'I had no clues as to who had hired me, or who had contacted Shane to hire me. For the one person that doesn't know, he's my handler. You heard Johnny mention before that he was on Max's payroll, he also does a nice side line in arranging hits. I'm sure anyone who had access to Max's rolodex could've located Shane's details, although I'm sure he wasn't listed under 'hit man for hire'. So that's how the initial contact was made and I never know who I've been hired by. Which meant I had to do some digging around. That's how I discovered about all the affairs, the gambling, the false imprisonment and whatever else you lot wanna throw into the mix but I could never get close to finding out who had hired me. I needed a lucky break and that came when Jody nearly shot Max. It gave me an idea, if you all thought Max was dead, then it would unsettle everyone and I hoped the person who hired me would call the hit off, what with Tim and Max the bodies were stacking up, we didn't need another one. It would be harder to pass of Magenta's death as an 'accident.' So we faked Max's death, Fly wasn't far wrong when he asked if we were playing a game. We were, but it was a game where if we lost, someone else would die. I wasn't gonna let that happen to Mags.'

'Oh my God, how did you manage to keep it a secret?' Savannah asked Magenta.

'I...I...I didn't, I didn't know Max was still alive. We went back to my suite,' she paused for a second as she looked over to Hunter, realisation fleeting through her brain. He knew they'd discover Max's 'body' the whole time they we're having sex in the other part of the suite. He set her up. She opened her mouth to speak, but he cut her off.

'For the plan to work, I had to keep her in the dark, because if my plan failed and I failed then I wasn't sure I'd be able to save her life,' he looked right into her eyes as he spoke next. 'Everything I did, every action I took was to save your life. If you think I was underhand with anything, then just remember one thing. I did it for you, la.'

Brooke frowned. 'La? What does that mean?'

Max sighed, finally finding his voice. 'It's that God awful scouse stuff she speaks, clearly Mr Cole must've picked it up too.'

'Wait,' Savannah jumped in excitedly. 'You said before you were each other's first loves, that means your scouse too. Oh my God, does that mean you're speaking in code?'

Magenta smiled and shook her head. 'No, it just something someone a long time ago used to say to me.'

'Oh for freaks sake you're all talking in riddles can we please just find out who wants Magenta dead? I'm sure it was quicker finding out who shot JR,' Fly complained.

Hunter carried on. 'After you guys came in here, I was still in the kitchen, but out of sight in the pantry, that's when someone pulled Shane to one side and told him to call off the hit.' There was a silence that filled the room.

'Brooke, do you wanna carry on the story?'

Logan gasped. 'Brooke? You hired someone to kill Magenta?'

She hung her head for a second, then raised her shoulders, head held high as she began to speak. 'Yes I did. I'd have been Mrs Maxwell if it wasn't for her. I deserved that role, I deserved to be that rich and successful.'

'Why Brooke? You had that with me? We we're rich and successful why did you want to throw that away?'

'I wanted more. I wanted to be famous, Max would do that for me, you couldn't. I was just your stupid little wife,' she turned to Magenta who was in total shock at this revelation. She knew Brooke hated her, but she didn't know she wanted her dead.

'You seriously would've gone through with this?'

'I wanted what you had, your fame, your fortune, your husband. I was always photographed as the hanger on in magazines, it was you they all wanted. I wanted my turn.'

'I knew you were always jealous but I didn't realise how sick you were. Like I said yesterday, you're welcome to him. I actually think you two deserve each other,' she stood up. 'I don't want to be anywhere near you,' she began to walk away.

'Wait, what's going to happen to me now? Are you going to call the police?' Brooke called after her.

'D'you know what. I couldn't give a shit what happens to you now. I've got a whole new life to go and live and strangely enough, it's down to you. So for now Brooke, just do one and don't ever be in the same place as me. 'Cos I swear on my life, cross me once, I'll let it go, do it a second time and you won't know what hit you.' Taking Hunter's hand she led him out of the drawing room, leaving the others to deal with the fall out.

Lying in Hunter's bed, her naked body against his, Magenta felt totally at peace. They'd gone straight from the drawing room to his room. He said they needed to debrief. The debrief he had in mind was a million miles away from any Army debrief. It was only now they were getting the chance to talk.

'You were great in there, a proper Columbo.'

He smiled, his fingertips lazily stroking her arm. 'Wouldn't go that far, I did quite enjoy it though, once I knew who had hired me and I knew you'd be safe I quite liked messing with their heads.'

'What will happen to Jody?'

'Probably nothing, she only injured Max, he could press charges if he wants but something tells me he won't do that.'

'It would be a different story if you hadn't taken the bullets out.'

'Well, just be glad I'm good at what I do.'

'So, when we finally defrost and can get out of here, we'll only have Tim's body to sort out and explain the accident to the police.'

'Mmmm,' he replied absent-mindedly. Yep Tim made a big mistake pulling him to one side and asking him who Jason Lomax was. Accidents will happen.

'You falling asleep there?'

'Nope, just enjoying finally getting to be with you properly.'

She flipped over onto her front. 'I think we should stay in here till we can leave. There is nowhere I need to be except here.'

Pulling her into his arms. 'That is the best idea you've ever had.'

She planted a kiss on his lips then pulled away. 'Talking about you being good at what you do...'

'At your service, ma'am.'

She frowned at him. 'What did we say about Americanisms?'

'Sorry, girl,' he grinned. 'I bloody well love you, la.'

'Love you too, la,' she kissed him softly then whispered 'Jason.'

EPILOGUE

MAX MAXWELL set up his company Phoenix but it crashed and burned as did his fleetingly brief relationship with Brooke. The media had cast him as the villain of the piece for his break up with Magenta after it emerged about his affairs with Brooke and Jody. He tried to sell a story about Johnny Kidd really being involved in the car crash that saw his brother go to jail, nobody believed him. He released his autobiography, this can now be found in the bargain bin at most good book stores. These days he can be found at his modest condo working on new ideas for TV shows. So far he is still waiting for his ex-contacts to get in touch. His fall from grace has been well documented.

LOGAN HUDSON paid off his gambling debts and threw himself back into work, he re branded Maximum

Corp. as Hudson Int. It is the most successful music company in America. Under his guidance the 'Starmaker' brand has gone global and the top ten is full of his artists. He is now only second to Barack Obama as the most powerful man in America. He doesn't return Max's calls and he spends a lot of time with his new personal assistant, he fell in love with the English accent when he was in Liverpool, so he hired an English girl. They are very happy.

BROOKE HUDSON thought she had it all for about five seconds, she got Max, he had a new company but as soon as the bubble burst she high tailed it out of there. Despite what Logan had said, she did get a fairly good pay-out from her divorce and he pays their son Dexter a huge amount of maintenance. Probably to ease his guilt for having nothing to do with them. Still she couldn't really blame him. After that terrible time in England she has barely seen him and she still lives in fear that one day Magenta would get her revenge. She now lives in California and has found love with someone who was happy to raise Dexter with her. She doesn't return Max's calls.

JOHNNY KIDD is still racked with guilt for letting his brother take the blame for his mistake. Shane says it's better to let sleeping dogs lie and to channel the emotion into writing new material. Broken Arrow have just released their latest album and his duet with Magenta was number one across the world. He is still the world's most eligible bachelor. He is about to go on tour with the band. Shane is going with them as a roadie. He doesn't return Max's calls.

FLY MACFLY is psyched to go back on the road, the band is bigger than ever and he is looking forward to meeting all the lovely ladies. He doesn't return Max's calls.

JODY STANLEY is slowly rebuilding her life. She moved to California and has a job working for Hudson Int. Logan felt sorry for her, he knew how manipulative Max could be and he figured everyone deserves a second chance. She works in a small office and is making new friends, ones she's very careful never to meet the boyfriends of! Besides, she has her eye on the guy who lives in the apartment next to hers. She never returns Max's calls.

SAVANNAH ZAGGER's career hit the stratosphere and under Hudson Int guidance she is churning out hit after hit. She is also a role model, as an openly gay pop star her profile has never been higher. She lives in California and is happily settled with Brooke and co-parenting raising Dexter together. She still sees Johnny when they bump into each other, some things are just too good to forget. She never returns Max's calls.

MAGENTA VALENTINA decided to take a back seat from being a pop star. She released her duet with Johnny then a cover of an old 90's song – I love you always, forever. Now she has more time she is doing what she's always wanted to do – write songs. She's been so successful at it that over the summer five of the songs in the top ten had been written by her. She enjoys being out of the spot light. She divides her time between New York, LA and her penthouse in Liverpool City Centre. She likes having more time to spend with Trina who she has employed as her PA and pays a ridiculous wage to, but it makes her feel less guilty about the whole 'knee caps' situation which, Treen being Treen, was totally ok with. That's what you call true friendship. Liverpool is where she really feels is home, because home is where your heart is and her heart firmly belongs to Hunter. After seventeen years apart and an assassination attempt they are finally together and couldn't be happier. They enjoy wandering around the Albert Dock, going out for long lunches and spending a lot of time in bed...they have seventeen years to make up for. She never returns Max's calls.

HUNTER COLE is blissfully happy, not only did he save the girl but he got her too. Mission accomplished. He has discovered a love of writing and has released some SAS style novels under a pen name...Jason Lomax.

THE END

Thanks for reading my book, if you've enjoyed it, don't forget to leave a review!

ABOUT THE AUTHOR:

Bev Dulson has written stories since she was old enough to hold a pen, she lives in a constant dream world and genuinely thinks her characters are real.

She lives in the North West of England, where sometimes the sun actually shines. She is married to her ex-rugby playing husband and has two adorable, well behaved (sometimes) daughters.

As well as writing she loves reading, whodunits, dancing around a disco ball in her friend's kitchen, anything purple, chocolate, Jon Bon Jovi and of course Prosecco.

Printed in Great Britain
by Amazon